I0718205

# BETRAYED

## *The Cuvier Women Book 2*

# BY SYLVIA MCDANIEL

# Books by Sylvia McDaniel

## *Contemporary Romance*

### *Standalones*
The Reluctant Santa
My Sister's Boyfriend
The Wanted Bride
The Relationship Coach
Her Christmas Lie
Secrets, Lies, and Online Dating
Paying for the Past
Cupid's Revenge

### *Anthologies*
Kisses, Laughter & Love
Christmas with you

### *Collaborative Series*

### *Magic, New Mexico*
Touch of Decadence

## *Western Historicals*

### *Standalones*
A Hero's Heart
A Scarlet Bride
Second Chance Cowboy

### *The Cuvier Women*
Wronged
Betrayed
Beguiled

### *Lipstick and Lead*
Desperate
Deadly
Dangerous
Daring
Determined
Deceived

### *Scandalous Suffragettes*
Abigail
Bella
Callie
Faith

### *The Burnett Brides*
The Rancher Takes a Bride
The Outlaw Takes a Bride
The Marshal Takes a Bride
The Christmas Bride

### *Anthologies*
Wild Western Women
Courting the West
Wild Western Women Ride Again

### *Collaborative Series*

### *The Surprise Brides*
Ethan

### *American Mail Order Brides*
Katie

Betrayed
Published by Virtual Bookseller

Cover Design by Lyndsey Lewellyn
https://lyndseylewellen.wordpress.com/

Edited by The New York Publishing House

Formatted by Laurelle Procter
laurelleprocter@gmail.com

Copyright © 2013 by Sylvia McDaniel
This book and parts thereof may not be reproduced in any form, stored in a
retrieval system, or transmitted in any form by any means—electronic,
mechanical, photocopying, or otherwise—without prior written permission
of the author and publisher, except as provided by the United States of
America copyright law. The only exception is by a reviewer who may
quote short excerpts in a review.

Short Description: Nicole discovers that her husband has been
murdered, and there are two other women claiming to be his
wife. Pregnant, and now a widow with a plantation on the verge
of bankruptcy, Nicole needs a temporary husband.

ISBN: 978-1-942608-18-9 (paperback)
ISBN: 978-1-942608-19-6 (e-book)

{Victorian Historical Romance – Fiction}

www.SylviaMcDaniel.com

# Synopsis

Nicole Cuvier went to New Orleans to share wonderful news with her husband only to discover him in a hotel room murdered, with two other women claiming to be his wives. It seems there are three Cuvier Widows and each one is suspected of murder.

Pregnant, unmarried, and now a widow with a plantation on the verge of bankruptcy. Nicole needs a temporary husband. Someone to save Rosewood and give her child a last name. Enter a handsome drifter, Maxim Viel, who agrees to marry her, but unbeknownst to Nicole, wants more than a temporary arrangement. Can his strong arms, tender caresses and heated kisses heal her shattered heart? Or could the price of his love, be more than Nicole is willing to give?

# Table of Contents

# Chapter One

*New Orleans, 1895*

**F**or the first time in their marriage, Nicole Rosseau Cuvier disobeyed her husband Jean. Though he told her never to come to his office in New Orleans without him, the news she had simply could not wait. And his office was just several hours by boat down the Mississippi River.

Yet her joy dimmed when she arrived at her husband's shipping company, and the clerk mysteriously informed her that Jean was ill and gave her his room number at the Chateau Hotel.

In the entire four years they'd been married, Jean Cuvier had never been ill.

Nicole burst into the hotel room, uncertain what she would find. Her gaze swept across the open room to a man dressed in a shabby suit in conversation with a refined lady with dark hair and smoky-gray eyes. "Where is he? Is he all right? They told me he was ill."

The man stepped between Nicole and an open door where she could see uniformed men standing around an unidentifiable body stretched out on the floor. Who could that be lying on the floor?

"Who are you?" the man asked, blocking her path.

"I'm Mrs. Cuvier," Nicole said anxiously. "I went by my husband's office and they sent me over here. Is the doctor with him?" she asked, trying to peer around the man to see into the other room.

"Good Lord, another one?" the man muttered, gazing back at the lady he'd been speaking with.

"Who did you say you were?" the woman inquired as she stared at Nicole, her gray eyes large and questioning.

Nicole didn't have time to chitchat with this woman, whoever she was. If Jean were ill, he needed her. "I'm Mrs.

Nicole Cuvier, Jean's wife. Now where is my husband?"

The man in the shabby suit coat glanced at the other woman and then turned his gaze on Nicole. "Jean Cuvier is dead."

Nicole felt as if someone punched her in the stomach. With a trembling hand she clutched her throat, trying to hold back the scream that seemed to swell and lodge itself in her throat. The room swayed precariously as a dizzy spell overcame her, the words reverberating through her mind. Her beloved husband was dead.

"No. No," Nicole cried, tears rushing to her eyes, hysteria bubbling up, threatening to overwhelm her. "Dear God, no. He can't be! Let me see him. Please tell me this is a mistake. Where is he?"

"I'll take you to him," the man said, taking Nicole's arm and gently guiding her. "I'm Detective Dunegan, with the New Orleans police."

Nicole heard the words, but her mind didn't comprehend what he was saying. Police detective? What was a detective doing here with her husband? He led her into the bedroom where the same body she'd seen earlier lay sprawled on the floor, surrounded by people.

*Please, God, that couldn't be Jean.*

She caught a glimpse of dark hair tinted with silver, the color of Jean's hair. The man wore pajamas the same dark brown that Jean loved, a silk robe wrapped around his still form.

At the detective's motion, they moved aside and let her in close to see the man she loved, who lay twisted on the floor, his skin an odd pinkish hue that looked unnatural. She knelt beside him, her hand reaching out as her fingers touched his cold flesh. Quickly, she drew her hand back, the sensation confirming that her husband's lifeblood no longer flowed, his warm, loving touch now just a memory. A sob tore from her throat as she gazed at Jean, feeling as if this couldn't be real.

Gently the detective helped her up from the floor and led her back into the main room of the hotel suite. Nicole sobbed for her husband, who'd taught her so much about life. Their short time together had been filled with love and laughter, and even today she'd come bringing him such joyous news.

"I think we need to remain calm, sit down, and find out what happened," the officer said, his voice firm and reassuring.

Calm? How could she remain calm when she'd just found out her husband was dead? That no longer would he hold her in his arms or his smiles brighten her day.

"What—what...happened?" Nicole sobbed, tears streaking down her face. "How did he die?"

"Poisoning. We suspect that his wi—the woman we found him with poisoned him."

Nicole spun around and glared at the finely dressed woman through tear-streaked eyes. Could she be Jean's killer?

Her large gray eyes returned her gaze unflinchingly. "Not me. There's another woman."

"What do you mean, another woman?" Nicole asked, confused.

"You're not the only Mrs. Cuvier in this hotel suite," the woman advised her.

Another Mrs. Cuvier? What was she talking about? Nicole didn't understand. The only other Mrs. Cuvier was a distant relative of Jean's who lived hundreds of miles away. Why were they lying to her?

"I don't believe you," Nicole said, fear making her almost hysterical.

The detective took Nicole by the arm and motioned for the other woman to follow him. They walked into an adjoining room where a young woman sat staring off at the horizon, her dark eyes glazed and distant.

"Layla," the detective said, releasing Nicole. "Tell these women how the man you're suspected of killing was related to you."

She turned her oval-shaped face toward the door. Hair black as night was swept up off her neck in a coiffure that left wisps of curls swirling around her pale face. She turned dark, censorious eyes on the detective and raised her brows in a disdainful look that was both elegant and disapproving. "I told you I did not kill my husband."

Nicole moaned, the woman's words confirming her worst fears, yet she couldn't believe this was happening. There had to be a mistake. "What are you saying? No! You lie. You can't be married to Jean."

The girl glanced briefly at Nicole, not responding.

"Did you marry Jean Cuvier?" the distinguished woman asked her.

"Yes," the young girl said, her voice starting to tremble. Her bright red lips pouted.

"That can't be. He married me. He's my husband," Nicole said, her voice rising, the pain and hurt audible in her voice, unable to control the fear that raged through her.

"And mine," the woman said quietly as she sank down onto a nearby chair. "I'm Marian Cuvier. I married him twelve years ago at Saint Ann's Cathedral."

Nicole turned abruptly and stared at her in disbelief. "No. That's impossible." She paused, comprehension as fleeting as the wind. "No. We were married four years ago. I don't understand. He would never do something so horrible."

"And I married him a year ago," Layla whispered, her face turning ashen.

"Impossible. Jean loved me. That's ...that's bigamy!" Nicole said, shaking her head from side to side. Jean would never hurt her this way. He loved her. He told her over and over how he loved her more than any other woman.

"Yes, it is bigamy. We're all married to the same man," Marian replied, her voice sounding uncaring and cold. "And now we're all Jean's widows. The Cuvier Widows."

Nicole sobbed. Dear God, she'd come to town to tell Jean that after four years she finally was expecting their baby. And instead she'd learned that the father of her child, the man she loved with all her heart, was a bigamist—and he'd been murdered.

~

Nicole stood in the attorney's office waiting, barely able to recall the previous days since Jean's death. Somehow she'd attended his funeral in disguise. In a crowd of people, she'd sat all alone through her husband's eulogy and finally his entombment. Tears streamed down her cheeks, her thoughts on the child she carried who would never know his father.

Later she'd made her way back to her hotel room only to find a swarm of reporters waiting for her. Their questions were rude and the headlines the newspapers printed sensational. This morning's headline read, *WHO IS THE REAL MRS. CUVIER?*

Her reputation was in tatters and she knew the baby she carried, if known as Jean's child, would never live down the scandal his father had created.

How could the man she loved have done something so painful and wrong? How could he feel affection for her and marry other women? How could he hold her in his arms and tell her she made his life worthwhile, when everything was such a lie?

A door slammed, snapping her attention back to the present. Mr. Fournet, Jean's business partner, shut the door firmly behind Marian Cuvier, Jean's first wife. "I'm locking the door, Drew," he called. "The press knows we're here."

"Quick thinking, Louis," Drew Soulier, Jean's attorney, replied. He'd been kind enough to let Nicole and Layla, Jean's third wife, sit in on the reading of the will.

Dark and regal, the attorney looked like a serious lawyer, except for the twinkle in his green eyes he couldn't seem to hide. "Mrs. Cuvier, how are you?"

Nicole felt a twinge of envy. She was Mrs. Cuvier too, though the law didn't recognize her marriage. No one seemed concerned she'd lost her husband in more ways than she'd ever dreamed possible. How could the man she cherished have been the same person who married all three of them? It just didn't seem possible.

"I'm fine, Mr. Soulier," Marian said, and then glanced about the room, her gaze falling on Nicole and Layla.

Nicole stood off from everyone, facing the opposite direction from Layla. Neither of them had moved since they'd walked in the door. Their backs faced, trying not to notice one another, yet Nicole was very aware of her husband's third wife, just the same.

Drew whispered to the legal Mrs. Cuvier something that Nicole could not hear, his eyes fixed on them, and suddenly she felt certain they would be asked to leave.

"No," Marian said quickly. "Let us all hear Jean's wishes at the same time," she said, loud enough to make them aware of her decision.

"All right. As you wish," Drew replied, and turned toward the other women. "Ladies, tea and refreshments are in my office; please, go inside so we can get started."

He motioned for them to proceed ahead of him.

Marian entered first, and then Nicole and Layla followed into the dark paneled room.

Refusing to be cowed, Nicole entered the room with her head held high. She'd done nothing wrong, except to fall in love with a man who obviously didn't believe in monogamy. If she'd known Jean was married, she would never have accepted his proposal.

Layla entered her eyes downcast, refusing to look at anyone. Jean's death appeared to have stunned them all and Nicole couldn't help but wonder what would become of them. How could Jean bequeath them anything when Marian was the legal wife?

Drew closed the door, enclosing them all together. Tension seemed to emanate from the women filling the tiny room.

Nicole nodded her head in Marian's direction. "Mrs. Cuvier."

Marian returned her head bob, then turned her attention to Layla, who stood with her back straight, her eyes fixed on a distant object. She appeared so young and fragile, and somehow Nicole felt envious. Jean married Layla after he married Nicole. Why? What kind of charm or spell could Layla cast to entice her husband away from her?

"Mrs. C-Cuv ..." Layla stumbled over the name.

"I think it would be so much easier if we dropped the formalities and called each other by our given names," Marian said, glancing at each woman.

Layla nodded. "Please, I intend to assume my maiden name again."

"I think that's wise," Marian said curtly.

How could Nicole go back to her maiden name? Her baby would have no father, no name. She swallowed back the tears that threatened to flow from her eyes. She couldn't think about that now.

A tense silence seemed to hang suspended in the air. Marian walked around the desk until she faced the other wives.

"This is an extremely awkward situation we find ourselves in. The press is outside just waiting for us to succumb to arguing over whatever crumbs Jean has tossed our way." She sighed and stared at them. "Ladies, I have no desire to come to blows over a man who deceived me like my... our dead husband. I only wish to take care of my children and live in peace without them being tarnished by their father's scandal."

The sight of Jean's children at his funeral had left Nicole feeling wretched. How could he treat his children to such a scandal of this proportion? What of her own child?

Marian paused and gazed at each of the women, drawing Nicole back from her thoughts. "Keep in mind, I shall certainly do what I must to protect my babies."

Nicole couldn't blame her; she felt the same regarding her own unborn child.

Layla let out a long sigh. "I understand. But Jean lied to me as well."

Nicole removed her hat from her blonde hair that she had carefully coiffed that morning and laid the bonnet on a table nearby. "Excuse me, but *I* loved Jean very much. Though I can't help but wonder why he didn't tell me the truth." She took out her handkerchief and dabbed her eyes. "It's so unfair that he died knowing all the reasons he did this but keeping them from us. Surely there's an explanation."

"I'm sure he could give you one, but why do you care? He lied to all of us. If he were alive, he wouldn't tell you the truth. He would just invent some new excuse to protect himself," Marian said.

*No, no,* Nicole wanted to shout, but the words seemed stuck in her throat. Her husband was an honorable man. He would never have lied to her this way. There had to be another explanation. Nicole shook her head in disagreement. "But I loved him."

"We all did at some time in our life," Marian said, her voice heavy with sarcasm.

"I hated him," Layla stated, her voice quivering with emotion.

The room became silent as they all stared at the prime suspect in Jean's murder, the last person to see him alive. The woman's hate seemed almost visible and Nicole wanted to dislike her, but suspected she was a victim of Jean's lies just like herself.

But did she hate Jean enough to kill him?

"Ladies, we need to get started," Drew said, standing beside the door, ending their impromptu confessions. "Why don't you all take a seat?"

The lawyer seated the three women in chairs placed strategically apart, while Louis Fournet stood at the back of the room, his arms folded across his chest Drew cleared his throat. "Before I read the will, I want to acknowledge some facts and let you all know why I invited Louis Fournet. He is co-owner of Cuvier Shipping and for that reason I requested his presence here today." He paused, looking at each of them. "I must clarify my position in this difficult situation. If I had known of Jean entering into any legal act of marriage with more than one woman, I would have advised against such an unlawful arrangement. I knew nothing of your supposed marriages."

Nicole felt a sinking sensation in the pit of her stomach. Jean had lied even to his lawyer.

Drew glanced down at the will he held in his hands, holding them all in suspense. "According to Louisiana law the only legal marriage the State recognizes is the first one to Marian Cuvier. I'm sorry to say, Nicole, that your marriage and Layla's are not binding and therefore, unless he names you specifically in the will, you will receive nothing."

Nicole gazed at Drew, her eyes widening. Somehow part of her had been holding on to hope that she would at least be entitled to part of Jean's estate.

"If you had been his mistress and he'd named you in the will, then you would inherit. But as an illegal spouse, you receive nothing unless you're named in the will."

He cleared his throat and turned to Layla. "Jean wrote this will four years ago." He paused and gazed sympathetically at the young woman. "I'm sorry, but the will was written before your marriage."

A gasp came from Layla as she opened her mouth, the words seeming to hang suspended before she finally managed to speak. "I have nothing?" she asked, perplexed. "What will I do? Where will I go?"

She stood, her eyes glazing over. "You don't understand! Jean bankrupted my father's business. My father made him marry me just so I would be taken care of. Our shipping company had been the family business for over three generations before it was taken over by Cuvier Shipping. I have no means of support I have nothing!"

Drew swallowed and shook his head. "I'm sorry, Layla. Legally, everything belongs to Jean's estate including the house and the business."

The girl swallowed and glanced around the room, her eyes wide with disbelief. "I have to leave my home?"

"Yes, it's in Jean's name."

Layla's eyes pooled with tears as she tried to absorb this startling revelation. Nicole felt so sorry for her, yet her own body grew cold with this information. Jean had bought the plantation for her. Could they take away the home she'd wanted for years?

"How long before I have to get out of the house?" Layla asked, visibly trembling.

"Jean appointed me executor of his will. I'll give you thirty days to find another residence. Is that all right, Marian?" the lawyer asked, his green eyes dark with worry.

"Yes, please give her all the time she needs to find another place to live," Marian said sympathetically.

"Thank you." Layla stood, her face completely ashen. "I have to leave...I can't stay...I have to think about what

I'm going to do. I must get out of here."

Flinging open the door to Drew's office, she ran out into the entryway. A sob echoed in the hall as she fumbled with the lock and then yanked open the outside portal and disappeared as the door slammed.

"Someone should go after her," Marian said, her voice sounding stilted. "We can't just let her go like that!"

Drew stood up and walked to the door. He yelled a young man's name. The clerk came from the back of the building.

"Eric, go after that young woman and make sure she makes it back to the hotel safely."

"Yes, sir."

The lawyer shut his office door again, and returned to the chair behind his desk.

"This is dreadful," Marian said, and Nicole couldn't help but agree with her.

She couldn't stand it any longer.

"What about me?" Nicole asked. "The plantation is in my name," she said. Her voice broke and a sob escaped. She couldn't lose the house.

"If it's in your name, then your home is your own," Drew said, taking a deep breath. "Let's finish this."

Nicole felt a small sense of relief. At least she wouldn't lose Rosewood.

Drew proceeded to read Jean's last will and testament; Nicole sat waiting expectantly for the moment of revelation, when Jean would leave her some of his wealth. The moment when they found out they were wealthy widows.

After several minutes Drew paused and looked at Louis. "'Regarding Cuvier Shipping...I entrust the running of the business to my partner Louis Fournet until my son Philip Cuvier reaches the age of understanding. My son's guardian, his mother Marian Cuvier, will vote or act in my son's best interest until he reaches the age of eighteen.'"

Drew finished reading the will and laid it down on the desk. He'd not mentioned her name. A buzzing noise like hundreds of small bees started up in her brain. This couldn't be happening. How could she support Jean's child if he didn't leave her a small amount of money?

"That's it?" Nicole asked. "He left me nothing?"

"I'm sorry, Nicole," Drew said.

The buzzing noise increased. She was broke except for the money for the house expenses Jean had given her this past month.

"But...but I was married to him. I loved him. We were—" She jumped up, and like a lamp being turned down, the world around her receded into darkness. She crumpled to the floor in a dead faint

Several minutes later Nicole could hear voices around her, but she couldn't see them or understand what they were saying. All she could think about was that the baby would be fatherless, penniless, and illegitimate. Just like herself. God, she'd promised never to do this to her child and now history was repeating itself.

"Get some smelling salts!"

Nicole moaned. "No ammonia. I'm all right. Just give me a moment to clear my head. I must have stood too quickly."

She moved, trying to sit up, but Louis touched her shoulder. "Lie back and give yourself a few more minutes."

She gazed up at Marian, seeing the concern on Jean's wife's face. "He left me nothing? I didn't dream that part, did I?"

Marian looked away and swallowed. "No, he didn't"

Finally Nicole rose and dusted off her skirt. She felt shaken and defeated as she glanced around the room and sighed. "I'm going back to the hotel. I can't believe he did this to me. That bastard left me nothing."

"I'm sorry," Marian whispered.

For a brief moment, Nicole felt like Marian did understand. After all, he'd been her husband for many more years than he'd been Nicole's. She not only had to face the humiliation of Jean's scandal, her two children needed her protection. Two children who at least carried Jean's name, unlike Nicole's own unborn, fatherless child.

Nicole gazed at Marian, feeling the need to get as far away from this scandal as she could. "Mrs. Cuvier, this must be extremely difficult for you."

Marian nodded. "No more than it's been for you." The corners of Nicole's mouth turned up in a smile, though she knew the feeling didn't reach her saddened heart. "I must be going. Good-bye."

She walked out of Drew's office, her head held high, her back straight and her heart numb. Jean had left her with nothing but a plantation she couldn't afford to run and a baby growing in her womb.

~

Nicole lay on the bed in her friend's town house and tried to rest, knowing she needed to be careful not to overtire herself. A severe case of bleeding the day after the reading of Jean's will had kept her in New Orleans, close to the doctors. She wanted this baby so badly.

A friend had offered Nicole the use of her town house while she was away, along with her servants. They had kept Nicole very comfortable, but she longed for Rosewood and worried about the growing sugarcane crop. Her future and her baby's lay in the success of those fields of green.

For six weeks she had lain in this bed, worrying whether her baby would live or die, worrying about how to protect him from the cruel blow that fate had dealt them both.

All her life the vicious label of illegitimacy had

stigmatized her. Her father had never married her mother. He'd never seen Nicole, and he'd never even given any support to her mother. They had lived off a seamstress' earnings and her grandparents' generosity until the day her mother died.

Poor Ava's little girl. Her father never loved her, never wanted her enough to marry her mother. Nicole had sworn her children would never have to deal with the ugly issue of not being wanted by their father or the terrible stigma of illegitimacy. Yet here she was, expecting a child and unmarried. She laid her head back on her pillow. It wasn't fair to her child. It wasn't fair to her, though she'd done everything the proper way. She'd waited until she was married to have relations with a man, yet her unscrupulous husband had betrayed her and now she felt cursed as history repeated itself.

*What would she tell her child? Sorry, your mother did the best she could, but you're still illegitimate?*

No! She couldn't let her child face the ridicule, the pointed looks, the ugly whispers she herself had endured her whole life. No one knew of her pregnancy. All they knew was that her marriage to Jean was not legal.

Surely there was something she could do to save her child from disgrace. Surely she could find a way to keep him from being born a bastard.

Though as much as she loathed the subject after Jean, she needed a husband. She needed to remarry quickly. But who? Who would marry a woman whose belly was already swelling with another man's child?

And after her marriage to Jean, she never wanted to let anyone get that close to her again. She never wanted to trust someone and give them her heart only to have them shatter her hopes and dreams again. No, this time when she married, it would be only for their name and there would be no hearts involved. No dreams of ever after. This time she only wanted their name, and then they were free to go wherever they chose, just as long as they left her and the child alone.

Sure there would be talk and speculation, but that would die in years to come, while the stigma of being illegitimate would follow a child throughout its life. This way, her son or daughter would not have that blemish on their innocent head. She would make sure that they were free from Jean's deception.

Where could she find a man who would marry her and give her child a name, then quietly disappear, never to be seen or heard from again? All she needed was his name.

Ridiculous. What man would say yes to such an agreement?

Nicole swung her feet to the side of the bed and sat up. She rose and walked to the closet where her clothes hung and pulled out one of the black mourning dresses she'd worn since Jean's death. The color made her appear even paler. She gazed at the dress and then tossed it onto the bed.

Today she was going home to Rosewood. The doctor had released her for the trip and she could hardly wait to leave behind this city and all the memories it now held. She pulled another black dress out of the closet and her gaze fell upon the gold band that encircled the finger on her left hand.

With a heavy sigh, she sank back down to the bed. With the fingers of her right hand she touched the smooth band of gold, the memory of the small ceremony where Jean had placed the ring on her finger coming back with a painful twist. She could see him smiling and leaning down to kiss her, just like it was yesterday.

With a cry, she yanked the ring off her finger. "No more," she said aloud. Her hand rubbed the hard mound of her abdomen. "I promise you, I'm going to find you a father. I promise you, we will be all right just the two of us."

She tossed the ring into her open trunk and reached into her closet for a pale yellow dress that reminded her of sunshine. From this day forward, she was no longer in mourning, and look out, because she was actively hunting for a man to marry her and give her child his name.

# Chapter Two

**M**axim Viel tried to blend in with the people on the streets of Plaquemine, Louisiana, as he watched the blonde woman he'd followed into town. Dressed in a blue shirtwaist, Nicole Rousseau Cuvier appeared a soft, gentle woman, though he knew she had a stubborn streak. After numerous attempts by his firm of lawyers to purchase Rosewood Plantation, he'd decided to try the personal approach.

For the last week, he'd followed Nicole wherever she went, in an effort to determine her strengths and weaknesses and use them to his advantage to acquire Rosewood.

The information he gathered on Nicole Rosseau— or whatever name she chose to go by these days, since the death of her supposed husband—would determine how to proceed with the offer for the plantation that belonged in his family. How the second widow of Jean Cuvier had obtained the plantation he didn't know.

The front page of every newspaper in Louisiana had carried the story of "The Cuvier Widows." How a man could sustain three separate households both emotionally and financially, with three different women, was beyond Max. And when the papers revealed the illegal wives would inherit nothing from their bigamist marriages, Max felt certain that Nicole Rosseau would want to sell the plantation he was determined to own, just to escape the gossips in the bayou country.

Yet every offer his lawyers presented had been rejected. Now two months after the death of Jean Cuvier, Max arrived in Plaquemine to present his latest bid in person. He'd come once before with his father only to learn she'd not returned from New Orleans. Rosewood was his destiny and he could now afford to take back the land his family once owned.

He watched as the fair-haired woman descended from the carriage she had driven into town. The fact that she was alone surprised him.

The morning sun shimmered off of the dirt road, beating down with intensity this early in the day. Max pulled a handkerchief from his pocket and wiped the sweat from his brow. Though he stood beneath an oak tree, the sweltering humidity could make even the desert sweat.

"Good morning, Mrs. Ashland," he heard Nicole call to a woman hurrying along the walkway.

Max watched Nicole in sympathy as the woman turned her face away, refusing to acknowledge her. The good women of Plaquemine would want nothing to do with a woman who had lived in sin with a man for four years, even though she believed in her vows of matrimony. Nicole Rosseau Cuvier was soiled goods, much too tainted to acknowledge or greet.

Nicole lifted her chin and hurried into the mercantile as Max crossed the street and followed her inside. He stepped into the store and went to the next aisle, where he pretended to be looking at some canned goods as he watched her comparing bolts of fabric.

Three women dressed in the latest fashion stood at the front of the store in a small gossipy cluster, whispering and staring at Nicole. Their voices grew louder, every word suddenly becoming clear.

"The paper said the law only recognized the first wife's marriage. The woman accused of killing him and our own Mrs. Cuvier, their marriages didn't count. Can you imagine finding out your husband already has a wife?"

The women giggled a nervous little twitter, though the woman's words were anything but funny. "And she thought she was so high and mighty, moving into that big house on the river. Why, she's no more than a common whore, living in sin with that man. I bet she knew they weren't really married."

For this very reason, he hoped the widow would be ready to sell Rosewood. He could offer her a chance to start fresh in a new town away from the scandal of her marriage.

Max watched as Nicole seemed to sway on her feet for a moment and then he saw her turn and walk toward the door, her steps in a halting, hesitating manner, her head held high. Her blue eyes were clouded, her expression was glazed, and her face had paled to a translucent shade of white.

Quickly he followed her out the door, and just as she reached the humid outside air, her legs began to crumple. He ran and caught her, just before she hit the ground. His left arm cradled her against him as his right hand grabbed her jaw. Gently he shook her.

"Come on, don't faint on me," he said, peering down at her creamy complexion set in a heart-shaped face. Up close her long dark eyelashes lay against pallid skin and he couldn't help but think she was a beauty.

Her lashes fluttered and then opened. She stiffened in his arms. "Oh, my. I felt so dizzy. Did I faint?"

"You started to, but I caught you." He held her in his arms for a few moments, letting her orient herself. Slowly he stood her up. "Here, let me help you into your buggy, where you can sit and relax for a moment" He lent her a hand up, as she gently sat on the cushioned seat in the shade.

"Thank you. I knew I shouldn't have come into town alone today, but I wanted so badly to get a few items at the store." She looked sadly back at the mercantile. "I should have known better."

"Is there something I can go in and purchase for you?" he asked.

Her soft cherry lips turned up in a smile, lighting up her gentle face, which suddenly brightened giving her more color. Stunned, he stared, her beauty taking him completely off guard.

"That's kind of you to offer. I'll just send a servant later to purchase what I need," she said. Her eyes held a hint of sadness and he realized she probably grieved, though she wore no mourning clothes, which surprised him. Maybe she *didn't* mourn the husband who had deceived her.

She swayed in the seat for a moment and he reached out to steady her.

"Put your head down and lean over if you feel dizzy. It will help," he said, watching her closely.

"I'm fine. I just feel dizzy occasionally."

"How far is it to your home?" he asked innocently, knowing the drive would take at least thirty minutes by buggy.

"It's not too far," she said. "I live out on the River Road. I can make it"

"I think I better drive you," he said, thinking this would be a great opportunity to win her trust before he asked her to consider his offer for Rosewood. "It's very humid today; you might have another spell and then you'd run the buggy off the road. You could be hurt."

The pale skin of her forehead drew together in a frown. She seemed so petite, so fragile, yet he sensed fierceness within her, a stubbornness that he needed to avoid colliding with at all cost.

"You seem very nice, but I don't know you," she said, gazing at him. "I hardly need more gossip circulating about me riding off with a drifter."

So the old clothes he'd worn to help him blend into the countryside led her to believe he was a drifter. Max held out his hand and enclosed her small gloved fingers in his palm. "Let me introduce myself. I'm Maxim Viel."

He released her gloved hand, his conscience reminding him of her comment, though he refused to correct her. He'd told her the truth regarding his name, but he would let slide her comment about him being a drifter. He wasn't ready to tell her he was the buyer whose lawyers kept sending her proposals to purchase her property. A drifter would be a nice cover until the negotiations began in earnest.

"I'm Nicole Rosseau Cuv—" She hesitated, unable to finish. "Please call me Miss Rosseau."

"Miss Rosseau, I don't think you need to be driving. Do you mind if I drive you home?" he asked. "I intended to head out in that direction and check out a small church that needed a carpenter. I would be willing to take you to your place."

She hesitated and then looked back at the mercantile where the ladies were still inside. "I thank you for your kindness, but I can't let you do that."

He shrugged. "I just wanted to make sure you were all right."

She leaned over to grab the reins and he watched as she swayed in the seat.

Max seized her by the arm, keeping her from falling. "Steady. Is there someone else who could drive you home?"

Her face was once again a pasty shade of white. "I'll be all right, I think." She paused for a moment and looked back at the mercantile, then leaned over and dropped her head low. "I should never have come without my servant."

He nodded in understanding, but couldn't help thinking how lucky for him that she was alone. "Could I get you a drink of water or anything?"

Slowly she rose up, took a deep breath, and relaxed. "A glass of water would be lovely."

For some reason, she reminded Max of a gentle flower drooping in the heat and he had the insistent urge to take care of her. Though he had to admit that his offer to take her home wasn't completely honorable. If she agreed, the time they spent in her buggy would help him assess how to convince her to sell Rosewood to him.

Max hurried into the mercantile where a bucket of well water sat nearby and poured her a small cupful. He carried it back to her. "Here, this should make you feel a little better in this heat."

She put the cup between her lips and drank until her thirst was quenched. With the tip of her tongue she swiped the last drop from her wet lips. That small gesture and the look of gratitude she bestowed upon him gave him pause as he forgot to draw in a breath.

"Thank you. I do feel a little better, I believe," she said.

He reached up to take the cup, and as his hand brushed against her fingers, he wondered at how small and fragile she appeared. He took the tin cup in to the storekeeper and when he returned the heat seemed to have wilted her even more.

"If you don't mind, I think I will take you up on your offer to see me home," Nicole said. "This heat is draining me completely. I don't know if I could make it home safely."

"It's my pleasure," he said, thanking his good fortune.

After tying his horse to the back of the buggy, he climbed up beside her, wondering how to gain her trust before he told her of his intentions.

She smiled at him. "Are you sure you don't mind? I'd ask someone else, but, well...there's no one."

"I don't mind at all," he said, storing away the bit of information she'd just bestowed.

He clicked to the horses and the wagon lurched. She grabbed onto the side as they started down the road and he glanced at her, noting the dark circles beneath her eyes. "You have to be careful not to overexert yourself when the humidity is this high. In the hottest part of the summer the heat can suck the life right out of you."

Nicole nodded her head, but did not respond.

"So where are we going?" he asked.

"Rosewood Plantation," she said as he turned the wagon onto the road that ran beside the Mississippi River.

The wide river meandered through the trees, occasionally making splashing and gurgling noises. A steamer chugged up the river, its big paddle slicing through the water.

"I've heard of that place. The home was built by a family of pirates, they say."

She laughed. "That's the story, but it wasn't my family who built it. My hus ..." She paused. "I've only lived there in the last four years."

"It's rumored there are secret passageways," he said, knowing that it wasn't true, but wanting to test her knowledge of the place.

"I doubt it. I suppose there could be and I just don't know about them. A few of my neighbors have told me several things about the house. And then a few of the old slaves are still around, but they don't talk much about the previous owners."

"You say you've only lived there four years?"

"Yes," she said. "As a little girl I dreamed of owning one of the big homes along the river. So before I married, my husband bought the home for me and gave it to me as a wedding gift."

"I would think that's a gift you both could enjoy." She shook her head. "No, his office was in New Orleans and he was gone a great deal of the time."

"You say 'was' as if your husband is in the past tense," he said, knowing the truth, but wanting to hear her response.

She sighed. "Yes, he's dead now."

"I'm sorry," Max said, and turned his attention back to the road. They drove along in silence, the cicadas singing their lonesome song as they called to one another in the hot breeze.

She turned and gave him a long assessing look. "I don't know why I've been telling you all this, except for the fact that you've been kind to me. In fact, I think you're the first person to tell me you're sorry for my loss." She gave a queer little laugh. "And you're a stranger."

For a moment he felt uneasy as he saw her eyes tear up, but he didn't say anything. She took a deep breath and gained control. "See these green fields? That's our second sugarcane crop. We were so excited about this crop. It would determine whether the plantation would be profitable or not and now he's not here to see it through with me."

Max gazed at the sugarcane and couldn't help but have mixed feelings about the green stalks. The success of Rosewood would be talked about for years, but her financial success would make her less likely to sell. And he wanted her to sell him the land.

"You know, I have this belief that those we love who have gone before us, watch over us. I bet he knows how that field is doing."

Nicole started to laugh. "Mr. Viel, I'm sorry, I'm not laughing at your belief. I'm laughing because if my husband can see from hell, he wouldn't be worried about how well the crop is doing. There are other matters he left unfinished that certainly should take more of his attention."

Max didn't know how to respond, so he said nothing. He couldn't blame her for being bitter. His lawyers had informed him on all the ugly details of how Jean Cuvier had married Nicole Rosseau and the way he had lied to and cheated on each one of the Cuvier Widows.

"Sad as it may sound, since his death the success of this

plantation is the most important thing in my life. If I lose Rosewood, then I've lost everything I ever dreamed of." She paused and gazed at him quizzically. "I've told you more than I have anyone in the last few months. You're a stranger and here I sit telling you personal details."

Max felt a sinking sensation in the pit of his stomach. How could he convince her to sell to him if the plantation was her life, her dream? She could take his money and find herself another dream. Another plantation. But he doubted she would see it that way.

He gave her a reassuring glance. "I'm a good listener. And sometimes you can tell strangers things that you'd never tell someone you care about."

She nodded her head. "True, but you don't want to hear my problems."

They rode along in silence for a few moments before he turned to her. "Do you have children?"

"Not yet," she said. "I hope to someday."

"But you're a widow. You'll have to remarry," he said. She looked at him, her brows raised, her blue eyes gazing at him curiously. "Yes, I will."

The thought crossed his mind that maybe he should consider courting the lovely Miss Rosseau.

"See those big oak trees? The house sits back among them. The original owner planted those trees and they shade the house nicely during the summer. The lane that leads to the house is coming up."

"It must be nice to look out your window and see the river in the distance," he said, already knowing everything that she'd told him, since he'd passed the house several times in his youth and had even followed her into town this morning, keeping a discreet distance back.

"I enjoy it very much," she said.

He turned the buggy down the lane.

"You know, Mr. Viel, I've talked about myself, but

you've hardly told me anything about yourself. Do you have a wife and children?"

"No, ma'am. I'm not married. I guess I just haven't found the right woman or the right place to settle down," he lied. The home he wanted to settle in loomed in front him, massive oak trees shading the porch that surrounded the Creole mansion. The soil he wanted to cling to his hands stretched out before him. She owned what he wanted most, and he was determined to somehow wrest it from her.

He'd worked toward this goal since he was a boy and now it appeared before him, just out of his grasp. "Your home is unusual," he said.

"Rosewood was built by a Creole family. The house is divided by a main parlor. The downriver side is considered to be the male side of the house and the upriver side is the female side, with the main parlor in between. Each side has its own entryway that leads through the respective bedrooms."

"How interesting," he said, though his grandfather had told him about the house many times.

Max pulled the buggy to a halt in front of the house he longed to go inside and see, but knew he couldn't. He glanced at the home, the sound of clanking bottles tinkling in the air, though hardly a breeze blew. "What is that noise?"

"That's the spirit bottles hanging in the oak trees. The servants believe that the noise made by the water- filled bottles keeps the evil spirits away," she said, watching him.

"Oh." He glanced at the bottles hung by their handles from the tree, all filled with different levels of water. He turned to face the woman sitting beside him. "Well, we're here. Are you feeling any better?"

"I feel much better now. Though I do think I'll go in and rest for a spell," she said, gazing at him, her sapphire eyes appreciative. "Thank you."

"You're quite welcome," he said, climbing down from the buggy and coming around to help her alight "I think I will go find that church that needed a carpenter and then return to town."

He lifted her from the buggy and set her gently on the ground. A wisp of white material with the letter N embroidered upon the cotton lay on the buggy seat. Quickly he scooped up the frilly material and shoved it in his pants pocket when she wasn't looking. It was her handkerchief and somehow he couldn't help but think it might be useful later.

"Have a safe trip, Mr. Viel," she said, and he watched her walk toward the curving stairs that led to the living quarters on the second floor.

A more beautiful woman he'd never met, and he couldn't help but wonder if she would sell him Rosewood. She mentioned the plantation being the most important thing in her life, and suddenly he had doubts she would ever sell.

A servant came around to take the horse and buggy and Max untied his own horse from the back. He climbed on his horse and then watched as she walked up the stairs and entered the house that had belonged to his family for generations before the war. He wanted the plantation back, yet the woman who lived there now seemed to belong with the house and its mysteries. Like the house, she seemed unusual, and he liked unique women.

~

Nicole watched the handsome, dark-haired man ride away from inside the safety of her home. His emerald eyes had shone with kindness and he'd been gentle as he helped her. She tried to remember the last time someone seemed concerned or even cared about her since Jean's death and the only other person had been Marian Cuvier, before

Nicole left New Orleans.

Nicole had lost her mother to pneumonia when she was ten years old and her father... all she knew about her father was that he'd been a wealthy man who never married her mother and never once offered them any support. Nicole grew up always referred to as Ava's daughter, the silent words of poor little, unwanted child somehow attached to her societal tag of illegitimacy.

Now, her own child would face that same fate, through no fault of her own. Always aware of what could happen when a woman lay with a man outside of marriage, she'd never given in to temptation and waited until her wedding day, only to find out her vows of devotion were a farce.

With Jean's death and his deception, Nicole found herself just like her mother, unwed, pregnant, and alone. And her child would suffer the same fate as "Ava's daughter." The cruelty of the past repeating itself wasn't fair, but she meant to change the course of history. She would take action to keep her child from being illegitimate.

She needed a husband. She needed someone to give her child a name, though she no longer wanted any part of marriage and wedding vows. If only she could find someone to marry her so her child would be accepted and not carry the tag of illegitimacy all his life.

But who would wed one of "the Cuvier Widows"? Who did she know that would stand up beside her and give her baby his name? She ran down the list of possibilities, realizing that since the move to the small community of Plaquemine, she knew very few people. No one well enough to ask to marry.

She sighed and stepped away from the window. Still, the idea was worth considering, though the problem would be finding the right man.

The image of Max Viel came again to mind, a drifter with no ties, and no connections to keep him in this area.

Would he consider marriage with someone for a short time, and then be free to continue with his travels? Nicole worried her bottom lip. He seemed kind and caring. Would he give her child his name?

Six months of being man and wife was all she needed. Just until her child was born and then they were free to go their separate ways.

Maybe sometime in the next few days she would go into town once again and see if she could find the handsome drifter. If he were still in town, then maybe she could summon the courage to ask him to marry her.

~

Three days later, riding his horse down the River Road, Max took Nicole's handkerchief out of his pocket and put it close to his nose. The lingering scent of roses filled his senses and the image of Nicole Rosseau came to mind. Slowly he returned the scrap of material to his pocket. The last few days she had never been far from his mind. After her confession of how much the plantation meant to her, he wondered how he could obtain the River Road home from the beautiful widow.

The thought of somehow taking the land from her left him feeling uncomfortable. Yet his family depended on him, and since the time he was a small boy they had made it clear that this was his duty in life, to restore the family fortune and home. So far he'd accomplished the fortune, but the family home was turning out to be much more complicated.

Today, as he turned his horse down the lane to Rosewood, he was bringing her handkerchief back and checking to see how Miss Rosseau felt.

He also intended to make her an offer on the plantation, though somehow he felt certain she would turn him down. Yet in the last few days, Max had learned from his firm of lawyers that if Miss Rosseau did not have a successful sugarcane crop that fall, she would be forced to sell the home she loved. Since her husband's death less than two months ago, the cash had ceased to flow into the bank and the widow had no obvious means of support.

Maybe she would consider his offer, though the thought of her moving away left him oddly sad.

Max's horse trotted up to the front of the house and he swung his leg over the side and dropped to the ground. He tied the animal out front and then ascended the stairs that led to the men's side of the house. The windows were open and the doors stood wide, drawing in the cooling breeze from the river.

The sound of the spirit bottles clanked in the breeze, melodic and somehow soothing.

His great-great-grandfather had built the house in the traditional Creole style, with one half the men's quarters and the other half the women's. Max felt nervous as he knocked on the door of the men's side.

A servant answered the door and gave him an odd look.

"Yes?" the black woman asked.

"I'm here to see Miss Rosseau," Max answered.

"Follow me," she said. She led Max through a man's bedroom into a parlor that ran between the two sides of the house, where she left him. The room was a centrally located gathering place that held a sofa, two chairs, and a bookcase along one wall, with ceiling to floor windows along the front. Sheer drapes fell gracefully to the floor and were tied back to allow the breeze to blow through the open windows.

His first trip inside the house and he couldn't see enough of where his ancestors had lived. Awe filled him to think of his family residing here.

Nicole strolled into the room, her blonde hair pulled back and up off her neck. The blue material of her dress flowed from her hips, the color accentuating her eyes and making them sparkle. She came into the room, a look of surprise on her heart-shaped face when she saw him.

"Mr. Viel, what a pleasure to see you," she said. Two small dimples appeared in her cheeks when she smiled.

"How are you feeling?" he asked. "Any more dizzy spells?"

"No, I think the heat must have affected me that day. But I haven't gone back into town alone either."

She motioned for him to sit, and he took a seat on her couch, his hat in his hand as he gazed about the room.

"You've got a real nice place here," he said.

"Thank you. I love sitting out on the verandah and watching the boats go up and down the river. I often wonder where they're headed. In the evening, that's my favorite pastime."

Just the thought of being under the stars and listening to the sounds that came from the river sent his mind places with this woman that he needed not to go.

He reached in his pocket. "By the way, after you went in the other day, I found this handkerchief lying on the seat of the buggy and picked it up. I wondered if it belonged to you."

As soon as she appeared more relaxed in his company, he would spring the idea of buying the plantation on her. But first he needed her to feel comfortable and trust him. At the moment she seemed nervous, and he didn't know why.

She took the piece of material from him and glanced at it. "Yes, this is mine. Thank you for returning it."

With her hand she absently smoothed the wrinkles in the cloth, her eyes refusing to meet his gaze. He sensed she wanted to say something, but was having trouble with the words.

"Mr. Viel, I'm glad you stopped by today. I need to talk

to you about a delicate matter," she said, finally raising her sapphire eyes to gaze at him. She stood and began to pace the family parlor. "Have you heard of 'the Cuvier Widows'?"

Why would she want to discuss her dead husband's other wives with him?

"Aren't they the three women that were all married to the same man?"

"Yes, Mr. Viel." She turned and faced him, the curtains billowing behind her. "I'm one of those widows. My husband was Jean Cuvier."

While he already knew this information, he tried to appear stunned. He waited a moment before he responded. "Well, that certainly explains why you seemed angry at your deceased husband."

"Yes. But there's a bigger complication. One that affects more than just me," she said, her gaze meeting and holding his. "I'm expecting a child. A child that through no fault of its own will be considered illegitimate."

"I'm sorry," he said, unable to keep his eyes from going to her waistline.

"I need a husband, Mr. Viel. I need someone who will give their name to my child and be here through the birth. Then you could leave and either seek a divorce, or just never come around again." She paused, watching him as he sat on her couch, realizing suddenly that she *wanted* to marry him. "Since you're an unmarried drifter with no ties to this area, I wondered if you would consider marrying me and giving my child your name."

Max sat there, stunned. She was with child. This was a complication he hadn't anticipated. He sat there staring at her, staggered at her news. She was so desperate that she'd marry a stranger? It took him several minutes to recover and when he glanced at her, her face was ashen.

"Are you all right?" he asked, feeling concern for

Nicole. His mind raced with this new knowledge. "You're looking pale again. At least now I understand why you were so dizzy."

Nicole sighed and sank down into the chair. "I never thought that I would be asking a man to marry me. I never thought I would need to find another husband. I never meant to burden a child with the stigma of being illegitimate."

He couldn't help but gaze at her and wonder how a man could deceive her so cruelly. And now she was expecting a baby.

"I know this sounds crazy, but I don't want my child to be born without a last name. I don't have a lot of money, but I have a sugarcane crop in the field that is doing very well and should bring me quite a bit of cash. What if I promise you half the money from the crop if you will marry me and share your last name with my child?"

He sat there feeling astounded at what she was proposing, realizing how truly desperate she was to protect her child.

"What about after the baby is born? What do we do then?"

She shrugged. "I don't know. I'll give you half the crop for your last name for my child. After the baby is born, you're free to leave, go wherever you want to go, as long as you don't expect me to give you the plantation."

For a moment he considered being honest with her and telling her he wanted the plantation. Though if he were truthful he risked her not marrying him and losing his chance completely. Then she could possibly find someone else and complicate things even further. But later, when she learned the truth, how would she accept his deception if he married her now on her terms?

He looked up at her and stared into the velvety blue of her eyes. She certainly was a stunning woman, but did he want to spend the rest of his life with her? Yet he was duty bound to obtain the plantation back for his family.

Quickly he made up his mind, determined this was the quickest way to get his hands on Rosewood. He would have to somehow convince his new wife their marriage should be permanent during the months before the babe was born.

"I'll marry you and give your baby a name. Just name the day and the time, I'll be there," he said, uncertain if what he'd just agreed to was wrong or if it was right. Only certain that he would now have Rosewood.

# Chapter Three

**N**icole spent a restless night thinking of her impending marriage to Maxim Viel. She'd met the man twice and was taking a huge risk by marrying him. What if he saw this as an opportunity to move from being a drifter to a planter? Sleep had been elusive as she'd thought of ways to try to protect her child and the plantation she loved. Finally, early that morning, she'd reached a decision. Now if only Consuelo would help her, she thought she'd found a way to safeguard both her child and the plantation.

After breakfast, she searched and found her trusted servant and friend, Consuelo Salvador, in the dining room, her gray head bent checking the silver, making sure that the servants had cleaned it correctly.

"I do declare, no one knows how to clean silver properly anymore," Consuelo said, rubbing a rag over the intricate carvings in the handle of the spoon she held. She looked up at Nicole, her dark eyes suddenly narrowing. "You feeling all right? You look a trifle peaked."

"I'm fine. I just need to talk with you." Nicole stepped into the room and shut the door behind her. She walked around the long walnut table, running her hand along the linen tablecloth. "How long have we been together, Consuelo?"

"Going on fifteen years. You were ten years old and had just lost your momma when your grandfather hired me. Seems like yesterday." She rubbed another spot on the silver and glanced at Nicole, studying her. "You know all that. So why are you asking me?"

"We're both without family and you've pretty much taken the place of my kin since my mother and grandparents died," Nicole said, staring at the older Spanish woman, noticing for the first time that her hair was more gray than dark now.

"I guess so," Consuelo said, peering at her intently.

"You know everything about me, including my background."

"Yes," Consuelo said as she laid the silverware down, along with the polishing rag. She tilted her head to the side. "What are you leading up to? I know you've been troubled since you returned from New Orleans. Why are you asking me all these questions?"

"I'm getting there, just let me finish." Nicole held up her hand and took a deep breath, needing to show the older woman how she'd arrived at her decision. Knowing she wouldn't like any part of what Nicole had decided.

"You and I both know how it feels when everyone in town knows you're illegitimate. My mother was the local schoolteacher until the school board fired her because she was pregnant and unmarried. I don't want my child to grow up being laughed at because his father tricked his mother."

Consuelo reached out and laid her hand on Nicole's arm. "Honey, neither one of us were accepted because of our illegitimacy, but I think we're stronger women because of our birth. Your child will learn to accept his heritage, just as we have."

Nicole shook her head. "If you accepted your birth, why did you never marry?"

The older woman picked up the polishing rag and began to clean again, rubbing the silverware until Nicole feared the silver would come off. "That's an unfair question that you know the answer to. But it was different for you. You thought you were married, and you've wanted this baby for so long. Don't tell me you're considering giving it up?"

"No. I could never give my baby up, but I can make sure my son or daughter has a last name."

"How are you going to do that?" Consuelo asked,

gazing at her like she'd lost her mind.

Nicole smiled. "I've found someone to marry me."

Consuelo shook her head. "Oh, no. I don't think I like this. Who is this man who wants to marry you? Where did you meet him?"

"He brought me home from town the other day," Nicole said, knowing the older woman would need a few minutes to accept her reasoning.

"What? You told me he was a drifter. I warned you about letting men you don't know bring you home, and now you're going to marry him?" She paused, dropping the silverware back into the drawer with a clang. "I think you've gotten the fever and I need to send for the doctor."

"Consuelo, he's a nice man. He's agreed to marry me and give my child his name. Our marriage will be in name only, and after the birth of the child, he's free to disappear."

"What about the child? This drifter is willing to give the baby his name, but what if he decides to stay? Everyone will think it's his baby."

"No, he knows this marriage is not permanent," Nicole replied, wanting people to think that the baby was Max's.

"Are you certain you can trust him to keep his word?"

Nicole thought of Max and remembered the green of his eyes and the way he'd taken care of her that day. Her instincts told her he was trustworthy—yet she'd been wrong before.

"I have no choice but to trust him to keep his word. I'm giving him half the crop as payment, so I would hope that would keep him honest."

"Sounds like you've decided this is what you're going to do. So why do you need my help to carry out this foolhardy plan? Why can't you leave things as they are?" she asked, picking up a new piece of silver.

"I want to sign the plantation and all the land over to you as a precaution."

Consuelo's eyes widened and she stared at Nicole, her dark eyes intense. The spoon she'd been holding slipped from her hands and she didn't even glance down at it. "You have gone loco. Since Jean died you've not been yourself and I need to send someone for the doctor."

"No, Consuelo. I'm fine. Don't you see the beauty of this idea? My baby will have a last name, but my new husband will not be able to take my land away from me. It's just a precaution. Just in case ..."

"What am I supposed to do with Rosewood?"

"You're going to hold on to it until the baby is old enough to take it over or Max is permanently out of our lives."

"This is crazy."

"No, it's a safeguard to keep me from having the land go to my new husband. This way I know the baby will inherit"

"I don't know, Nicole." Consuelo stared at Nicole, shaking her head slightly. "Yet it would solve the problem of the baby being illegitimate. It seems so drastic. Are you certain of this?"

"Yes, I am. But not unless you agree to help me. I'm not willing to risk the plantation my child will someday inherit, with a man I hardly know."

Consuelo frowned. "You know I love you and would do anything I could to help you and the babe. You're like a daughter to me."

"You're the only person I would give Rosewood to, Consuelo. I know that you will hold on to it, until I want it back."

Consuelo hugged Nicole. "Thank you. I'll do this to help you, though I'm worried about this man you're marrying. It's so sudden. You hardly know him." Nicole returned the older woman's hug.

"I know, but I can't wait. People will already be

questioning who the father of my baby is. But this way, my baby will have a name, and someday Rosewood, too. We'll go into town tomorrow and take care of the paperwork."

~

Max pulled the buggy he'd rented to a halt in front of the Creole mansion. Today was his wedding day and though he'd often wondered whom he would marry, he'd never considered the ceremony would be before a justice of the peace. Where didn't matter, however, only that this marriage would certainly guarantee his right to Rosewood Plantation and fulfill his family obligation.

The memory of his grandfather recounting to him the numerous tales of Rosewood were as fresh today as his first recollection somewhere around the age of four. At the end of each story, his grandfather would remind him by saying, "It's up to you, boy, to get our home back."

Even as his grandfather lay dying, he'd reminded his grandson of his obligation. "Get the family home back, boy. I lost it. You reclaim Rosewood." And so today he made the final sacrifice to obtain the land, thus fulfilling his obligation.

It wasn't as if he minded what he perceived to be his duty for his kin. He wanted the family home back just as much as the rest of them, but marrying a woman who had no clue of his intentions troubled him. There would be no divorce, no separation after they were joined as man and wife. He intended to somehow convince Nicole that their union would become permanent and everlasting.

Yet their life together would begin based on lies, and that disturbed him more than he cared to admit—not to mention the fact she thought this a temporary arrangement. He'd been attracted to her from the very beginning, so consummating the union wouldn't be an issue, but she thought him a drifter, a man without wealth or direction, and he'd let her believe her misconceptions. Once she realized he was never leaving, and then he could be honest with her and tell her about his family. But until then, it seemed best to keep her in the dark.

He had very few doubts she would make him a good wife, yet her heart had been broken by a deceitful man, and now their own life together would begin based on dishonesty.

Many marriages begin like theirs, two people needing something from the other, but he'd never thought his bride would be a stranger. And he'd never considered he'd deceive the woman he would wed just to get what he wanted. If only she'd sold him the plantation, then he wouldn't be forced to take such drastic measures.

There was still time to back out, to walk away, still a last chance to be honest and tell Nicole the truth regarding his reasons for marrying her. There was always the possibility she would sell him the plantation outright this time, though she'd turned away every offer his lawyers had presented. But being honest with her was too big a risk and marrying her would guarantee the property would return to his family. Unless he intended to give up his family obligation, he had to go through with the wedding.

A cool breeze blew off the river as he climbed down from the buggy, determined to go forward with his promise to his grandfather. He hurried up the steps to the big house and paused to glance around at the beauty of the land, the way the tall oak trees shaded the house, and the wisps of moss that hung from their leaves. In the distance he could see the sugarcane rippling like a green wave in the breeze. No wonder his grandfather insisted he restore the land to the family.

A sense of rightness and belonging overcame him. This land belonged to the Viel family and would soon be returned to them. And Max felt good about keeping his promise to his grandfather.

Nicole met him at the men's entrance. Her beauty outshone the splendor of the land so, he couldn't think for a moment as he stared at her. Her dark iris-colored eyes gazed back at him, trepidation shining from them like a beacon. Her blonde hair was piled on top of her head, the curls cascading down like a waterfall shimmering in the sun. Stunned, he couldn't help but think in a bit of awe that this lovely woman would soon be his wife.

"Good morning. I saw you drive up," she said.

"Good morning," he replied, noting how her pale blue dress brought out the color in her cheeks. "We'd better get going so we can get you back before the heat becomes unbearable."

"Yes," she said nervously. She gazed at him, her expression thoughtful, as if she feared what she wanted to say. He stared into her soft blue eyes, waiting patiently for her to voice what troubled her.

"Are you sure about this?" she asked, her face tilted to the side. "I mean, you can back out if you'd like."

He nodded his head. "Yes, I'm certain. How about you? Have you changed your mind?"

"No," she said quickly. "My baby needs a name. I won't let my child be thought of as illegitimate. I just can't. But you must understand that this is just a temporary marriage, nothing permanent."

"I understand. We need to get going," he said, despising lying to her, yet trying to reassure her. "The justice of the peace is expecting us."

She sighed and gripped her reticule tightly in her hand. "All right, let's go get married."

~

"I now pronounce you man and wife," the justice of the peace said, smiling at them like they were a happy couple instead of two people coming together to solve a problem. Nicole stood beside him, with a fake smile on her face. "You may kiss your bride, Mr. Viel."

Max hadn't thought of this moment before now. He turned to Nicole, feeling awkward as she gazed at him, her blue eyes large and apprehensive. Her feelings were so easy to distinguish on her soft face. She hadn't considered this part of the ceremony, either. There were a lot of things that neither one of them had thought of as they rushed to get married.

Max leaned forward and pressed his lips to hers. The sudden urge to linger surprised him as he tasted the sweet dew of her mouth, but he quickly ended the kiss.

"Congratulations, Mr. and Mrs. Viel. Just sign the marriage license and the register, then you're all set," the man said, but Max stared at Nicole, surprised at how tender her lips had felt against his own. He'd been attracted to her the moment they met, but he was a little shocked at her kiss.

Finally he turned to the justice of the peace and placed his signature on the license. Then Nicole leaned over and signed the document, making it official. They were man and wife, for better or worse.

"For an extra three dollars we can take a photograph of this special occasion," the clerk said.

"Oh, no, I don't think that's necessary," Nicole said, shaking her head.

Max thought for a moment and realized that this was his wedding day, and no matter what, they were married until one of them perished. Shouldn't they have something to remember their simple ceremony by?

"We'll take it," he said, removing his money clip and paying the clerk for the picture and the ceremony.

"But..." Nicole began, gazing at him with a questioning glance.

"Come on, honey, it's our wedding day," he reassured and took her by the arm. "We can afford one small luxury."

She glanced at him awkwardly and then the two of them posed for the traditional wedding photograph in the small office. Max sat in a chair and Nicole stood behind him, her hands resting lightly on his shoulders.

The clerk poked his head under a dark cloth that draped the equipment, and peered through the lens at them. "Looks good. I'll count to three. One, two, three."

A large flash and a pop recorded the day on glass plates. The smell of sulfur filled the room and Max couldn't help but wonder how they would look back on this photo in the years ahead.

"If you want you can pick this up sometime tomorrow. It will take me a little while to process it," the clerk said as he stepped out from under the cloth.

"I have to come back into town tomorrow anyway. I'll pick up the picture then," Max assured the man.

The wedding was over, the marriage complete. Max looked at the woman who now was his wife. What did they do now? They weren't the typical couple that could hardly wait to be alone.

Yet, if given the opportunity, he couldn't say having sex with his wife would be unwelcome. In fact, he'd jump at the opportunity.

"Well, you're all set," the justice's wife said, moving them toward the door. "Best wishes."

"Congratulations," the clerk called.

Max took Nicole by the arm and they walked out of the justice of the peace's office in awkward silence. The door shut behind them and a strained hush enshrouded them, leaving Max uncertain as to what to do next.

"Is there any place in town you'd like to go?" he asked her, as he helped her up into the buggy. She was extremely quiet and he worried that she regretted her quick action.

"No; could we just return to the house? It's beginning to get warm and I don't want to chance getting sick," she said, her face seeming pale and drawn once again.

He'd thought of suggesting lunch at a local cafe to celebrate their nuptials, but realized the heat, a full stomach, and a bouncing buggy could have terrible results for a woman with child. Nicole was right; they should get back to Rosewood. While she rested, he could explore the house he'd heard so much about "All right. I thought I would move my things from the hotel I've been staying at tomorrow," he said, going around the other side of the buggy to climb in.

Nicole glanced at him from beneath her long dark lashes. "Oh, I hadn't even thought about you moving in. I mean, I knew you would, it's just that it all seems a little strange. One day we're strangers and then a week later we're married. Dear God, I'm so nervous I'm rambling."

For the first time since he'd known her she appeared frightened and he wanted to reassure her that everything would be fine.

"It's all right Nicole," he said, using her given name for the first time.

She glanced at him, her forehead wrinkling in a frown. "Yes, everything will be just fine. While you're gone tomorrow, I'll clean out Jean's things. You can have his old bedroom."

She stared at him, her head tilted to the side, worrying her bottom lip. "Why did you have the clerk take a picture?"

Suspicion shone from her gaze and he swallowed nervously. More lies. How long could he possibly keep the information from her when he hated not being truthful?

"I don't know. Maybe someday the baby would want to know what the man who gave him his name looked like," Max said, thinking quickly on his feet.

He'd wanted the picture because he knew this marriage would last until death did them part. Though doubtful their marriage would ever be a love match, he hoped they could live together in a somewhat happy union. And if they ever had children, he would like them to know how Nicole and he had looked on the day they wed.

He only hoped he hadn't just made the biggest mistake of his life.

She nodded and seemed to relax. "Thank you. You're right. I hadn't even thought of that. He probably *will be* curious about what you look like."

Max smiled at her, relieved she'd believed him. Until she knew the truth, he would need to be more cautious. "Come, Mrs. Viel, let's get you home before the heat becomes unbearable."

~

Nicole stood in the window of her bedroom and gazed out the window at the stars that filled the midnight sky. Dear God, what had she done? She'd married a complete stranger today, just to give her baby a name. A common drifter with sparkling, kind emerald eyes and hair as dark as midnight slept just a few doors away, and now she carried his last name.

A knock sounded on her door. "Who is it?"

"It's Consuelo. I saw your light on and wanted to make sure you were all right."

"Come in," Nicole said.

The door opened and Consuelo walked in. "Are you feeling all right?" she asked, concern causing her forehead to furrow in a frown.

"I'm fine. I just can't sleep," Nicole said, gazing out the window, pulling her wrapper around the small bulge in her abdomen protectively. This baby meant so much to her.

"You need your rest," the woman said, her voice filled

with concern. "Would you like me to fix you a glass of warm milk?"

Nicole shook her head. "No." She gazed at the woman. "Thank you for the lovely supper, Consuelo. It was very nice."

The woman shrugged. "It's the least the servants could do to celebrate your marriage. Mr. Viel seems nice, not at all what I expected."

Nicole nodded. "Yes, he is, though I hardly know him."

"There's speculation among the servants about why you would marry so soon after Mr. Cuvier's death, but I didn't say anything about the babe. They'll find out soon enough."

"Thank you, Consuelo. I want my son or daughter to have a chance to grow up without some horrible stigma being attached to them."

"I understand about negative names being attached to you." She straightened the bedding and pulled back the sheets. "I must say I was prepared to dislike your new husband, but he seems very polite. Makes you wonder why a man like that hasn't settled down."

"Yes, it does," Nicole said, frowning as she looked out at the darkened sky, listening to her friend saying the words she feared out loud. Could Max be a criminal or a man on the run from the law? Just what did she know about him?

"What's wrong? You seem worried," her friend said. "Are you already regretting this hasty marriage?"

"I'm frightened, Consuelo." Nicole gave an awkward laugh. "How can I trust my judgment where men are concerned? As I lay down to sleep tonight, I suddenly realized what I've done. I married a man I know very little about, just to give my child a name. What if he's married to someone else?"

The servant shook her head. "No one could have such terrible luck as to marry a man who is already married a second time. Not even your luck is that bad."

"Then tell me, why did he agree to this marriage?" She sighed. "Maybe I'm just overreacting. The day has been fraught with tension. As I stood beside Max saying I do, I couldn't help but feel strange. I was pledging forever to a man who will only be here through the end of the year. Yet somehow when he looks at me, he calms me. With just a glance I feel that everything is going to be all right."

Consuelo shrugged. "You married him for your baby's sake. He married you for a chance to have a clean bed at night and home-cooked meals. Some men, it doesn't take much to satisfy them. Not to mention the money from the cane crop."

Nicole shook her head. "Maybe, but suddenly I felt like a fool as I realized I know nothing about a man who is now my husband. Who is sleeping under my roof and has access to my bed, to everything I own. Was I foolish to try to protect my unborn child?"

The servant pulled the gauzy curtains closed and let the night breeze stir the material that draped the windows. She shook her head. "It's an honorable sacrifice. Your child will not suffer the same fate as you. He will be accepted by the other children and not whispered about."

"But why would a man like Max marry a woman like me, unless he thinks that I have money." She laughed, the sound chilling in the semi-dark room. "If that's what he thinks, he's in for quite a shock."

Consuelo frowned, her brows drawing together as she considered Nicole's words. "While you rested this afternoon, he walked out to the barns and was seen inspecting the sugarcane fields."

Nicole pulled the curtains open enough to see the stars in the sky. So Max had visited the fields this afternoon. "Well, maybe the crop is the reason he married me."

For a moment there was silence as Nicole felt somehow saddened at the thought Max had married her just for the crop. She gave herself a mental shake at the absurdness of her thinking. Of course he'd married her only for the money he would gain from the sale of her sugarcane.

Consuelo cleared her throat. "Have you thought about what you're going to do once the baby is born? I mean, will you stay here?"

Nicole frowned and shook her head. "Everything is dependent upon the sugarcane crop. If I don't make enough for us to live on, then I don't know what's going to happen. All I can do is pray that the crop earns enough money to support us."

The older woman started walking toward the door. "Try to get some sleep. You need to concentrate on the little *niño.* I'll spend some extra time in prayer tonight and pray to the Blessed Virgin Mother to help us."

Nicole smiled sadly. "What would I do without you, Consuelo?"

~

Max woke the next morning, surprised at his surroundings. He glanced around the master's suite at Rosewood Plantation and gazed at the walls, thinking of his ancestors. His great-great-grandfather had built these walls and he couldn't help but feel in awe at what his family members had accomplished.

He rose from the bed and quickly dressed, knowing that he needed to get into town as early as possible.

Max stepped into the dining room centered in the large house.

"Where's Mrs. Viel?" he asked a servant hurrying out the door.

She stopped and gazed at him nervously. "Mrs. Cuv— Viel is taking her breakfast outside on the verandah."

"Thank you," he said, trying to make the older woman feel more at ease with him. "Could you please bring me a cup of coffee out to the verandah?"

"Yes, sir, and breakfast will be out shortly."

"And what is your name?" he asked.

"Marie, sir."

"Thank you, Marie," he said, and walked back to his bedroom and then outside to the verandah.

Nicole sat sipping her coffee, watching a boat meander down the Mississippi River, the breeze softly blowing a curl that twirled about her face.

She turned and saw him walking toward her. "Good morning," she called. "I trust you slept well."

"Very well, thank you," he replied, thinking that this radiant-looking creature was his wife and hoping that someday she would accept him as her husband. "How did you sleep?"

"I tossed and turned most of the night," she said. "Won't you join me for breakfast? It should be out soon."

"Yes, I just spoke with one of the servants and she said breakfast would be served shortly," he said, pulling out a chair to join her at the table.

They sat across from one another, tension permeating the morning air. Sparrows called to one another in the trees, filling the silence.

"So, you're going into town today?" she asked.

"Yes, is there anything I can get you while I'm out?" She shook her head. "No, thank you."

"I thought I would get my things out of the hotel and pick up our wedding picture."

"How is it you can afford a hotel?" she suddenly asked, looking at him in puzzlement Max paused for a moment. "I did some carpentry work for them and we managed to work out a deal for me to stay there."

"You're definitely resourceful," she said.

He smiled, but didn't respond, thinking once again he'd almost given away his secret.

She frowned and lifted her coffee cup. "There is something I need to discuss with you."

"What?"

"It's about marriage. I just want to make sure that you agree and understand you're free to leave any time after the baby is born, or you can leave now, but return when my time gets closer. I just want you here when the baby is born so there will be fewer questions about the father."

He shrugged and lied to her. "Of course, I understand. Our marriage is in name only for the sake of the baby." He watched as Nicole visibly relaxed. "Why this question now?"

"I couldn't sleep last night and suddenly I realized that you never really explained why you agreed to marry me," she said.

"Simple," he said, needing time to figure out a reason for his consenting to the marriage. After all, he couldn't be honest and tell her it was for the plantation, could he?

"Why, then?" she said, looking at him with a questioning expression. "What are you getting out of giving my baby your name?"

He frowned, not liking the turn of this conversation. "Well, I'm getting to spend at least five months at a working plantation, and while I'm here, I hope to learn as much as possible about raising a sugarcane crop. I'll get three meals a day, a nice roof over my head, and—not to mention—the money you're paying me."

She frowned at him as though she was puzzled at his response.

"Did I say the wrong thing?" he asked.

"No. It seems natural the way you said it, but as I lay in bed thinking about this last night, I couldn't seem to find a single reason that didn't seem self-seeking and I wondered what you would tell me when I asked. Everything happened so fast. I asked, you accepted, and a week after we met, we married."

"Your reaction is reasonable considering what you've gone through with Jean's death," he assured her.

"Maybe. But I suddenly realized I know nothing about you, and last night I began to question why you agreed to marry me," she said, a quizzical expression on her face.

He shrugged. "There were a lot of reasons why. As for knowing me, ask your questions and I'll answer." She frowned. "Where were you born?"

"I don't really know," he lied, knowing his birth occurred in her very bedroom. "My parents never told me."

"Where does your family live now?" she asked. "They live in New Orleans. My mother's name is Audra and my father is Charles. What else would you like to know?"

Nicole looked puzzled as she sat there staring at him. "I don't know. You've given me the basic information about yourself, yet I don't feel like I know you. I guess I want to know more about you than your name."

He nodded his head, wishing somehow to end this conversation quickly or at least change the topic. "You're not going to know me overnight, Nicole. It's going to take time for both of us. In the meantime, I'm going to make sure that our sugarcane crop is doing well and see what I can do around the plantation to help you out while we await the arrival of your baby. After I go to town."

She smiled. "You're right. I just had a bad case of nerves last night I've been betrayed once, and I don't want to get hurt again."

Max's conscience twinged and he pushed the feeling of guilt away. He was doing her a favor by marrying her and giving her baby a name. He shouldn't feel remorse; they were helping each other out. He didn't want to hurt her, but he needed her property. Yet he also realized that if the truth were known, he wouldn't mind having *her,* too.

Max watched as one of the field hands climbed the

stairs. "Excuse me, Mrs. Viel, but the field hands have been standing around with nothing to do, waiting for Mr. Frank to show up to work this morning."

"Where is Frank?" she asked.

"I don't know, ma'am. He's not in his cabin or in the barn. I've looked everywhere and I can't find him.

I hate for these men to stand around doing nothing, so I thought I would come to you."

Max watched this discussion with interest. How could the overseer just disappear and leave the men with nothing to do?

"Thank you, Noah. Would you please make sure that the cane is well watered and I'll speak with Mr. Frank as soon as I see him."

"Yes, ma'am. We also should probably think about starting to fertilize the fields, ma'am," he told her.

She smiled at him. "Would it be better to fertilize the fields when they're wet or when they're dry?"

"I was always taught to fertilize and then water the fields, ma'am," he said, holding his hat nervously in his hand.

"Then that's what we'll do," she said. "Fertilize the fields and then water them well."

"Yes, ma'am. That will certainly keep the men busy." He nodded his head and walked away.

Max couldn't help but think there were a lot of things he could start working on at Rosewood; while Nicole busied herself preparing for this baby, he would ingratiate himself into the running of the plantation. And the first thing he wanted to look into was her overseer. It appeared the man wasn't doing his job.

~

Max rode into town to the hotel where he'd been staying. He sat down at the desk in his small room and quickly penned a letter to his mother, telling her he'd acquired the property and a bride, but not to come just yet. He couldn't explain, but he didn't need his mother here telling Nicole the reason he'd married her. He needed some time to convince his new wife how he would be good for her permanently, and then his mother could come to Rosewood. But until then he advised her to stay away.

He asked his father to make sure his son was being cared for properly. At the age of twelve, Paul could almost raise himself, yet Max paid Desiree, the boy's mother, on a regular basis to feed and clothe the child. Though he didn't trust her to use that money on his son.

Max sealed the envelope and collected his belongings from the hotel room. He'd accomplished what he'd set out to achieve, only not in the manner he'd expected. But maybe marrying Nicole would be a positive experience. And maybe not....

# Chapter Four

**A** week passed and Nicole sensed a change around the plantation. Though she'd spent the better part of the week resting and sitting on the verandah, more work seemed to be getting accomplished in the fields and even near the house since Max's arrival.

Several days after their wedding ceremony, she'd begun to spot again. When she'd gone to bed, Max had agreed to take over the running of the plantation while she rested, praying that she wouldn't lose the baby. After marrying this unknown man, she'd be so distraught if she lost this child she'd waited so long for.

Now as she sat on the verandah and watched Max work with the men in the field, there seemed to be more energy and vitality in the field hands. Max had put several men to cleaning the flower beds and grounds around the house, and another couple of the workers were busy fixing the back door that she had begged her overseer to repair months ago.

A new awareness of work and needed repairs around the plantation seemed contagious and somehow she felt almost jealous at what Max had achieved that she hadn't been able to accomplish.

Nicole watched Max as he strode about the plantation with a sense of purpose, his white shirt open to reveal dark chest hairs, brown pants clinging to his shapely legs. The climate seemed to fit him as he kept the men working day after day until dusk, repairing the fence, doing yard work, and preparing the equipment for the sugarcane harvest, which was still months away.

Though from all appearances Max seemed like the perfect companion, something about this man made her uneasy. In so many ways he seemed ideal except for the fact he lived the life of a transient. She wondered why he'd never settled down with his own land and built a business the way Jean had. Yet did she really want to compare him to Jean and find they were similar in any way? The thought of finding another man like Jean made her shudder.

She had loved Jean; his commanding personality and charm drew her more than any man she'd ever known. But she'd always recognized that a ruthless side to her husband existed, a side she had chosen to overlook. Somehow, Jean had identified exactly what she lacked in her life and he'd given her those material things, and now look where her blindness to his faults had led her. Her marriage had been considered illegal and her child would have been illegitimate— just as her own birth was—if not for Max.

She glanced out at the land that surrounded the Creole home Jean had bought her. He'd known she pined for a place on the river, a home to call her own, a place where she felt she belonged and could bring their children into this world and build the dynasty she'd always dreamed of. Now everything she wanted seemed to be slipping through her fingers except the child she'd longed for, who would depend on her to take care of him. For this reason she clung tighter to the land and the child that grew within her. She'd lost Jean, but she'd be damned if she would lose the land or her baby.

That's why she sat here in the shade of the house, trying to make it through a difficult pregnancy, willing to let Max run the plantation while she concentrated on her child.

Voices raised in anger came from the barns, drawing her attention to the sound. She stood and walked around the verandah until she could see who was shouting.

At the back of the house, near the barn, she saw Frank, her overseer, and Max in a heated debate.

"If you're going to work for me, don't you ever treat any of my animals this way again. I will not accept sloppy care, do you understand?" Max shouted, his face red, his green eyes flashing.

"They were only saddle sores. Easily treated," Frank replied, his own face red in the heat.

"No, the animals lacked proper care and feeding, plus the horse had saddle sores, which shows neglect. They're treatable, but only when someone puts salve on them."

Frank stood there. "The horses are not ridden that much around here."

"If you don't like the way I expect your work to be completed, then you're free to pack your bags and leave."

She'd never seen Max angry before and somehow he seemed more imposing and looked less like the drifter she knew him to be. Whatever gentleness she'd seen in his demeanor before was hidden by the imposing man who now stood before Frank. Was Max another man with a hidden side?

"I doubt that Mrs. Cuvier would like my leaving," her overseer said in an arrogant tone of voice as he leaned in close to Max.

For a moment Nicole felt certain fists would start flying and she waited to see which man would throw the first punch. She started to intervene and then decided to see how Max handled the man who managed her field hands.

"You mean Mrs. *Viel,* my wife," Max said pointedly.

The overseer said nothing, but stared at Max, his expression clearly not happy but defiant. For a moment Nicole felt a twinge of anxiety as she feared the man would leave. What would she do when Max eventually left if she had no overseer? Someone must help her run the plantation, as she couldn't do it alone.

"I expect the animals in that barn to be treated with fresh hay and water every day and I will require you to make sure that the sores on that horse are doctored. Are we clear?" Max asked his voice stern.

"Yes, sir," the man said, not looking at Max.

"Good."

Nicole watched Max turn and walk away from the man into the cool shade below the house. She hurried down the back stairs and into the storage area beneath the house, surprised at how neat and tidy the small room appeared. The last time she ventured in here the area had been cluttered with lumber and empty wine casks. She'd asked Jean about having the workers straighten the space, but he'd said not to worry, he'd take care of it. Now the place looked neat and orderly with everything in its proper place, and she knew Jean had never pushed the servants to have it cleaned.

"Who did this?" she asked in awe as she twirled around the aboveground basement.

Max looked up from going through a trunk of tools. He raised his brows. "Me and several of the men organized everything almost two days ago."

Nicole stared at the man in front of her, that feeling of uncertainty coming back again. For a man who was just here for a few months, she would have assumed he would ask before he took control, but somehow she knew that wasn't his personality. Yet it disturbed her that he seemed to be acting more like an owner than a visitor. Or was she just experiencing yet another case of pregnancy nerves?

"I wish you would have told me before you cleaned this area," she said, knowing she should be grateful but frightened of the significance of his actions.

"Why?" he asked. "Would it have made a difference?"

"No, but I would like to have been included in the decision," she said, feeling somehow left out.

"Everything that I threw out is sitting right outside in a pile, if you'd like to go through it," he said, agitated. He picked up a wooden plank and began to use a rectangular metal blade on the wood.

"No. No, I just wish you had told me you were going to do this," she said, knowing that it sounded silly, but still feeling the need to be involved in her plantation. Just because she had remarried didn't mean she no longer participated in the decision-making regarding Rosewood.

Rosewood belonged to her and this marriage was mainly a farce that existed to protect her child.

His eyes glanced at her and darkened as he gazed at her, studying her face. "I didn't think it necessary for me to ask your permission if I'm going to work while I'm here."

She shrugged, the feel of his annoyed gaze on her making her uncomfortable. Maybe he was right in that he didn't need to ask her consent, but was it asking too much to want to be involved? "You're right. Just tell me what's going on, so that I know."

He bent his head and went back to sanding.

Nicole walked around the room looking at the shelves that he'd built, the way everything had a place.

"Where did you get the lumber?" she asked, knowing she owed money at the lumber mill in town and doubted they would extend her a loan with the publicity of Jean's death.

"I found it around here," he said, not looking at her as he picked up a new piece of oak and began to scrape the wood with the cabinet scraper.

She couldn't remember seeing any lumber just lying around, but then she'd been gone for two months so maybe Max found a stack she knew nothing about.

She touched the cabinets, running her hand along the smooth woodwork. "This is very nice."

"Thank you," he said, gazing up at her, and then returned his attention to the board he scraped.

"Why were you yelling at Frank?" she asked, finally getting to the question that caused her to follow him into the dark, musty room.

The muscles in his forearms stood out hard and strong as he moved the cabinet scraper back and forth along the board, smoothing out the rough edges. "Who said I yelled?"

"I heard you on the verandah," she said.

He stopped rubbing the scraper against the board and stared at her. "There were several horses in the barn that had been neglected. None of the stalls had been cleaned in days and the animals needed feed. No one treats my animals with such disrespect"

"Oh," she said. "Your animals?"

Max frowned at her and wiped the sweat from his brow with the back of his hand. "So they're yours. But while I'm here I won't allow the mistreatment of any animals under my care." He stood there staring at her, his gaze uncertain. "Why all the questions?"

She frowned, realizing her fears seemed unfounded, but expressing them just the same. "In the last week, you've done so much around here that one would get the idea you intend to stay. I just want you to understand that you are only needed until I have the baby."

"We've gone over this before. I understand. But also recognize that while I'm here, I'm going to do a good job of helping you with your plantation. I don't believe in doing something halfway and, excuse me for saying so, but, most of your workers have been cheating you."

Nicole stood there, stunned for a moment, as the man she barely knew made candid accusations about her field hands and foreman. Part of her thought she should be grateful for his forthright disclosure, but part of her wanted to hold tightly to the power she felt slipping through her fingers. She reminded herself he would only be here until the baby was born, and if she could convince him to leave and then return, that would be even better.

"Are you saying I don't know how to run a plantation?"

she asked, feeling the hackles on the back of her neck rise.

"No, I never said that. I said your workers have an even lazier foreman and were taking advantage of the situation. But not for long."

"What makes you think that they're lazy and that Frank hasn't done a good job?" she asked perplexed.

His gaze met and held hers. "Because a good overseer would have already taken care of the things I've done this week. I shouldn't have to tell them to clean the flower beds, repair the doors, and clean the horse stalls. Those things should be done automatically. He should lead the workers to get those items taken care of."

"How do you know? Have you worked as an overseer before?"

"No, but I know I would never accept sloppy work from any worker."

She knew he was right, but that didn't mean she liked the truths he revealed. In fact, she'd known that Frank had a lazy streak, but hadn't wanted to search for a new foreman.

"Frank is still here only because I didn't think I should fire him without your say-so. But it won't take much more for me to let him go without your permission," he said, his frustration evident in his voice.

"I would prefer that you didn't. I'll need him once you're gone," she said.

"You could find a better man," he said.

"Maybe, but I'm not ready to find out," Nicole said. "This is my plantation and you won't be here all that long."

"Why would you want someone who isn't doing his job properly?" he asked. "Your profits will improve if the plantation runs smoothly and your workers work."

"Look, up until a year ago, I couldn't hire enough workers," she said. "It wasn't until the Louisiana Sugar Plantation Association became involved that we could find enough men to do the job. It's taken me three years just to learn about the planting side; I'm still dealing with the issues involved with field-workers."

"You should have worked on them first. Usually one of the men knows the trade and can help you." He looked up at her, his gaze setting her heart to pounding. "Without a good overseer, you usually don't get enough work out of your workers."

Max returned to his woodworking as Nicole walked around the new cabinets and ran her hand along the smooth wood, ignoring his last comment. Jean had never seen to the plantation. He'd said it was all hers to run, though she had never been in charge of field hands and knew very little about running a plantation. But she loved this place, and she was still learning some of the details that made it run smoother.

"You know, you don't have to stay here until the baby is born. You can leave and return before I have the child," she said, thinking maybe that would be best before Max became too involved.

He smiled at her and wiped the sweat from his brow with the back of his hand. "I know, you've told me. Are you trying to get rid of me so soon?"

"Oh, no. I just didn't want you to feel that you had to stay here the entire time and toil. If there was someplace you needed to be, you could always return later."

"And leave that sugarcane crop to that bumpkin of a foreman you have?" he asked. "I don't think so. I want my share of the profits."

She stared at him, a sinking sensation in the pit of her stomach. Somehow she'd hoped that he wouldn't be so intent on earning his share to stay here and protect it, but then again, she doubted that he'd ever seen the amount of cash the crop could bring in and he wouldn't dare leave it now. And maybe that was a good thing for both of them. For she needed that money as badly as he.

"I guess I'm glad you feel that way, because that crop is very important to this plantation," she said, not willing to trust him with the knowledge that without a good sugarcane crop, she would be forced to sell.

He stared at her, his eyes dark and warm. "If I didn't feel that way, it wouldn't do either one of us any good."

"No, you're right. It's difficult for me to let someone just take over."

A smile lit his face and then he turned back to running the scraper along the wood. "Who knows, you might get used to it and actually enjoy a man being in charge."

She felt a brief moment of fear. "Doubtful, since I never intend to let a man have that kind of control over me ever again. I married you for your name, not your looks, or your brain, or even your management abilities. Just merely your name for my child."

He smiled. "Better be careful, Mrs. Viel. What you just said could become a challenge to most men, just to prove you wrong. Just to show you that having the right man take care of you and the plantation would be enjoyable."

~

The next morning before the sun heated the inside of the house, Nicole took Consuelo and together the two of them went into the spare bedroom where the servants had piled all of Jean's things and began the ugly task of sorting through his clothes, jewelry, and other belongings. Nicole had put this off as long as possible, but suddenly she knew she needed to remove Jean's things from the house. She'd been home going on almost four weeks and remarried for a little over a week. She needed to get on with her life, though barely two months had passed since she'd learned of Jean's betrayal. The pain still bled like an open wound, while her sorrow had been transformed to near hate at how he'd deceived her.

"Well, Consuelo, I guess the best thing to do is to start sorting. I'm going to donate all of his clothes to the church, but I'll need to look through his jewelry and things. Most I'll keep for the baby, and whatever's left, I'll send to Mrs. Cuvier in New Orleans."

Nicole gazed at the pile of things in front of them, including a locked trunk she'd never seen before.

"Where did that trunk come from?" she asked.

Consuelo looked at the small wooden steamer trunk. "Noah found it in the back of Jean's armoire."

"Do you know where the key that unlocks it is?"

"I've never seen this trunk before the day Noah found it."

"You know, I bet we could break into it pretty easily," she said, her hand running over the lock.

"I'll get one of the men to break the lock for us." Consuelo hurried out the door.

Nicole stared at the clothes and remembered the times she'd seen Jean in the different garments. She felt a pang of heartache as she picked up one shirt and held it to her nose, his smell faint upon the cloth. How could she have fallen in love with a man who never valued marriage? Why hadn't she recognized his total disregard for the sanctity of marriage before he disgraced her? And how could he keep such a secret from all his wives?

Tears pricked her eyes and she threw the offensive garment in a pile. Quickly she moved to the next one, going through each item, tossing them into separate piles.

Consuelo returned and in a matter of moments, Noah had the lock open. After the field hand left the room, Nicole lifted the lid and started to go through mementos of Jean's childhood. She saved a few things for her child and the rest she decided to pack up to send to Mrs. Cuvier's children. At the bottom of the trunk lay an old blanket. When she reached under the woolen cloth she found a book. She picked up the torn and spotted leather- bound volume and glanced at it.

"Look at this," she said.

She opened the journal and the spine fell to a rose that had been pressed between the pages. With interest she read the entry.

*Today was a most joyous day as my lover came to visit and we walked to the park on Magnolia Street.*

*He gave me a rose and promised me that soon we would be together forever. If only his naive wife would realize that she's no good for him and let him go, but he refuses to leave her until their children are older. I've yet to tell him that soon we will have our own child and that our love will know no bounds. I fear what my brother will say when he learns of the child. These last few years since Mama and Papa's death, he's been so kind to take care of me and I feel like I've betrayed him by falling in love with someone who is unable to be open with his love. Someday our love will be obvious for the world to see. Until then, I will care for our child. If it's a boy, I'll name him Jean after his father.*

Nicole dropped the book, her fingers tingling with awareness.

She reached down and picked up the journal again, flipping back to the front of the diary where the owner's name should be written, only to discover the jagged remnants of the missing pages that had been ripped from the book. Nicole thumbed through the pages looking for any other evidence of the woman's identity, but the names she saw were unfamiliar.

Dear God, another woman! Yet this one had known of his marriage. But did she know he had not one extra wife, but three?

In a fit of anger, Nicole threw the book against the wall, hating Jean because he was nothing like the man she'd loved and married. Nothing about her life with him had been real.

~

Nicole sat in the cool shade of the verandah, the diary open on her lap. She hadn't been able to read the pages as she watched a schooner making its way down the river. She could see the men working on deck as they passed Rosewood, her thoughts on the woman in the diary. She couldn't stop thinking about the woman's journal and her relationship with Jean. How another woman had believed the lies of that scoundrel she'd once been married to.

The young woman's memoirs began ten years ago, when she was a young debutante of seventeen. Filled with hopes and dreams and the events of a society girl's life, Nicole found the account hard to read, knowing that at some point in the story, her life would cross with Jean's and be forever changed. Just like Nicole's life would never be the same.

"Mrs. Nicole, I hate to disturb you but..." Consuelo stood at Nicole's side, wringing her hands.

Nicole glanced up at the woman who had been her servant since childhood. "What's wrong, Consuelo?"

"Your husband, Mr. Viel, the field hands say that he fired Mr. Frank," she said, visibly upset at the news.

"What?" Nicole said, stunned as she swung her legs over the side of the chair. "Why would he do that? Max knows I depend on Frank."

This is what she got for marrying a man she hardly knew. A man who, for all appearances, seemed very passive, yet in the week he'd been here, had managed to create quite a sensation. Even Jean's occasional trips home had never created this kind of stir.

Nicole stood and started for the inside of the house, Consuelo following her. "They say he caught Mr. Frank stealing, but I don't know what he took."

When Max left she would need an overseer she could trust. As far as she knew, Frank had never stolen from her before. Surely this was a mistake, a misunderstanding.

Nicole felt a moment of pure rage at the man she called husband. Frank had been with her since the very beginning and Max could just find him and bring him back to Rosewood. Why would Max do this without consulting her? Because this rambler liked things done his way and he especially liked being in charge.

The memory of Max telling her that her foreman was lazier than the field hands suddenly came to mind. Still, she needed someone to direct the field hands. And she certainly wasn't going to be in any kind of condition to oversee the men after the baby came—or even before.

"Where is Mr. Viel, Consuelo?" Nicole asked, marching into the house, her fury increasing with each step. This was her plantation, not some common drifter's who she'd married just for his name. He needed to learn his place. He needed to consult her before he made changes that affected her and the plantation.

"I think he's in his room," Consuelo said as she followed Nicole into the house. "Please, Mrs. Nicole, don't get all upset over this. It's not good for the babe."

Nicole put her hand to her abdomen and worried. She'd yet to feel the baby move and feared that something could be wrong for the child not to have stirred. But still, she must protect their future, and while she tried to calm down, she knew her anger only smoldered.

"I'm all right, Consuelo. I just need to speak with my husband," she said, going to the men's side of the house and knocking on his door.

"Who is it?" he asked.

"It's me," Nicole said. "May I come in?"

"Certainly," Max replied.

She walked in to find him stretched out on the bed in his clothes, his long frame taking up much of the space. For a moment she stared, stunned to see him lying there, and quickly averted her gaze. The room looked completely different from when Jean occupied it. There was more of a masculine coziness that exuded warmth, with the smell of pine permeating the room.

The rage she'd been filled with seemed to deflate at the sight of him lying on the bed, leaving her startled.

"Yes?" he asked.

"I ...I ..." She returned her gaze to his and couldn't help but gape at him lying there. "I heard that you fired Frank," she said, wishing he would get up. Her throat seemed to close up at seeing him lying in bed.

"Yes, I did," he said matter-of-factly, gazing at her with no remorse. "You deserve better."

"I think you're forgetting your place. You have no right to fire my employees. You're only here temporarily," she said, turning her back on him and walking across the room, trying not to think of him lying in that big four-poster bed watching her. "Frank has been with me since the very beginning and I depend on him to handle the men in the field."

She took a deep breath, steeled herself for the sight of Max, and turned around to face him. He wore a smile on his face, which flamed her fury once more. "I insist that you go find him and ask him to return."

"I can do that if that's what you wish," he said, sitting up and swinging his legs to the floor. "But I'll warn you. I've been going over Frank's payroll books for the field hands. I can bring him back if you're willing to lose more money. It seems that Frank had a hard time paying the wages the Louisiana Sugar Planters' Association set for the field hands. So he set his own wage and kept the difference for himself."

Nicole stopped her pacing and stared at Max. "How did you find this out?"

"I spoke with several of the hands and realized that he was cheating them and you."

"Well, why didn't they come to me? I would have made sure that they received the correct pay."

Max stood and walked toward Nicole. He stopped and placed his hands on her shoulders. "They spoke with Jean, who did nothing."

Nicole stared up into the warmth of his green gaze, shock dousing the small flame of anger that still burned. "I don't understand.... Why didn't Jean do anything to stop Frank? If you're right, we've probably lost hundreds of dollars to his stealing. Money that, if the Louisiana Sugar Planters' Association found out we weren't paying our workers, could have gotten us expelled from the organization. No wonder we could never keep good field hands. They were all going to other plantations to earn more money."

Max shrugged. "So, you still want me to go find Frank and bring him back?"

Nicole ignored his question as she gazed at him, her feelings still raw, though he'd proven his actions had been justified.

For a man who traveled from place to place, she couldn't help but wonder where he'd learned how to manage a plantation and question the employees.

"Where did you learn how to run a plantation?" she asked.

He smiled. "I've never been on one until now. But my grandfather used to own one and he always gave me tips. One of them was you should run a big place just like a business. And his leading suggestion was watching your overseer. He said never trust the man, always double-check his figures." Max paused. "I guess Grandfather was right"

"You, a drifter, have never been on a plantation before now? Where did you work?"

"Oh, around," he said, not being direct.

"You're not wanted by the law are you?" she questioned.

He laughed. "It would be a little late to be asking that question, don't you think? No, I'm not wanted by the law."

She gazed at him, trying not to be suspicious of him, but so afraid after what Jean had put her through.

"Mr. Viel, I would like to remind you once again that you will only be here until my baby is born. Then you're free to go—so don't get too attached to my plantation or running it"

He tilted his head and smiled at her. "You know, the more I think about this arrangement of ours, the more I have a question for you: Just how are you going to explain that this child's daddy was here for his conception through his birthing, but just disappeared after the baby's birth? Won't that appear suspicious?"

She frowned. It wasn't as if she hadn't already thought about this and come up with several scenarios. It bothered her that he'd considered what she would do. Why was he suddenly taking such a keen interest in how she would resolve their marriage?

"Yes, but at first I'll tell people you're away on a trip. Then after several months I'll say that I haven't heard from you, and then eventually we'll deck the house in mourning and pretend that you died," she said, watching his face with interest.

He frowned. "What if someone sees me in another town?"

"I'll tell them they're mistaken, that my husband is dead," she replied, staring into the emerald of his gaze.

"You've got this all thought out, don't you?"

She folded her arms across her chest. "I want my child to be protected."

"You're depending on me to go along with your plan. What if I don't? What if I told people of your plan?" he asked.

Fear rippled through her. "Then you wouldn't receive your half of the proceeds from the sugarcane crop. And you would be hurting an innocent child. A child who has no father to protect him."

He smiled and lifted a blonde curl from her shoulder. "There is another option we could consider. We could make this into a real marriage and I would never leave."

She laughed, suddenly feeling very nervous, and stepped away from him. She couldn't think of him as a real husband—she couldn't think of any man as being in her life on a permanent basis ever again. And especially not a rambling man who made her heart quicken at his touch.

"Thank you for the offer, but I'd like to stick with our original setup. I've already been married once—and, well, we both know how that turned out."

Nicole stepped around Max and walked to the door of his bedroom, fighting the urge to run, trying to retain her outward calm appearance, knowing the shell would crack very soon.

"The next time you go to town, please place a notice on the bulletin board at the mercantile for a new overseer. I'll talk to anyone who has previous experience," she said, as though they were still discussing business and not marriage.

He gazed at her; his dark eyes seemed almost hypnotic, and he watched her closely. "I'll take care of it." Nicole nodded and then stepped out of the room, shutting the door firmly behind her. She leaned against the portal and gave her emotions free rein. Her body began to shake while tears surged to her eyes.

She was losing control of her gentle, passive husband and she wondered if she'd been right to marry this man. Had she made things better or worse for her child by marrying Max? Or had she only complicated an already tough situation?

# Chapter Five

The next morning, Nicole stood in front of the house waiting for the stable hand to bring the wagon around. The feelings of losing control of her home had stayed with her all night long. She worried about what she should do to prove to her short-term husband that she did not intend to relinquish the management of this plantation entirely to him. Yes, she had let him manage things while she was ill, but she felt much better now and she couldn't surrender complete power to a man who would only be there until the birth of the baby. Where would she be once he was gone if she'd become dependent on him?

And she worried about his last comment regarding their marriage. Could the drifter think that living here would be better than wandering from town to town and decided that he would convince her to let him stay? Did he mean to try to claim his position as husband in her household?

Had she so misjudged his character that hiding behind his smile was a man who suddenly thought he'd married someone with money and land?

She laughed out loud at the last thought. She'd been unable to pay the lumber mill this month, the mercantile in town would soon cut off her credit, and the workers fund would run out of cash to pay them before the crop came in.

The baby and the crop were due in the same month and she had to hold on until December. Max could leave in January and she'd start the new year, just her and the baby.

Jean's face swam before her eyes, and for the first time in months, she felt tears prick her eyelids. Not because she missed her dead husband, but more because of what he'd done to their child. For the first time, she understood how her mother must have felt. Nicole mourned the one person no longer on this earth who would have known how to help her cope. She'd been dead since Nicole was ten. Though Consuelo understood being illegitimate, still there were times when Nicole missed the comfort of her mother.

She blinked back the tears. Lately she felt so weepy, and today she was determined to show her strength. This morning she would regain control of her plantation. Just then the wagon came around from the stables and pulled to a stop in front of her.

"Ma'am, would you like me to drive you?"

"That's not necessary, Moses, I'll be fine," she said, knowing the sun would soon climb high in the sky and turn the land into a sweltering inferno. There would be little time before the heat became so unbearable it made her sick. But she would drive to the fields and show that she still managed Rosewood.

Moses helped her up into the wagon and then handed her the reins.

"Thank you. I'll be back shortly."

"Yes, ma'am," he said, and stepped back out of her way.

She clicked to the horses. The wagon jerked as she turned onto the road that led to the fields. Noah had told her they were working the largest field of sugarcane today, fertilizing the tall green stalks. Unfortunately, the largest field was located at the very back of her property and could only be reached by horse or wagon.

It didn't take long for the sun to roast right through her clothes, the high humidity sending sweat trickling down her back. A parasol would have at least protected her from the piercing heat of the sun shining directly on her, but nothing could deter her from visiting the fields today and showing the field hands she still was in charge.

Finally, she arrived at the cane field and noticed the men working in the fields, some without shirts, some with ripped shirts that allowed for the breeze to cool them as they hoed the field.

She pulled the wagon to a halt and climbed down. When her feet touched the ground, she felt the first wave of dizziness hit her, but she stood, holding onto the wagon and letting herself stabilize, hoping the feeling would soon pass.

"Nicole, what are you doing here?" Max called to her as he gazed toward her, his shirt open, his planter's hat firmly on his head. He looked strong and virile with the rippled muscles of his chest visible, his stance solid, his arms folded across his chest.

"I came to inspect the sugarcane and see how it's doing," she said, determined not to succumb to the heat once again.

He smiled and walked toward her and she knew he realized that she'd come to usurp his authority. "We're just finishing fertilizing this field. I was about to let the men take a break."

She let go of the wagon and walked toward him, feeling better.

"I'm surprised to see you out here," he said. "If I'd known you were coming, I would have said to bring a picnic lunch and we could have eaten together."

She frowned. Why did she feel like he was picking up right where he'd left things the last time they were together? Almost like he seemed glad to see her. Did he seem to be more interested in her as a woman than what she deemed wise?

"I only came out here to see how the sugarcane is progressing," she said, feeling rays from the sun beating on the top of her head and wishing she'd thought to bring her parasol. "It's so hot out here."

"Here, let's move you into the shade, out of the sun. I don't want you fainting on me again," he said, taking her by the arm and leading her into the shelter of a large oak tree that grew on the edge of the cane field.

A gusty breeze blew, but instead of cooling, the air seemed hot and blistering. Yet the shade helped and she thought she would be all right

"Who's doing Frank's job?" she asked, gazing at the workers in the field.

"I am until you hire someone new," he said. "I'm going to be putting up a notice in town and I thought I would speak with the candidates before you make the final decision."

This wasn't going at all as she'd expected. He was conceding to her that it was her decision and she'd expected to have to demand that he let her choose the next overseer. She'd planned on showing the men that the plantation still belonged to her, but Max didn't seem to be making any claims that she wasn't the owner.

She gazed at him warily, trying to decide if he could really be this honest and gentle, or if it was just a facade.

"All right," she said hesitantly.

"Do you want to see what we're doing?" he asked.

"Yes, I'd like that," she said, following him, unable to keep from noticing the way the back of his pants fit snug around his buttocks. She raised her eyes, wondering how she could even be thinking of such a thing.

They stepped inside the rows of cane that stood taller than Nicole and all the hot air she'd felt before died away, leaving behind a thick pocket of humid, pungent air. When she tried to take a breath, her lungs felt heavy and constricted.

"All we're doing is...putting a scoop of... around each plant," Max said, walking close to her side, reaching out occasionally to steady her.

Nicole tried to listen to him, but her attention remained focused on her breathing, the sharp odor thick in her nostrils, her stomach rising at the caustic odor.

She took a deep breath and the smell of manure was overwhelming, causing her to gasp. A new wave of nausea hit her and at that moment she knew she should never have come. "Oh, no, I think I'm going to be sick."

Max turned and looked at her. He took her by the arm and quickly led her between the rows of cane, trying to find his way back to the edge of the field.

She stumbled and he wrapped his arm around her, steadying her.

"We're almost out of here," he said.

"I'm not going to make it," she whispered, halting, feeling sweat trickle down her back, the breeze almost nonexistent among the rows of tall cane. There was nothing she could do to stop the nausea from rising, filling her throat. "I'm going to be sick."

Nicole turned away from him, mortified to lose the contents of her stomach in front of him. Tears sprang to her eyes as her knees went weak and her abdomen began to heave.

He slipped a comforting arm around her waist and a gentle hand rubbed her back and she wanted to tell him to go away, but couldn't. All she could do was make a retching noise as she bent over and lost everything.

When she finally stopped, he handed her his handkerchief.

"Here, wipe your face with my handkerchief. It's clean," he said gently.

Nicole, humiliated past the point of caring, took the scrap of cotton and wiped the tears from her eyes and her mouth and nose. She didn't want to look at him, to face him after her humiliation, but finally she glanced into his emerald eyes and was surprised to see his worried look. "I hate being sick. No one has ever seen me be sick except Consuelo."

"Well, there are first times for everything," he said, his

voice soothing. "Come on, let's get you back in the wagon and I'll take you home."

"No, I'll be okay. You need to stay here with the men," she said, realizing how stupid she'd been to have come all the way out here when she knew the heat wilted her.

"I am not going to let you drive yourself home. Seems as if we've had this argument before," he said, his voice rising in agitation. "Sometimes you're a very stubborn woman."

"Thank you," she said. "I mean to be."

"Well at least your sense of humor hasn't left you."

Walking back to the wagon, with his arm around her waist supporting her, she stopped and looked up at him. Suddenly she swayed and he reached down and scooped her up in his arms like she weighed little or nothing. Nicole felt too weak to argue with him.

Gently he set her in the wagon. "Why did you drive out here today, anyway? Were you just trying to show me that this is your plantation?"

"I don't have to show you; it *is* my plantation," she said with the last little bit of defiance left in her. "But I wanted the field hands to see that I still controlled Rosewood. I guess I really didn't accomplish what I set out to do."

He chuckled. "Not really. Come on, Mrs. Viel. Let's get you home and settled in the cool shade of the house."

"Please," she whispered, mortified. She wanted to be strong, but felt so weak. Yet how could she be angry with Max when he'd been so kind and caring? Jean would never have stayed and soothed her while she retched. Max appeared to be a decent, kind man and twice now he'd helped her when she felt ill. She only hoped his compassionate nature wasn't an act that hid a much viler disposition, just as Jean had hidden his evil behind his charming temperament.

~

The sun hung low in the evening sky as Max made his way to the house. He couldn't help but worry about Nicole. He'd brought her back to the house and put her in Consuelo's capable hands. He'd left Consuelo scolding Nicole the way that Max wanted to, but thought unwise. The woman frightened him, almost fainting in the cane field that way. He'd been afraid for her and the baby. She had no business coming out there, even if she was concerned about him taking charge of the plantation. She had the baby to think about.

He'd worried about Nicole and the child all afternoon. When he reached the house he searched until he found Consuelo.

"How is Nicole?" he asked the little Spanish woman.

"She's better. I put her to bed and made her rest all afternoon, and she has more color in her cheeks now." Consuelo frowned at him. "She can't be allowed to do that again."

"I know. I've told the stable hands they are not permitted to hitch the wagon for her or saddle a horse during this extreme heat. Mrs. Viel is not to leave the plantation unless someone is with her," he said as he sat down at the large dinner table all alone.

"Good," Consuelo said, watching him.

"Has she eaten anything?" Max asked, thinking that he dreaded having his meal alone and would miss her company.

"No. I was going to fix her a tray and take it in," Consuelo said.

"I'll take it to her," he said, standing up, eager to check on her. "That is, if you think she's up to having company."

Consuelo stared at him, a furrow in her brow. "She's told me about your marriage," she said, pausing and gazing at him, her dark eyes watchful. "You seem concerned about her."

He frowned, wondering what Nicole had told Consuelo. And yes, he was worried about Nicole.

"Of course I'm concerned, she's expecting a child. I don't want anything to happen to her or the baby."

Consuelo nodded, her observant eyes staring. "It would be good for her to have dinner with you. I'll put both of your plates on a tray and you can take it in to her."

The servant hurried out of the room to prepare the plates. Max had yet to figure out her role in the household, though it seemed as if Nicole listened to the older woman.

Max glanced around the large dining room. The table could easily have seated thirty people, with a sideboard along one wall where the food could be placed. A cord controlled a large punkah fan over the table that could be pulled by a servant, keeping the dinner guests cool during the hot summer months.

For a moment, Max imagined his grandfather and grandmother entertaining in this room and he could almost hear the sound of their laughter. Rosewood should have been his inheritance and now it would be his son's.

"Here is the tray," Consuelo said, coming through the door from the area that led to the pantry, bringing his thoughts back to the present. "Are you sure you don't want me to carry it in?"

He smiled. "I won't drop it," he promised. "Just open the door to her bedroom for me."

Consuelo gazed up at him with a look that left him feeling as if he'd been warned to keep his distance from Nicole, but dutifully followed him to her bedroom. With a rapid knock, she swung the door open and Max stepped into Nicole's room.

Pale yellow curtains hung from the windows, with a matching yellow coverlet on the bed. Mosquito netting surrounding the bed had been pushed to the side.

Nicole sat in bed, reading a book, her wrapper covering her nightgown. He stopped at the sight of her blonde hair cascading down to the pillow, past her shoulders, almost to her waist. He hadn't realized the length of her hair.

He swallowed and tried to think of something cool and refreshing, because looking at Nicole definitely raised his blood until he felt scorched. His wife didn't realize her beauty and how it affected him. And if she saw his lust for her it would frighten her away.

"Good evening. I hope you're feeling better," he said as she gazed up at him, her blue eyes shimmering.

She smiled. "Much, thank you."

"Are you hungry?" he asked.

"Actually, I'm famished. Whatever you have there smells wonderful."

"Well, you can thank Consuelo. She fixed the plates. I hope you don't mind me coming in, but I didn't want to eat alone and I wanted to check on you," he said, unable to tear his gaze away from his wife.

The more he knew her the more he liked her gentle spirit, her soft smile, the more ashamed he felt at deceiving her. She deserved so much better and yet he had no choice. Regaining Rosewood was his familial obligation.

Max placed the tray on a small table and pulled it close to the bed. "There you go. I even brought napkins."

He started to tuck a napkin in her wrapper and then caught himself. She gazed at him, her blue eyes dancing with mischief. "I'm not an invalid, Max. Just expecting a baby."

He nodded, and a smile flitted across her face. For the next few minutes they sat enjoying their food, each one watching the other, a comfortable silence between them. Sometimes he felt like he'd known her for years instead of only weeks.

"You seem to be feeling better. You've eaten quite well," he said, watching her.

"I'm starving. This is the first meal I've had since breakfast and I didn't realize how hungry I was," she said.

"I'm glad to see you're recovering from this morning," he said, noticing the color in her cheeks.

Nicole reached out and touched him on the arm. "Thank you for taking care of me and bringing me home."

He smiled at the feel of her hand on his arm, soft and warm. "You're welcome. But promise me you won't drive the wagon or buggy without bringing someone with you."

"No, I guess my driving days are rather limited— until after this baby comes."

Max sat back and contemplated Nicole, watching her finish her dinner. "Do you mind if I ask you a question?"

She glanced at him and shrugged. "All I can do is say no; if I don't want to answer it, I won't."

"Why did you marry Jean?" Max asked the question that he couldn't help but wonder about these past few weeks. Had she loved Jean Cuvier?

Nicole stared at him, stunned for a moment. "Believe it or not, Jean Cuvier was wonderful at convincing a woman that she was the most important person in the world to him. I mean, after all, he persuaded all three of us that we were the only women in his life and we trusted him. I didn't question his absences, little things that I should have noticed. I blindly believed whatever he told me."

She shook her head. "We had a wonderful life together and I thought we were very much in love. We wanted children, we wanted to travel, and we wanted a big family that could gather here at Rosewood."

She sighed, the sound heavy in the early evening light. "But someone poisoned Jean and that's when we wives all found out the truth about our husband." She paused and gazed at Max. "Funny, I thought Jean and I were happy, but little did I know that everything was a lie."

Max shrugged, wondering how he could overcome her resistance to trust after what Jean had done. "You're going to have a problem trusting someone again."

"Wouldn't you?" she asked, gazing at him from her bed.

"Yes," he said, thinking of how his own manipulation would hurt her. Sooner or later, she would become suspicious when she asked him to leave and he refused. Soon, he would tell Nicole that temporary marriage to him meant until the end of time. Soon she would realize that their lives had become one; but until that time, Max had to build her trust.

"I could understand if he had tried to make me his mistress, but to marry me ..." she said, her voice filled with hurt and anger.

Max stood and placed both of their empty plates back on the tray, then walked over to the window and leaned against the wall, facing her. He put his hands in his pockets and crossed his ankles.

"I'm not offering excuses, but maybe he knew he couldn't marry you, but loved and wanted you," Max said, thinking any man who didn't want his wife would be crazy. A beautiful, gentle woman, Nicole had put her trust in the wrong man and paid dearly.

"But that's so unfair to me, to our child, and even to his real wife, Marian. They had children together. How did he think this would affect them?" she said, her voice filled with anger and resentment.

Max nodded. "I'm not saying what Jean did was right. It was morally wrong, but sometimes where a woman is concerned men don't always make the best decisions."

Nicole stared at him, her eyes darkening at his words as she contemplated them. "Have you ever made a bad decision regarding a woman?"

He almost laughed out loud as he thought of Desiree and his son Paul. One moment of reckless abandonment had brought a life into this world. And the verdict was still out on whether marrying Nicole had been a wise choice or an act of folly.

His breathing seemed to quicken as he gazed at Nicole lying in bed. He remembered the simple kiss they'd shared at their wedding ceremony and the urge to taste her red-wine lips once again almost overwhelmed him.

"Only a half a million times," he said, trying to lighten the mood. He couldn't let himself think of her lips or the way her wrapper clung to her full breasts or the fact that she only wore a nightgown beneath those sheets. He couldn't let himself think of any of these things, because Nicole was expecting a baby. And she expected him to depart as soon as the child arrived. She had no plans to consummate their marriage.

But her plans and his were not the same.

She laughed. "I find that hard to believe, Max. You don't seem like a man who makes wrong decisions very often."

He gazed at her and wondered if she realized what she'd just said. He smiled. "You're right I don't like to be wrong. I like knowing where I'm going and that I'm doing the right thing."

"Is that why you married me?" she asked.

"Partly," he responded, knowing the much bigger reason she wouldn't want to hear.

Nicole gasped and gazed down at her belly, placing her hand on her stomach. She looked at him, a smile of relief spreading across her face. "He's alive. I think the baby just moved. I felt a little flutter of movement"

She laughed out loud and closed her eyes, relieved. "Thank God, the baby is alive. I've been so worried." He gazed at her, feeling anxious, and then crossed the room to stand beside the bed. He moved the table out of the way and sat down next to her on the bed. She giggled delightfully. "Here, feel it"

Nicole grabbed his hand and placed it over her abdomen and he felt a faint flutter like a butterfly wing, barely discernible through her nightgown.

He moved his hand, suddenly realizing where she'd placed it.

"Did you feel it?" she asked excitedly.

"I can't feel anything," he said, feeling awkward about sitting on her bed, touching her so intimately, being this close to Nicole. Though they were married, thoughts of her that he knew he shouldn't be thinking skittered across his mind. None of which had to do with motherhood.

He stood and picked up the tray of dirty dishes. "I'll take these back to the kitchen so that you can rest" She looked at him, still excited, yet oddly disappointed. "All right. Thanks for being here, Max. I don't think I've told you, but I appreciate you marrying and taking care of me like you have."

His conscience twinged as he walked toward the door.

"You're welcome," he said, not glancing back at the woman in bed. His mind filled with images of her lying naked in that bed with him beside her. Images that somehow he seemed to think of way too often lately

# Chapter Six

Late the next day, Max looked up from the field, stunned at the sight of his son riding horseback alongside his father. Fear that something dreadful brought the two of them here seized him and he ran to meet them on the road.

They reined in their horses when he reached them. "Papa, Paul, hello. What are the two of you doing here?" he asked, slightly out of breath. "Is Mother all right?"

Charles glanced at his grandson, and then at Max. "Your mother is fine. But there's a little problem that Paul needs to talk to you about. His mother sent him to live with you after he ran away."

Max frowned at his twelve-year-old son. Desiree must have a new man in her life. "What? What happened, Paul?"

The boy frowned and raised his chin defiantly. "I got tired of Mother's gentlemen friends and ran away."

Max absorbed this news and couldn't say that he was surprised at the appearance of his son on his doorstep. The boy's mother breezed in and out of Paul's life on a daily basis and Max knew someday the boy would see the difference in how his parents lived their lives.

"I want to live with you. I don't want to stay with my mother anymore," Paul said, his young face stern and rigid.

"Climb down off your horse and let's sit in the shade where we can talk," Max told the boy, watching as he swung his long legs over the side of the horse and slid down to the ground. At twelve years of age, Paul's tall and lanky frame had not yet filled out. Somehow his muscles seemed to have fallen behind his bone structure, making him appear skinny and lean. Charles Viel, Max's father, climbed down and approached his son.

"You're looking fit. Living in the country must agree with you."

"Thanks, Father. How is everyone at home?"

"Your mother is her usual belligerent self. We'll talk about it later."

Max didn't ask, afraid of what his father meant by that statement After Paul ground tethered his horse, the boy turned and shook his hand. "Good to see you, sir."

"And you, boy." He hugged his son, not caring that he felt stiff in his arms. "Let's go sit in the shade and you tell me why you ran away from your mother."

While the boy's mother's faults were many, she managed to keep him fed and cared for. Somewhere along the way, Paul had learned decent manners and seemed to have a good head on his shoulders, so Max was surprised to learn that Paul had run. This was the first time that Max knew of his being defiant or causing his mother any trouble.

The three of them sat down under a large oak tree—grandfather, father, and son.

"Go ahead, boy, and tell your father what you told me," Charles Viel said.

The boy glanced at his father and took a deep breath. "Mother has a new boyfriend who has money and doesn't want me around. She didn't believe me when I told her that he told me to get lost. He even offered to pay me to leave. But you know how she always is when she has a new gentleman friend. She thinks he's wonderful and doesn't want to hear anything bad."

"That will only last until either the money I send is all gone or her new boyfriend disappears," Max said with a frown.

He sighed. Paul was the result of Max having a schoolboy affair with an older woman. A woman he later learned had several children out of wedlock. When Desiree informed him she was with child, Max felt a responsibility for the child she carried, but he'd refused to marry her. He couldn't. Over the years, he'd always made sure that his son had food and clothes, which was more than some of the boy's brothers and sisters received.

"Sir, you've always told me that if I wanted to come live with you, I could. I'm tired of my mother and her boyfriends. If I can't live with you, then I will run away somewhere no one will find me," Paul said dramatically.

Max loved this child and wanted to be involved in his life; he wanted to give Paul a good start, even if he'd been unable to provide him a stable home. But keeping him from Nicole would be difficult.

And though the timing could have been better, Max couldn't turn his back on the boy now when he needed him.

"Okay, son, you can stay with me, but for a while you're going to have to sleep in the barn. Things are not what they seem right now, and later I hope I can explain everything to you. Just trust me on this and stay away from the main house until I can get things straightened out."

"Yes, sir. I don't mind sleeping in the barn," the boy said. "It'll be fun."

Max smiled and shook his head. "Only a kid would think that sleeping in a barn could be an adventure." He looked at his father. "I'm afraid the same goes for you, Papa. I can't risk you going to the big house just yet"

Charles shrugged. "I don't particularly want to be in that house. Jean Cuvier lived there and you know my feelings regarding that scalawag. Until your mother forces me, I don't want anything to do with that house."

"Papa, your new daughter-in-law was once married to Jean and loved him. You're going to have to accept Nicole."

"I don't have a problem accepting her. But that doesn't mean I have to like her dead husband," he said defiantly.

Max shook his head, knowing the subject of Jean always made his father angry, though Charles would never say why.

"Come on then, let's go into town and have dinner."

"Your new wife, she won't mind you going with us?" his father asked.

Though Max would miss dining with Nicole, he knew he couldn't risk his father and his son being found out, so tonight he would take them to town.

"She'll be fine," Max said, and glanced toward the big house, hoping that she wouldn't be on the verandah and see him with his father and Paul.

"Come on, they have a restaurant in town that you'll both enjoy. I'll treat," he said, wanting to get them out of sight before the sun cooled enough that Nicole would wander outside. Right now he didn't want to answer any questions regarding Paul to Nicole.

~

Later that night after Paul had finally fallen asleep, Charles and Max sat outside the barn, far enough away from the big house that they wouldn't be detected, and gazed at the stars visible in the late night sky.

"How's Mother? I'm surprised she didn't insist on coming with you," Max said, glancing over at his father in the darkness.

In the last few months his father's hair had turned completely gray and new lines had formed around his mouth and eyes. Charles had buried his only sister, Max's Aunt Blanche, four months ago, and since that time his father had aged considerably. His drinking had increased and Max feared for his health.

Charles laughed. "Well, she's been a little upset with me. Your mother told me to leave town for a while and not return. I know she would have come with Paul, but when she received your letter she agreed to wait. I give her about a month and then she'll be beating down your door, insisting that you take her in."

"That doesn't give me much time. But I'm sure you're right, she's wanted this house back for many years," he said with a sigh, knowing he couldn't waste any time in convincing Nicole to make their marriage real.

"So why did she tell you to leave, Papa? What did you do that sent her into a snit this time?" Max asked, not sure he really wanted to know, but thinking that maybe it might be better to be forewarned.

"Nothing more than the usual, except this time I came home drunk after being out all night, and she smelled another woman's perfume on me. It was nothing. I've been staying in touch with Blanche's lady servant, Colette, and she gave me a hug goodbye. Your mother didn't believe me," he said, dejected. "She's pretty mad at me, especially since I stayed out all night and came home drunk."

Max shook his head and stood up. Since the death of his father's sister, his drinking had grown progressively worse until now seldom a day went by that he wasn't drunk.

"Your drinking is getting out of hand, Papa. I know you miss Blanche, but she wouldn't like what you're doing to yourself."

"My drinking is my business," Charles said, and glanced away from his son.

"That may be, but I don't want to watch you slowly kill yourself," Max said into the darkness.

Charles shrugged and Max knew from previous experience with his father that the subject was closed. For a few moments they sat in the darkness and listened to the night sounds. A mosquito buzzed Max, and he reached up to slap the pesky creature.

"When do you have to go back, Papa?" Max asked.

"Tomorrow morning, but I'm going to go by the cemetery first and check on Blanche's grave. Make sure it's being kept up and bring some fresh flowers."

Max nodded, seeing the sadness still in his father's eyes, not knowing how he could help with his grief.

"I need to ask a favor, Papa," Max said, knowing that soon they would be forced to go inside or be carried away by the nasty bugs.

"What, Son?"

"I'm glad you brought Paul to me, but try to keep his location from his mother. Once her new gentleman friend disappears and she no longer has money, she'll come running to get him back."

His father nodded. "I feared as much. She doesn't want the boy so much as she does the cash."

"True. Otherwise she would have given him to me years ago," Max said as he thought of the woman he'd been so foolish to become involved with.

His father nodded. "Paul's a nice kid, he deserves better."

"Desiree only looks out for herself, and right now Paul is not useful to her. But once this new man has ditched her, then he will once again be one of the few of her children she receives money for." Max hated the situation but had felt powerless to change it. Now the boy was in his safekeeping and the time even seemed right to have his lawyers arrange to have Paul placed in his custody. After all, his mother had released Paul to his father. Why shouldn't Max take advantage of the situation?

"Keep both Desiree and Mother away from Rosewood for as long as possible. I'm hoping to resolve the situation with Nicole soon, but it's not going to happen overnight. Soon, very soon, Mother can come spend as much time as she wants in the house. Tell her I said so," Max told his father.

"Does your wife know that your great-great-grandfather is the one who started this plantation?" his father asked, his eyes widening in the darkness. "That you married her to regain Rosewood?"

A stiff breeze blew off the river, sending the spirit bottles to rattling in the night air. They clanged together, their sound tinkling with the breeze.

Max cleared his throat. "Not so loud. The night has ears, and I don't want that information making its way back to her just yet"

"So when do you intend to let her know that you want the land back?"

A cricket chirped close by as Max sighed, the sound heavy in the night air. "I don't know. We're married and I keep hoping that with time she'll agree to make this marriage work. I just need some time to help her adjust."

"You know your mother. All I can say is you better hurry because she'll be knocking on your doorstep before the weather cools."

"Well, you could help me by keeping her at home. Court her like she was a young girl again. Just do something to keep her from coming to Rosewood," Max pleaded, knowing his mother could ruin everything.

Charles snorted. "Courting is for fools. She hasn't been interested in me for the last twenty years. What makes you think she would be now?"

"With that kind of an attitude, she probably gave up on you. Just once, if you treated her like the woman you loved instead of tolerated, maybe she would look twice at you. Frankly, I don't know how she's put up with you all these years."

Silence filled the air. "Since the day she learned I couldn't save Rosewood for her, she's hated me. I've never done anything right for that woman, so what makes you think that's changed?"

Max shook his head, knowing he fought a useless battle that he could never win. "You're both in the wrong most of the time, but you'd think that with almost thirty years of marriage you'd care enough about each other to be concerned. Sometimes I wish you'd both agree to live separate lives, just so I wouldn't have to listen to the two of you argue." Max paused, anger filling him at the way his parents acted.

"I think I've said more than enough for one night. I'm going to bed and will see you in the morning." He walked away from his father, leaving the barn behind, and strolled toward the big house. The years had taken a toll on his parents' marriage, leaving them miserable, disillusioned, and downright hateful at times.

Knowing the way his mother felt about Rosewood, he was almost certain his father was right. Soon, very soon, she'd be here, and if Nicole hadn't agreed to make their marriage permanent, he'd be revealed prematurely.

~

The next afternoon Nicole sat reading the diary on the reclining couch in her bedroom, when a knock sounded on her bedroom door.

"Come in," she said, glancing out the front window where she could look out and see the river flowing by in the distance. The sun had driven her indoors and she'd spent the rest of the afternoon resting, reading the diary she'd found.

Consuelo came into her bedroom and shut the door behind her. "I picked up the new deed at the lawyer's office, like you requested. Everything's been taken care of."

"Good."

Consuelo frowned at her. "The lawyer and I, we also drew up a new will just in case anything should happen to me, so the land would revert back to you and the child."

"You didn't have to do that," Nicole said. "You'll probably outlive me."

"Well, I wanted to do it...just in case."

"What about the material I asked you to pick up? Did you find any baby cloth that we could make blankets from?" Nicole asked, wanting to start on a coverlet for the nursery.

"Yes, I bought you several yards of a soft cotton and even some yarn in case you wanted to crochet a blanket," Consuelo said, handing her the brown paper-wrapped package.

Eager to see the cloth, she tore into the package and admired the material. "Thanks, Consuelo, I can't wait to get started sewing."

"You're welcome." Consuelo frowned. "I asked about the bill, but Mr. Johnson said not to worry, that it had been taken care of. Did you pay it?"

Nicole stopped fingering the soft cotton material and glanced up. "What are you talking about? I didn't pay Mr. Johnson. In fact, I feared he wouldn't let you purchase the things we needed."

"No. He said your bill had been paid."

Nicole frowned. "That doesn't make sense. Who would have given him money?"

Consuelo raised her brows. "Then I went down the street to the lumber mill because Leon needed some nails. I checked first to see if they would let me buy them and they told me I could put as much as I wanted on the account. It seems that bill has also been paid."

"What?" Nicole said. "Did you find out who is paying my bills? Please tell me you asked?"

"Yes, I asked, and was told that your new husband, Mr. Viel, paid your bill. It appears that he took care of your bills at the mercantile, the plantation store, and the lumber mill. You owe no one in town anything," Consuelo said as Nicole peered up at her in total shock.

A trickle of uneasiness went through Nicole. How could Max pay her bills? The total was not an enormous sum, but still, almost fifty dollars for all three places. How could a drifter come up with that kind of cash?

And why hadn't Max said anything to her about paying her creditors? He'd kept quiet about what he'd done, and that concerned her. Where did he get the kind of money needed to pay her debts?

She would insist on repaying him as soon as possible. But how could she afford to let go of that kind of cash? Especially now, when her bank account balance looked more like egg money.

"What are you going to do?" Consuelo asked.

"I don't know. I just don't understand why he did this. And how could he afford to pay those bills?" Nicole asked her trusted friend.

Now she was indebted to Max and she didn't like that one bit

"I don't know. If your marriage was going to be lasting, then I think he's doing his husbandly duty by taking care of you. But he knows yours is only a temporary arrangement, doesn't he?" Consuelo said.

Nicole nodded, contemplating her trusty servant's words. "So if he knows our marriage is not going to last forever after, then why is he doing this?"

She sighed, suddenly feeling fearful of the reasons for Max's actions. Why had she thought an arrangement like theirs could ever work? How could she have trusted Max to keep his word?

"I think I need to speak with Mr. Viel," Nicole said, suddenly rising from her resting place. "He owes me some answers."

## Chapter Seven

Even though Max could hire any number of carpenters, he enjoyed the sense of accomplishment that working with wood gave him as he pounded a nail into the cradle he was building. The aboveground basement of the house provided him a cool, shady place to work out of the late afternoon sun. A refreshing breeze blew through the open doors and he felt a sense of peace working with his hands. In this place, he could ruminate about the situation with Nicole and plan how to help his wife realize he wanted their marriage to become a lasting union of two people who worked toward a common goal. Not a love match, but they both wanted Rosewood and this was a good compromise.

Max picked up the cabinet scraper and began to smooth the edges of the wood. He'd decided to build a cradle as a gift for the baby. Not to impress Nicole, but rather because he wanted the child to have something from him. Given the chance, he would raise this child as his own and never tell his family any different. Now instead of having one child, he'd have two, and hopefully more.

"Moses," he heard Nicole call. "Where is Mr. Viel?"

Before he could hide the crib she walked into the storage area, her face flushed, and her eyes wide. The smell of lilacs permeated the small room like a breath of fresh air from the garden. Until Nicole, he'd never noticed the way a woman smelled, and the scents she wore were light and delicate, reminding him of springtime.

"We need to talk," she said, her voice strident as she hurried into the room, her skirts swooshing as she moved into the semi-dark, damp room. Her gaze dropped to his hands as he sanded the bare wood with the scraper.

"Oh," she said, gasping at the sight of the crib. Slowly she walked over to inspect the wooden cradle, her face holding a look of amazement. She glanced up at Max, her indigo eyes large and luminous, searching his. "Are you making this for the baby?"

He smiled, pleased at her response. "Yes. I thought you might like to use this while the baby is tiny."

"You built this for the baby," she said in amazement. She ran her hand over the oak, gave it a little push, and watched the cradle sway. "It even rocks."

"I still need to finish sanding it and then I thought I would put a light stain on the wood."

Max watched tears fill her eyes, surprised at the emotion he saw there.

"No one has ever made me anything like this," she said, looking at him in wonder. "Why are you doing this?"

He shrugged. "I wanted to do something special for the baby and I thought you could place it by your bed at night."

She sniffed back her tears. "Consuelo and I can make a small mattress and coverlet for it." She gazed up at him, her blue eyes warming him clear to his toes and making his breathing more rapid. "Thank you, Max. I don't know what to say. You continually amaze me."

He smiled, pleased at her response. "I enjoy surprising you. Sometimes I think you've never had a man who spoiled you before."

Nicole blushed and he could tell he'd taken her completely off guard. "I guess I never have."

"Didn't your father ever indulge you when you were a little girl?" he asked in a teasing manner.

She tensed, and he knew he'd said the wrong thing and he was sorry he'd somehow ruined the mood.

"No, my father never spoiled me." She seemed to gather and separate herself from the cradle. She walked away, her back to him, and when she whirled around, the emotional wall that divided them was firmly back in place.

There's something I need to discuss with you. Consuelo

went to town this morning and came back with some interesting information."

"Like what?" he asked, frowning, afraid of just what Consuelo knew.

"Someone has paid all my outstanding balances in town," she stated, her expression serious. "Did you pay my debts?"

He paused, wondering how he should answer her question. He'd hoped that she wouldn't find out until their life together was more settled. But he couldn't hold off settling the bills because he'd needed some lumber, and when he'd tried to purchase the material on the plantation account, he'd discovered Nicole owed money.

"I had some extra cash, so I went ahead and paid the bills," he said, not really being deceitful, but not being honest, either. He hated lying to her, yet he couldn't tell her the truth just yet. He couldn't tell her that her debts were minimal and he could pay them easily.

She frowned at him, her hands going to her hips. "How do you have extra cash? I'm sure you must have needed it"

"I told you that I did some work for that hotel," he said.

"But you also told me that they gave you free room and board in exchange." She watched him, her eyes narrowed in suspicion.

"Yes, they did. But the owners were so pleased, they paid me extra." He picked up the cradle and reminded her, "I do excellent carpentry work."

Silently he regarded her as she stared at him, distrust darkening her eyes. "Before you decide to do something that involves me or the plantation again, I wish you would consult me, since you're not going to be here that long."

He tilted his head to the side and gazed at her. "You seem upset about this. I'm only trying to help you."

"I don't want to owe you any more than I already do," she said with determination. "I'm sure you need the money just as badly as I do."

Something in her response caused Max to bristle. She assumed the worst about him and he couldn't help but wonder why. Or had Jean scarred her so badly she assumed the worst about all men?

"Do you think that I'm not worthy as a man? Did you just assume that I have no money?"

She stared at him, a frown between her brows. "I know very little about you as a man, except that you seem gentle and nice." She took a deep breath as he watched her contemplate her words carefully. "But most drifters never settle down in one place for long. They never put down roots and they never acquire much money. So yes, I thought you were the same way."

He stared at her, wanting so much to tell her the truth, but knowing that he'd be foolish to dispute her claim before he'd convinced her to let their marriage be everlasting.

Yet his pride was taking a beating. She thought him a bum siphoning off of her, taking advantage of her hospitality. He turned his back on her and went back to sanding the cradle in an attempt to control his response.

"I'll consult you before I pay off any more of your bills. You can pay me back when we settle up after the baby is born," he said, not looking at her, afraid to say much more.

A successful person all his life, no one had ever called him a vagrant or a drifter before and he didn't like it now. In fact, it took all of his self-control to keep from yelling out the truth to her. But he couldn't. There was so much at stake here besides his pride, yet he didn't know how long he could let her think of him as a loafer.

~

Three mornings later, Nicole sat across from Max at the breakfast table, sipping tea.

"How do you feel this morning?" he asked her.

The morning sickness seemed to have disappeared and as long as she had food in her stomach, she actually felt good. The baby moved now on a regular basis and her expanding waistline actually looked like she might be expecting.

"I've felt really pleasant these last few days," she said cheerfully, hoping the worst of her pregnancy was behind her.

"I'm glad to hear that," he said. "Then I think we should go into town today and attend the crawfish festival."

Nicole felt a moment of fear seize her as she remembered the day she met Max and how the ladies had snubbed and ridiculed her because of her marriage to Jean.

"I don't think I want to go," she said, rubbing her teacup nervously. "I don't particularly like crawfish and I have no need to travel into town."

Max raised his brows, his expression somewhat confused. "Don't you think we should be seen together before the baby is born? I know we put a wedding announcement in the paper, but if people don't see us as a couple, they won't believe the child is mine," he said, gazing at her, his green eyes warm with understanding. "We could wait until this afternoon, late, when it's cooler, and that way we could enjoy the music tonight."

The look he gave her made Nicole feel tingly inside, like thousands of nerve endings awakening to his gaze. She frowned, not certain she liked that feeling, not certain she wanted to feel anything as far as Max was concerned. Yet, he always managed to stimulate her, awaken a part of her that these last few months had seemed dead.

Contemplating his words, she knew he was right. How could she argue if his suggestion protected the baby? The afternoon heat would be dissipating and her last outing in a crowd had been Jean's funeral. Since then she'd avoided any social gatherings, and now even trips into town. Sooner or later, she would have to overcome her apprehension and become involved in community life once again, if for no other reason than the sake of the child.

"All right, I'll go for the baby," she said.

He frowned. "You need to go for yourself. It's important they think that the child you're expecting is mine, but you need to be accepted once again."

"I hardly think that one outing is going to repair the damage done to my reputation," she said. "In fact, I doubt that after Jean's death I will ever truly be received. I just don't want Jean's accursed bad behavior to taint our child. And that's where you're going to help me."

He raised his brows. "I can try to help you, but whether or not you're received again is mainly up to you."

"How?" she asked, feeling frustrated by his words, remembering her outing to the mercantile where she'd met Max. "By creating a scene every time one of the old society matrons scorns me on the street? Or should I get into a fistfight with the women who stand around tittering about me?"

All the anger that Nicole had carefully locked away returned in a flash of fury at the memory of how the townspeople treated her that day in town.

For a moment he said nothing. "No. We're going to become one of the most respectable young couples in town. We'll be invited to parties and everyone will be looking forward to the birth of our child. But you've got to smile and pretend that what you experienced previously never happened."

Nicole couldn't believe he would even suggest such a thing. How could she ever forget leaving the mercantile that day, her blood pounding with humiliation and shame? "You think that people are just going to forget all about my marriage to Jean and the fact that I suddenly married you, a stranger, out of the blue? Or the fact that my shape looks suspiciously like I'm expecting a child? Whose child is it? Yours or Jean's?" She paused. "I think you presume just a little too much, sir."

"No. People will talk regardless, but we're going to hold our heads high and smile and make them look petty when they don't want anything to do with us. Then we're going to be such an intriguing couple that soon everyone will want us at their parties," he said.

Nicole didn't know whether or not to laugh or be angry with him for such a ridiculous idea. "How much experience does a drifter like you have with genteel society?"

A shadow passed across his face and for a moment his eyes flashed with anger, but then he smiled. "It doesn't matter who you associate with; these are simple techniques that work on everyone."

She gazed at him, feeling suspicious. How could a man with a mind like Max's be a person who just wandered from place to place? And yet he didn't appear to be a shiftless, lazy man. Quite the contrary, really. He seemed to be comfortable being in control, as if he were used to running a plantation every day. He appeared very much at ease with people, a natural leader.

"So are we going this evening?" he asked, bringing the conversation back to his question.

"Yes, I'll go. But only if you promise me we'll be back at the house before it gets too late," she said, watching him stand to leave the table.

"Seems reasonable. Then we'll leave here about four o'clock. Wear your dancing shoes, as I expect to have at least one dance tonight, if not more," he said as he walked away.

~

The entire trip into town, Nicole feared she would make a fool of herself by throwing up once they reached the festival. But Max drove slowly and kept an eye on her. Consuelo sent along ajar of cool water and several sprigs of mint in case she felt ill.

When the buggy pulled into town a cooling breeze blew off the river, soothing the festival attendees. A *boucherie* was well underway with the pig roasting over a spit. Under an oak tree a group of men sat playing *La Bourre,* while off in the distance on a small stage, a band played, their instruments including a fiddle, an accordion, a scrub board and spoons.

People danced to the sounds of the band, while some women hurried around setting up tables of precooked food and chasing children away from the desserts.

At the sight of Anna DeChoskey, Nicole felt a moment of panic and wanted to tell Max to take her home, but knew that would be cowardly. The woman still wore the same sour expression she'd last seen in the mercantile that day the women had been all a twitter over Jean's scandal.

Nicole glanced over at Max, and he stared at her, waiting for her reaction. After several moments when she didn't say anything, he raised his brows.

"Are you ready?" he asked.

How could she disappoint him, when he'd been so patient and kind? He deserved to have some fun.

"Of course," she said, not about to admit to feeling faint at the sight of walking among the people who had scorned and ridiculed her.

Max climbed down from the buggy and came around to her side and lifted her off the seat "Then let's go make a good impression, Mrs. Viel."

He lifted the basket of food from the buggy that Consuelo had cooked for them and then took Nicole by the arm. They made their way through the crowds to where the women were busy setting out the food. Nicole clung to his arm, her hands shaking. She glanced at Max and he smiled reassuringly. When his lips turned up, her heart warmed at his smile.

Mrs. DeChoskey watched them approach and she raised a brow at Nicole, who wanted to somehow lower the woman's snob ratio just a tad.

"Hello, Mrs. Dechoskey, my husband and I brought some fresh cooked greens and a bread pudding to contribute," Nicole said, trying to cover her shaking hands and be friendly, though the memory of the woman's mistreatment remained fresh in Nicole's mind.

The woman took her basket, turning up her snobbish nose at the food offering, and gave Nicole a condescending smile. "Your husband?"

"Oh, yes, did you not see the announcement in the paper over a month ago? This is my husband, Maxim Viel."

Mrs. DeChoskey held out her hand, her face a mask of surprise as she gripped Max's hand. "Nice to meet you, Mr. Viel."

"Thank you."

"What part of the country are you from?" she asked, her brows drawn together in a questioning frown.

"New Orleans, ma'am."

An older woman walked up and stared at him. "Did you say your name was Viel?" she asked.

"Yes, ma'am, Maxim Viel."

The grandmotherly woman studied him, nodding her head. "I went to school with a girl who married a boy whose last name was Viel. I wonder if you're related."

Max shifted his eyes to Nicole. "Doubtful, ma'am. There's not many of my family left," he said without explaining. He took Nicole by the elbow. "If you ladies don't mind, we're going to walk around a bit, and my wife can introduce me to all the good folks of Plaquemine."

They walked a few steps farther where Max stopped

and Nicole introduced him to several of the men of the community. When they turned away, she heard one of the men say, "Hey, isn't she the woman who married that fellow who tied the knot with all those women?"

She tensed and couldn't hear the man's response.

"Smile, Nicole. Don't let them upset you," Max reminded. "Act as if you are a queen paying her subjects a visit."

"If I'm the queen, off with their heads!"

Max laughed. "You do have a sense of humor."

Nicole turned and glanced at him, noticing how his emerald eyes seemed to sparkle and glow in the fading light. How could just a look leave you feeling warm? "If I'm the queen what does that make you?"

"Well, I'm certainly not going to settle for anything less than your king," he said, tucking her hand inside his arm as they strolled about the festival watching the people.

"Do you think this stuff up all by yourself?"

He smiled and patted her hand. "Of course."

"I think I've married a crazy man," she said, pulling her shoulders back as they walked to the next group of people.

Max laughed and leaned closer to her ear. "Only when I'm with you."

His breath tickled the inside of her ear, sending a shiver down her spine, his words warming her. She turned and gazed at him, her breathing quickening at the heat she saw reflected in his gaze. How could she want something she knew was bad for her?

"Save your lines for other ladies, not me," she said, trying to remember that this marriage was in name only. She turned away, the look in his eyes leaving her tense and breathless in a way that she'd long forgotten.

"I think we need to find a table to sit at. They're beginning to serve the food," she said nervously, suddenly wanting to be with other people, anywhere but alone with

Max.

"We've got time," he said, nodding hello to a man as they walked through the crowds. "We're going to make sure that as many people as possible see us and then we'll go sit down."

"Have you ever done this before?" she asked suddenly, looking at him with new interest. "You know, you've never told me why you drift from town to town. Did something happen that made you not want to stay in one place?"

He smiled at her, his green eyes twinkling in the dying sunlight. "Nothing traumatic. But my grandfather always believed in belonging to a community. He's the one who taught me the value of being connected with people."

"So why haven't you settled down somewhere?" she asked, enjoying their stroll, enjoying being with this man who was her temporary husband. "Seems you would want to stay in one place."

"Is that an invitation?"

She laughed. "No."

"A guy can always hope." He shrugged. "I'm still looking for the right parish."

She thought of his response and something seemed vague and unbelievable. Why did she get the feeling that there was more to Max Viel than what he told her?

"Max, I hope you find the place you're looking for and that you'll be very happy," she said.

"Thank you. I will someday soon," he replied as he took her arm. "Come on, let's go get in line now. I think that we've walked through the crowds enough saying hello. Let's get something to eat and join someone at their table."

"Good, I'm famished," she said.

They heaped their plates high with food, including the *boucherie* and then joined a family at one of the tables.

The family happily made room for them and joined them in peeling the succulent crawfish. The couples exchanged names and enjoyed the meal prepared by the women of the community.

After dinner, the band began to play a Cajun tune and couples got up to dance. Though Nicole didn't want to overtire herself, she couldn't quite keep her toe from tapping to the music.

"Mrs. Viel, I think it's time we showed these couples how newlyweds two-step."

She laughed. "All right, Mr. Viel, but I'll ask you not to spin me too much."

They walked to the dance floor and as they two-stepped their way across the floor, Nicole couldn't remember a time when she'd had such fun, when she'd felt like she belonged. The people around her seemed accepting and she couldn't help but think that maybe Max was right about joining in. But always before she'd felt like people were whispering about her, wondering about her father, talking about Jean.

During their third dance, Max looked at Nicole, his eyes warm and unsettling. "Are you having a good time?"

She couldn't keep her smile from spreading across her face. "Yes, I am. I was afraid to come tonight, but I'm happy you talked me into attending."

He smiled and pulled her in closer to him. "I'm glad."

She could feel his solid chest against her and a sense of belonging overcame her that left her feeling unsettled. It felt good to be held in his arms.

As they walked back to their table beneath a large oak tree, the first cool breeze of the night whispered against her skin. "It feels so nice to be out here, dancing under the stars."

He halted and looked up at the stars; the full moon shone down brightly on them. "I've always heard of the term 'courting moon,' but I never believed in it until tonight."

The music played in the distance and the sound of people could be heard, but otherwise they were alone. She glanced at him in the darkness and her throat suddenly went dry. Even in the shadowy light, she could see the warmth reflected in his eyes, touching a place deep within her. That look awakened feelings she'd been trying to deny since the day he'd kissed her at their wedding. She wet her lips in anticipation of his kiss, a reckless urgency spiraling within her. She needed to feel his lips against hers, wanted to taste him once again, though she knew this could only mean disaster. But she'd longed for his kiss since that day in the justice of the peace's office.

He leaned toward her, his lips coming closer and closer to hers. "I enjoy dancing with you under the stars," he said, his voice whisper-soft, his mouth hovering right above her own until she thought she would beg him to kiss her. Her hands ached to reach up and pull his mouth down to her lips, but she resisted, fighting the primitive hunger surging through her, unlike anything she'd ever felt before.

Shadows danced around them like a ghostly parade, but Nicole didn't notice as she stood frozen in his arms, his scent enveloping her. Finally, she moved, just a tiny movement of her head, and he closed the distance between them.

His mouth covered her own, plundering hers with a definite insistence that left her knees weak. Liquid heat seared her mouth, stunning her with the pleasure that engulfed her. Potent and demanding, his tongue greedily sought the recesses of her mouth and she gladly opened up to him. Her hands slipped up to wrap around his neck and she clung to him for support, her limbs weak.

They were in a public place, kissing like lovers. The realization shocked her. What was she doing? This could only lead to trouble.

She broke the embrace, pushing out of his arms, her

breath sounding harsh to her ears as he released her. For a moment they simply stared at one another, as the disbelief of what she'd just done frightened her. Her heart pounded loudly in her chest and she resisted the urge to melt once again in his arms. She'd kissed him like no man ever before, including Jean.

She needed a few moments to collect her thoughts and let her body cool before she faced Max again. She needed to get away.

"Excuse me, but I think I need to find the privy," she said, feeling awkward and needing a chance to recover and gather her wits about her. She'd enjoyed the feel of his lips on hers. She'd liked the way his mouth teased and tempted her, making her want more. The warmth of his kiss infused her body, making her feel alive and leaving her more aware of him as a man than ever. Max Viel suddenly looked quite dangerous.

And she was married to him.

She whirled away, escaping to a tented area set on the edge of the festival site. Quickly she went into the tent designated for women and took care of her personal business. The night, the stars, and dancing somehow had enticed the two of them and she couldn't let herself ever be seduced into caring about a man again. There could be no more sampling Max's lips.

Though Max looked like sin and tasted of the devil, she could never let herself indulge. She'd only married him for the baby, and once the child was born, Max would be gone. And her heart had suffered enough aches for one lifetime.

As she stepped to the door of the tent, she overheard Anna DeChoskey gossiping with a group of women.

"Can you believe that hussy showed up here with a new husband?" she said, her voice loud in the night air.

Nicole sighed, not believing that this same woman would ridicule her a second time.

"Looks like she might have something cooking in the oven," a voice she didn't recognize said.

Nicole ran her hand over her abdomen, a feeling of protectiveness coming over her.

The women giggled, and a new voice chimed in. "Wasn't her mother the schoolteacher in Mrytlesville that the school board fired because she had a baby out of wedlock? I remember my mother talking about it. Maybe Nicole's following in her mother's footsteps."

'Yes, her mother was a complete disgrace. She refused to tell who Nicole's father was, so they fired her."

Nicole looked back at the slop bucket that she'd just used. She was tired of being a victim. Of being discussed as if she had no feelings whatsoever. Without further consideration, she picked up the bucket and strode to the door. With a lunge, she hurled the contents of the slop bucket out the tent, in the direction of the group of women.

Shrieks and screams filled the night air as she calmly set the bucket back in the tent and then proceeded to walk toward the women. They all watched her as she left the tent behind.

"Good evening, ladies. Enjoy the rest of the dance," she called. She walked past the women as they took their handkerchiefs and dabbed at the moisture that splattered their dresses.

She couldn't quite contain the smile that spread across her face. She'd never done anything so horrible in all her life, but she was tired of being the brunt of their malicious conversation.

When she found Max talking with a group of men, she joined them.

"Excuse me, gentlemen, but I think it's time for my husband and I to be going," she said, weariness overcoming her. Suddenly, all the fun of the day seemed to have caught up and drained her.

Max glanced at her, a worried expression on his face. "Sorry, gentlemen, but I promised my wife we'd get home early." He glanced at one of the men. "James, I'd like to talk more about the idea of a sugar co-op. Maybe you and your lovely wife could come to dinner sometime." He smiled at Nicole. "I'll let the ladies handle the arrangements."

"We'd enjoy coming out to Rosewood. It's been years since I've been out there. Until then, the Prudommes are having a party to announce the engagement of their daughter. I'll see if I can get you an invitation," the man said, nodding in Nicole's direction.

"Thanks," Max said, and waved good-bye.

After they walked away, Nicole frowned. "Why do you want to meet with James and talk about a sugar co-op?"

"We could save a lot of money if we all went together and had our sugar processed at one central mill," he said, helping her up into the buggy. "Though I won't be here for the next crop, your new overseer could take care of it."

She watched him walk around the buggy and climb in to take the reins. He released the brake, and with a snap of the reins the buggy began to roll. But the worry of how drawn in Max was with the plantation wouldn't leave her. "You seem so involved for a man who's only going to be here several months."

"I told you, I don't do anything without putting my all into it. I just can't."

She hoped that was all he meant by taking care of everything so well. After the baby was born, she didn't want to have to fight Max to persuade him to leave.

"Are we going to this engagement party?" she asked.

"Do you want to go?"

She thought for a moment, part of her longing to be involved in the community, yet so afraid of their not accepting her. But she needed to get over this fear. "Yes,

I'd like to go."

"Well if we receive an invitation, we'll go," Max said.

The buggy rolled along the dirt road, the frogs calling back and forth to each other near the river, the cicadas singing their song of loneliness in the dark.

Nicole sat and contemplated the night, thinking about the dancing, Max's kiss, and the way his mouth left her trembling, wanting more, knowing she shouldn't dwell on his kiss. She glanced at his lips in the darkness. How could the pressing of lips together make you feel so good?

Overall, the night had been fun, with the only tarnished spot of the evening, the loss of her temper. She wondered how Max would react to the news of her retribution.

"I did something tonight that wasn't very nice," she said. "I didn't act very queenly."

He glanced at her, surprised. "What are you talking about?"

"When I went to the privy, I overheard a group of women talking about me, and, well, I tossed the contents of the slop bucket at them."

For a moment Max simply stared at her, stunned, and Nicole was afraid he thought her a terrible person. She'd let him down and suddenly she didn't want him to be disappointed in her.

When had he become so important in her life that his opinion mattered?

He burst out laughing. "You threw a full slop bucket at a group of women who were talking badly about you?"

"Well, they said terrible things about my mother and I couldn't take it anymore. I'm tired of people thinking that my misfortune is something for them to talk and laugh about. I'm sorry if I embarrassed you, but I couldn't stand by and do nothing any longer."

For a moment, Max didn't say anything and Nicole wondered what he could be thinking. Then he chuckled softly. "Well, remind me not to talk about you while you're in the privy. I certainly don't want the contents of a slop bucket thrown at me."

For several minutes they rode along in silence, Max's attention focused on the murky river road. At night, the darkness seemed to go on forever, though Nicole knew the river lay not far to the left. If you listened closely sometimes you could hear the sound of the water lapping against the bank or gurgling on its way to the gulf.

She yawned and squirmed on the seat, trying to get comfortable, her back aching, and her mind unable to concentrate as their kiss kept intruding into her thoughts. Whatever had possessed the man to kiss her with such flagrant disregard to their agreement?

She watched him handling the reins of the buggy, the memory of his hands on her back, moving against her, pressing her closer etched like a photograph in her brain.

"Why did you kiss me tonight?" she asked him, the words seeming to slip out before she could restrain them.

He glanced at her and she watched his Adam's apple bobble in his throat. "Because I wanted to."

"But why?" she asked. "You know as well as I that there's no point in any romantic involvement between us."

"I kissed you because we were dancing beneath the moon while the stars twinkled in the night sky. I had a beautiful woman in my arms and the opportunity just seemed right. I kissed you because I wanted to and if the mood strikes me, I may do so again."

She gasped, his words leaving her aching with the memory. "You're serious."

"Yes. I am. If I get the urge and you're in my arms, why not? We are married," he said, glancing over at her, his voice low and sensual.

"I don't think that's very wise," she said, the thought making her nervous. She liked the feel of his lips way too much.

"I don't care whether it's wise, Mrs. Viel. Only that it feels right, and good, and I want to."

Nicole sat back, stunned at his response, and watched the road to the plantation, very aware of the man sitting next to her.

"I think I should stay out of your arms," she said, knowing it could only lead to trouble.

"Not if I can help it," he replied, never turning to look at her, his eyes focused on the road, his voice full of conviction.

A shiver went through her and she realized part of her could hardly wait to feel his lips on hers once again

# Chapter Eight

The dream seemed so real as Nicole watched Jean move toward her, laughing. She moaned and clutched at her abdomen, trying to hold onto her baby, even as her dead husband approached. He wanted the child. In her nightmare, blood trickled down her legs, and she woke with a start. The cramp tore at her again and she gasped, holding her breath until the pain passed.

Darkness surrounded her. All was quiet except for the sound of her breathing as she lay very still, hoping the pain had been part of her dream. Within five minutes, a cramp seized her again, tightening her abdomen until she wanted to scream. She panted, hoping it would soon pass, fearing what this meant.

Once the throbbing passed, she lay resting, praying that something she ate had upset her stomach, fearing this was the baby. It couldn't be the baby. Dear God, she'd been so careful since the scare in New Orleans, resting and taking care of herself, spending lots of time with her feet up. Except for the dancing she'd done tonight, but that was only three dances.

Again, pain snatched her breath away and left her hanging on as it ripped through her body and came at her once more. This couldn't be happening. Please, she didn't want to lose her baby. She wanted this child. The pains were coming faster and harder now, wrenching her in two, and drenching her in sweat.

When the next spell passed, she stood and went to the door. Dressed in only her nightgown, knowing she didn't have time to make it to Consuelo's room or even put on a dressing gown, she crossed the main parlor. She clutched her belly, in her long white nightgown, her bare feet treading hurriedly to Max's room. She knocked on his door and then entered before he replied. Panic swelled within her as she knew another pain would soon be upon her.

"Max!" she called, trying to wake him.

He sat up in bed. "What's wrong?"

Tears filled her throat, the fear she'd held at bay overwhelmed her, and she sobbed. "I think I'm losing the baby."

The throbbing began to come at her again, building until it consumed her, wringing a gasp from her lips as she doubled over, cramping. Max jumped out of bed dressed in only his underclothes and hurried to her side. He wrapped his strong arm around her and she leaned against him, his body absorbing her weight.

"Oh, Nicole," he said in a whisper, holding onto her until the pain subsided. "Let me help you to your room and then I'll send someone for the doctor. I'll awaken Consuelo, and we'll take care of you."

"I don't want to lose this baby," she cried against his shirt.

"I know you don't. Try to remain calm. We'll do everything we can to help you," he said, rubbing her back, holding her. He wrapped his arm around her waist as he helped her back to her room. Just as he got her into bed, another pain gripped her, holding her prisoner until she screamed. She clenched Max's hand until she felt certain she'd crushed the bones, but he said nothing.

When the pain passed, he leaned over and kissed her on the cheek, his lips comforting though she barely noticed.

"I'm going to wake Consuelo and send someone for the doctor, and then I'll be back.

Nicole watched him hurry out her door, yelling for Consuelo once he reached the dining room.

Tears streamed down her cheeks as she felt the first trickles of blood between her legs. All the love she'd formed with Jean was no more, including the baby they created.

~

Max anxiously paced the main parlor, wanting to be by Nicole's side, wishing he could fix the situation and make her happy. She'd seemed so fragile, so broken when she'd come to his room. God, he'd never felt so scared in all his life as when she'd doubled over with pain. He'd been so afraid that she would die.

After what seemed like hours, the doctor opened her bedroom door and walked slowly out into the hallway. He shook his head at Max. "She lost the baby."

Max sighed, all his fears realized, wishing he could spare her this pain. "Is she all right?"

"Other than being very upset and tired, I think she'll be fine. I want her on complete bed rest for several days, and if she starts running a fever, send for me immediately," the doctor said, rolling down his sleeves. "She's lost quite a bit of blood, but I don't think she's in any danger."

"Thanks for coming so quickly, Doc. I know we woke you early," Max said, running a tired hand through his hair.

The doctor picked up his hat and walked toward the door. "I'm used to it, Mr. Viel. Just make sure that your wife stays in bed and recuperates. She should be fine."

"Thanks again, Doc."

Max opened the door to the men's side of the house just as the first rays of dawn chased the night away, heralding a new day. He closed the portal behind the doctor and looked toward Nicole's room. She'd wanted this baby so badly.

He couldn't imagine the heartache she must be feeling at this moment. She'd already suffered so much, but now, to lose the one thing in her life that she'd wanted more than anything...

Slowly, Max made his way to Nicole's room, needing to reassure himself that she was all right. He knocked gently on the door, and Consuelo cracked open the portal.

"How is she?" he whispered.

"She's very upset, but she'll be all right," Consuelo said, watching him closely. Either the older woman didn't trust him or she didn't like him. She always scrutinized him, and her searching eyes left Max nervous.

"Can I see Nicole?" he asked, needing to be with her, be near her at this time, though he didn't understand why. In fact, he feared her first response would be to end their marriage—for the very reason she'd married him no longer existed. He didn't want their marriage to end. And he felt she needed him to give her comfort.

Consuelo nodded. "I'll leave you two alone. Try not to upset her."

The older Spanish woman walked out of Nicole's bedroom, her face drawn and tired. When she left, Max shut the door behind him and slowly approached his wife's bed. She lay on her side curled in a ball, her eyes open but dry. She turned and saw him, her blue eyes glazed, and then turned her face back to the wall.

"Please, go away," she said, her voice quivering.

He eased onto her bed and lay down beside her. She rolled toward him, her eyes questioning. He pulled her into his arms and held her. The feel of her body trembling in his embrace as he gently rubbed her back left him shaken to the core.

For Nicole to let Max hold her, in her bed, he knew the extent of her pain must be unbearable. And he wanted to console her, to offer her solace in the only way he knew how, which was to simply hold her.

Tears trickled down her cheeks, falling onto his shirt, but he didn't care. "I... I lost the baby."

"I know. I'm sorry, Nicole."

She sobbed and his heart ached for her. He grieved for her and the lost child. It didn't seem fair that she'd lost the child so soon after their marriage.

While the sun slowly rose in the eastern sky, Max held Nicole, wishing there was something he could do to soothe her pain, knowing how much this baby had meant to her. He held her, conscious there were no words of comfort he could offer that would make her feel better. So he offered her a strong shoulder and soothing arms.

Yet the entire time he embraced her, a sense of rightness of being where he belonged overcame him and he *wanted* to be her husband. Somehow he had to convince Nicole that they were meant to be man and wife. Maybe theirs would never be a love match, but they could live comfortably. They could have more children, raise their own family, and lead happy lives.

She might not think much of him as a man, but if only she would give him a chance, he could show her how different their married life together could be. Particularly compared to her life with Jean. For Max promised himself to be a good and faithful husband to Nicole, which was more than she ever received from Jean.

And he couldn't deny that the picture of his wife naked, her limbs entwined with his own, had entered his mind more times than he cared to be reminded of. Just the feel of her soft body pliant in his arms left him trembling. But those thoughts were better left for another day.

As she finally floated off to sleep, cleaving to Max, he knew more than ever before that he was determined to make Nicole his wife in every sense of the word, and gain his family's home in the process.

~

"Papa, I received a letter the other day from my mother," Paul told Max later that day as they worked together in the barn.

Max stopped currying the horse he cleaned and glanced

at his son, frowning. "How did she find out where you were?"

"Grandfather forwarded me her letter. She came around several times, trying to find out where I was, but he didn't tell her." Paul paused for a moment, chewing on his bottom lip. "She wants me to come home."

"Do you want to go back, Son?" Max asked, thinking how much he'd enjoyed being with his boy and how difficult it would be to let him return to his mother.

Paul considered his father's question, his brown eyes serious. "I like living with you, but I'm worried about Mother. I don't want anything bad to happen to her or my brothers and sisters."

"I'm glad you like living with me and I'd like for you to stay," he told his son, feeling relieved that Paul didn't appear anxious to return. Max knew it would be hard to let the boy return to Desiree. He wanted his son with him.

"What do you think could happen?"

"I don't know. In the letter, she kept telling me how much she depended on me. I was the only child that she could count on. What's going to happen to her?"

"Your mother is an adult. She'll be all right," Max said, thinking that he wished there was something he could do to protect the other children from their mother's neglect.

Max picked up the comb and began to curry the horse once again, reflecting how he could help his son, knowing full well that Desiree would use the boy's soft heart to lure him back. It wasn't the boy she wanted so much as the money that Max sent her to care for him.

"Did she mention whether or not her new man was still around?" he asked. "It seems to me that she didn't care that you were gone when he was there."

The boy shrugged. "She said that he turned out like all the others. Why can't my mother find a man who wants to stay with her?"

Max knew he didn't want to answer that question. No matter what, Paul loved Desiree, though he had yet to learn how his mother liked to manipulate a man to obtain what she wanted. It would be better for the boy to reach his own conclusions regarding his mother's behavior, when he was older.

"Your mother has followed a difficult path in life. Part of growing up is learning to make good decisions, something that I hope you will learn to do," Max told Paul, hoping he was vague enough that his son could realize on his own that Desiree hadn't made wise decisions. "If you decide to return to your mother, I'll take you," he said, wishing the boy would stay here with him.

Paul watched Max comb the palomino until the animal's coat glistened in the sunlight. "I'm not ready to go back to Mother. I like living on the plantation and I want to stay here longer with you. But I worry about the kids."

Max nodded, realizing that the boy hadn't said he would never go back to his mother, only that for the moment he needed more time to make his decision. And that was all right. The longer he stayed here, the more Max hoped to influence his son and help him realize that the best opportunities for him were with his father.

"It's okay to worry about them, but they're your mother's responsibility. So don't feel guilty for doing what's best for you." He glanced at his son, noticing for the first time the changes in his body. The boy seemed to have grown a couple of inches since he'd arrived at the plantation. Three good meals a day and the country air seemed to be agreeing with him. Max felt a rush of pride in his son.

He didn't want to send him back to a home where the mother stayed out all night and slept all day, while her eldest child cared for her children. Where new gentlemen friends never lasted more than a month and sometimes only a night. But she was the mother of his son.

"School hasn't started yet; could we wait until closer to September before I give you my answer?" the boy asked his father.

"That sounds reasonable," Max said, thinking he'd gotten a little more time with his boy. "Let's finish up these horses, and then, what if we go check to see if the fish are biting? We haven't done that since you arrived, and I feel the need to wet a hook."

The kid laughed. "That'd be great"

"Then let's clean up and go." Max slapped his son on the back as Paul led the horse back into the stall.

He felt lucky to have Paul. Though the kid's birth had been less than ideal and left him tied irrevocably to Desiree, he still loved the boy and was glad to be in his life.

Whereas Nicole had lost the child she so desperately wanted and Max could only imagine her anguish. Someday he hoped they would have a future together that included their children and Paul.

~

Later that evening, Max stood before Nicole's door and softly knocked. She'd been in his thoughts all day and he'd forced himself to stay away and let her rest Consuelo had been given strict instructions to let him know if her condition worsened.

"Come in," she said. Her voice sounded dull.

He opened the door and with one arm behind him, tiptoed in to see her propped up in bed, reading a book of poetry. Though her cheeks showed more color, her blue eyes seemed lifeless, as if the sparkle had been drained from them.

"How do you feel?" he asked, standing off to the side, where she couldn't see his hand.

"I'm all right," she replied, her voice laden with sorrow.

He held out his hand, filled with yellow field daisies, their fragrance floating through the room. "I picked these for you this afternoon and I thought that maybe they might cheer you."

It seemed lame, but he'd wanted to do something for her other than hold her this morning while she'd cried. The daisies were the only offer of condolence he could think of.

"Thank you," she said and looked away, blinking rapidly. Finally, she returned her gaze to his. "They're beautiful."

"Consuelo found the vase," he said, putting them in the ceramic holder and then pulling up a chair to sit next to her bed. "Are you in any pain?"

"No," she said.

The word hung in the air, reverberating with how much she didn't say. She must feel battered and bruised by the experience.

Max fidgeted in his chair, not knowing what to say, feeling useless but wanting to be with her just the same. She looked so pale, and he missed her smile.

Her eyes closed for a moment and then she opened them, looking directly at him. "Thank you for helping me this morning. I appreciated your sending for the doctor and getting Consuelo." She clenched her hands and then gazed directly into his eyes. "And for holding me after it was over."

He shrugged. "I wanted to do more, but I didn't know what else to do."

"I know," she said, a tear slipping past her guard to make its way down her cheek. "You've been very good to me. If you ever decide to settle down, you'll make some woman a nice husband."

He raised his brows, but didn't respond. Now was not the time to tell her that their vows were the forever after kind, and that he planned on being her husband until death did they part, for better or worse.

"So I guess you'll need to start the annulment proceedings," she said. "I'm sure you want to move on."

"Annulment proceedings?" he asked. "Even after the doctor came out and knew you miscarried? I don't think that's going to be possible."

She sighed. "I don't care, just do whatever it takes to end our marriage."

He watched the emotions on her face. She seemed so lost, and he didn't like the sound of her words.

"I guess what I'm trying to tell you is that you're free to leave now that the baby is..."

"We don't have to talk about this right now," he said, watching her struggle to get the words from her throat. He didn't want to think about leaving her. He only wanted to spend time with her.

She took a deep breath. "I know, but I need to tell you that you're released from our agreement."

Released from his duties? God, that was an awful way to describe being a husband. Somehow, he needed a quick way out of this discussion despite the fact she seemed determined to talk about this today.

Nicole ignored him and continued on. "As for the sugarcane crop, I can't pay you until it comes in, and since you won't be here when it's harvested, I don't think I should have to pay you half. I would think that a fourth should be sufficient"

The realization of what she'd just said startled him and gave him an excuse to stay. Here was the reason he could use to keep her from getting rid of him. But now still was not the time to bring this to her attention. She needed rest and he couldn't upset her, not after what she'd been through today.

"Let's not worry about this tonight, Nicole. You need to get better and once you've improved, then we can discuss how to handle this situation," he said, wondering if he gave Nicole some time, she would truly become his wife. "There's no need to change everything right away."

Nicole looked away and swallowed, struggling to keep the tears from falling. She laughed. "Change. I've certainly seen a lot of that recently." She wiped the tears from her eyes. "I don't know what to do with my life now. Nothing's the same, including my relationship with you."

Her words startled him. "How have things changed between us?"

"Isn't it obvious? I no longer need a husband." She said the words bitterly. "I no longer need your name."

For a long moment he said nothing as he sat there and mulled over her words. Somehow they left him disappointed, and then he realized she was hurting and he expected too much from her. It wasn't like he'd anticipated her to say he could stay, but somehow a small part of him hoped she would acknowledge that he'd made her life easier and he'd helped her. He wanted her to recognize that he wanted to take care of her.

She cocked her head, looking at him as if she were gazing into the eyes of a stranger. Afraid to push her, fearful of her fragile emotions and not wanting to endanger her health, Max let the subject go. There would be plenty of time in the weeks to come to discover what she thought about their relationship. "Nicole, just rest tonight. Let's not think of the past and what's happened today. Get well and then we'll discuss how we're going to handle our situation. Tonight, just sleep and let your body heal."

She gazed at him, the indigo irises of her eyes void of feeling, almost blank. She looked overwhelmed by the events of the day. He knew he needed to be supportive and give her time. She'd been through so much.

"I can't sleep. I've tried and every time I close my eyes, I think of the baby."

"Why don't I sit here and hold your hand while you try to rest"

Her brows drew together in a frown, yet she rearranged the pillows and lay down on the bed. "Thank you. I don't like being needy, but thank you for staying with me until I fall asleep."

"It's all right to be dependent occasionally," he said, watching her eyes get droopy, enjoying the feel of her hand tucked inside his own.

As he watched her drift off to sleep, a feeling of protectiveness so powerful overcame him, he would have died to look after her.

The emotions rattled him, leaving him startled and confused. How could this small woman have so quickly crawled inside his skin and caused him to care about her?

~

The grandfather clock had just chimed midnight when Max softly shut the door to Nicole's room. Darkness enveloped the old house and he started to walk across the main parlor toward his room.

"I was beginning to think you were going to spend the night in her room," Consuelo said, causing Max to almost jump out of his skin.

He took a deep breath. "Do you always creep around in the shadows of this old house scaring people?"

She laughed, clearly pleased that she'd caused him to jump. "No, I've just been sitting here waiting for you to leave her room so I could go in and check on her."

"She's asleep. I stayed with her until she fell asleep," he said.

He could feel the older woman's eyes on him in the dark "You know, for a man she only married for his last name, you seem to be taking real good care of her."

Max didn't say anything, instinctively realizing that

Consuelo would know if he lied. "Doesn't she merit someone to look after her?"

"She definitely deserves a good man who will care for her and stay with her. I'm still trying to figure out if you're the right man for the job or if you're just like Jean and only going to take advantage of her."

Max looked out the window at the darkened land, knowing he had to be careful with Consuelo. The old woman somehow seemed to have insight into people that most individuals lacked.

"Well, I'm not Jean, and though I have my faults, other women are not one of them. I know our marriage didn't start out as any love match, but I would like to see it become a partnership where both of us can live happily."

He watched Consuelo nod her head in the dark. "I kind of like you, Mr. Viel. If you'd told me you loved her, I would have known you were lying, but I think you care, and that's a good start"

"Thanks, Consuelo. I kind of like you too."

She laughed. "That's good, because I'm not going anywhere." She rose from the chair she'd been sitting in. "Now if you'll excuse me, these tired old bones of mine are ready for bed. I'll check on her in the middle of the night to make sure she's all right."

"Before you go, I want to let you know that I had the baby's body placed in the family tomb."

She sighed, a tired, heavy sound. "Thanks, Mr. Viel, for taking care of that for Mrs. Nicole. The baby was too young for a funeral and for sparing Mrs. Nicole the burden of a ceremony. As it was, I didn't think she'd ever let go of that tiny body."

Consuelo coughed, the sound deep and raspy. "This has certainly been a sad day. Good night Mr. Viel." The old woman shuffled out the parlor door and down the hall, leaving Max alone.

Max ambled out onto the verandah and gazed into the darkened night. He stared at the land his grandfather had loved and wished the old man could be here to see the lush fields of cane now. Since moving to Rosewood, he understood his grandfather's determination to find a way to bring the plantation back into the family. And though he didn't want to hurt Nicole, he couldn't turn his back on his legacy and walk away.

He glanced back at the house, remembering the way she'd fallen asleep with him holding her hand. She seemed so fragile, so lost right now, like everything had been taken from her. How could he seize the one last beloved thing that she had left?

He rubbed his hand across his face, feeling like a monster at the thought of forcing her to realize they were married, for better or worse. How could he tell her that he would never leave her side that he was here to stay?

Somehow he must convince her that he'd fallen deeply in love with her and that he wanted their marriage to last. Somehow, before his mother descended on his doorstep with the news of his family having once owned Rosewood. For Audra would be certain to let everyone know she'd returned and her family once again owned her beloved home.

But what would keep Nicole from leaving him when she found out that his family had once lived at Rosewood and wanted to do so again?

How had he ever thought that this marriage was the solution to obtaining the plantation? Instead, now he had a badly bruised woman he cared about, one who would certainly be hurt even more when she learned of his deceit.

# Chapter Nine

**T**hree weeks passed and with each day Nicole felt stronger both emotionally and physically. Though she had wanted Jean's baby more than her next breath, part of her realized the miscarriage was for the best. The child would never have to learn the truth regarding its father and the crimes he had committed. And though she would have loved the baby with all her heart and soul, she suspected she alone would never have been enough. Though her baby would have known who its father was, Nicole knew from personal experience that wondering about a missing parent meant gazing into the faces of strangers, questioning if they were your kin. The questions of *why didn't you want me?* never went away, and she'd vowed long ago that her child would never experience this kind of loneliness.

The morning sun had long since begun its climb in the eastern sky and Nicole didn't want to give up her place on the verandah just yet. She tilted her straw hat farther down to protect her face, shading her fair skin from the sun.

Consuelo came out and gathered her breakfast dishes. "Would you like me to bring you a glass of mint tea?"

"No, thanks," Nicole said, as she watched a young boy cross the yard toward the barn. She squinted and glanced at him again. "Consuelo, who is that young man? Do you know him?"

The older woman glanced at the grounds. "One of the girls in the kitchen told me that one of the stable hands said that Mr. Viel hired him." Consuelo shrugged. "He's been here about five weeks now. I don't know where he came from, but he's very polite."

"Five weeks! Why didn't Max tell me he'd hired him?" Nicole shook her head, her frustration mounting. "You know, since Max has been here, he's just more or less taken over. I think it's time he left"

She knew she was being irrational but she feared Max's staying would only prolong their marriage. And she didn't want to think of how quickly she'd become accustomed to his presence.

"Don't be too hard on Mr. Viel. He took good care of you while you were sick," Consuelo said. "He seemed genuinely worried about you."

"He treated me very nice. But the reasons for our original agreement are no longer valid, so it's time he left I don't need him to run the plantation," Nicole said, knowing that wasn't the only reason she wanted him to leave. Never had a man taken such good care of her, and his well-meaning ways frightened her. Max made her feel special and protected, and he seemed genuinely interested in her.

Max nurtured her like no man had ever taken care of her before.

Sure, she deserved to be treated well, but his friendship couldn't be real. A man like Max didn't exist, and she didn't want to rely on him only to discover his flaws. It would be better if he left before he broke her heart, before she became so attached that she didn't want him to leave.

Consuelo shook her head. "Mr. Viel works very hard. He's not like Mr. Cuvier, who never even ventured out to the fields."

"I think you like Max," Nicole said, surprised at the sudden realization. She gazed at her friend and servant, waiting for her answer.

Consuelo lifted her chin. "Yes, I do like Mr. Viel, but something troubles him."

"It's called the need to move on; and I've released him from his agreement to stay, so he should be leaving soon." She paused. The sooner Max left the sooner she could forget him and all the reasons for their marriage. "Maybe one of the reasons he's such a hard worker is that he's going to be paid for this crop."

"No, Mr. Viel is a man who likes to work. You can tell when you watch him. He's at ease being in charge and gives orders to the men like he's done this all his life," Consuelo said.

"That doesn't make any sense, Consuelo. He drifts from town to town, doing odd jobs, waiting for the right place to settle down."

She shook her head. "No, I don't know why, but for some reason that doesn't fit him. Maybe I'm wrong, but I think he is a man who knows exactly what he wants and goes after it. And I think that if you were wise, you would try to hang on to him."

"As what? My husband?" Nicole vehemently shook her head, feeling anxious. She couldn't risk caring about another man ever again. "No. He's not staying permanently. I don't care that we are married. He knew this would not last when he married me."

Consuelo picked up the breakfast tray. "Maybe so, but he's different from any drifter I've ever met. He has ambition, you can see it in his eyes. I don't know his story, but he's not always been a wanderer."

~

When Max came to dinner that night, he was pleased to see Nicole waiting for him beside the long formal table. He couldn't help but think that once again color suffused her fair skin and her intense blue eyes sparkled with more life than he'd seen in weeks.

She looked radiant in a soft mauve dress that accentuated her bust, ecru lace trimming a neckline that showed off the tops of her creamy breasts. The thought of pulling that lace down past her nipples and putting his mouth on her tasty rosebuds, suckling each one until she begged him to finish what he'd started, startled him. He swallowed and took a calming breath. Their gazes locked, and a warm sensation curled, tightening within him.

"Good evening," he said, hurrying to pull out a chair for her. "You look stunning tonight."

Thank you," she replied, sitting down as he pushed her chair to the table. "I thought the time had come for things to return to normal."

He walked to his side of the table, knowing how hard it must be for her to accept the miscarriage, wondering what normal meant in her life. With the death of Jean and everything else that had happened this year, what could normal be?

"It's good to see you up and around again," he said, watching the candlelight flicker across her high cheekbones. He'd missed her these last three weeks that she'd been in bed. They visited some each night but a tension that he'd never felt in her presence had been there.

The servants brought their dinner to the table, setting the fined chicken, bowls of squash and beans before them. Marie, the kitchen maid, served the food and then quietly left the room.

For a moment they ate in silence, the only sound the clatter of their forks against the elegant china. When they finished eating, Marie served the rich coffee the Creoles enjoy and they sipped the strong, flavorful brew.

"How are things with the crop?" she asked.

"The cane is looking very hardy. I'm hoping that we won't experience the insect problem that damaged last year's crop," he said, wishing he could pick her up and carry her to his bed, and then start by stripping the pins from her hair and finish when she stood naked before him. But that wouldn't be the end of their night, merely the beginning.

He didn't dare let his thoughts go past what he would do once he took down her loose blonde curls. She had just

suffered a miscarriage—he should be thinking of her
health.

She glanced up at him, confused. "How do you know
about the grasshoppers?"

He swallowed, realizing he'd just made a colossal slip
of the tongue by thinking about her instead of concentrating
on the conversation. His lawyers had given him a detailed
report of how the plantation had fared last year, so he'd
known all about the damage to the previous year's harvest.

"Most plantations in this area suffered the same
problems as Rosewood. Plus one of the field hands told
me," he said, hoping she would believe the lie, wishing he
could just end this silly masquerade and tell her the truth.
But he knew she wasn't ready, and that knowledge would
bring certain ruin. Once she accepted their marriage, then
he would tell her about his family and his deception.

She nodded. "Sorry, I guess I'm still a little edgy." For a
moment silence prevailed as they sat, the singsong of
crickets coming through the open windows. He could see
the moon beginning to rise over the sugarcane fields, the
wind blowing the green stalks like waves on the water.

"I saw a new boy walking around the grounds today. I
asked about him and Consuelo told me you hired him?
Why? What did you hire him to do?"

She'd seen Paul. He'd hoped to have more time to
prepare her for the knowledge of his son, but he couldn't lie
to her about the boy. It seemed ironic: he could lie about
the reason he married her, but he couldn't lie about his son.
If the truth were told, he didn't like lying to Nicole at all.

If they were truly to be man and wife she would need to
know that Paul belonged in his life. Max doubted that she
would ever accept his illegitimate son, but just the same,
the boy would remain in his life always.

"His name is Paul and he's my son," Max said,
watching her eyes widen in surprise.

"Your son?"

"Yes."

Nicole swallowed hard, her face suddenly becoming white. "Please tell me that you're not still married to his mother."

"No," Max said, for some reason not ready to tell her the circumstances involved with Paul's birth. "We never married."

She sighed, a deep, heavy sound. "Well this is certainly a surprise."

"I should have told you about him before now, but the time just didn't seem right."

"How could you have a son that age?" she asked, bewildered.

Max took a deep breath. "I got a woman with child when I was a young man."

Nicole didn't say anything for a moment as he watched the expression on her face change from contemplative to a frown. Her forehead drew together in a scowl and her blue eyes darkened with anger.

Most women didn't like other women's children, but he didn't expect her to become this upset at the news of his son.

"Where is the boy sleeping?" she asked indignantly. "If he's not in the house, where did you put your son?"

"I didn't want to distress you, so I put him in the barn."

"You put your son in the barn, like an animal?" she asked, her voice rising, her blue eyes widening in horror. "How old is this child?"

"He's twelve," Max said, confused by her reaction.

"You put a twelve-year-old child in the barn to sleep," she said, getting up from her chair and walking toward Max. "What if he gets hurt? What if he's afraid?"

"He can take care of himself. The kid wanted to sleep there and I didn't want to offend you," Max said, becoming indignant. He began to wonder if he could win in this situation.

"Did you think I was such an ogre that I wouldn't take in a twelve-year-old child?" she asked, her blue eyes flashing in anger.

"No, but you've been sick, I was trying to look after you," he said, his voice soothing.

"Don't worry about protecting me, Max. I can take care of myself, quite well, which is more than I can say for a twelve-year-old boy."

He frowned at her words. He'd been thinking of her and also trying to keep his son from accidentally revealing the identity of his family. Plus the boy wanted to sleep in the barn; he considered it an adventure, which certainly helped relieve the complications Max had foreseen. But he'd never thought she would become this upset when she found out Paul slept in the barn.

"I'm going down there right now and move him into the house," she said, heading for the door.

"Nicole, sit down," he commanded. "It's late, he's asleep, and you're upset. You'll frighten the kid."

She halted at the door, but she didn't return to her chair as she glared at him. "How?"

"Just let him sleep. If we move him now, he's going to be wide awake and have trouble going back to sleep. The kid works hard; let him rest tonight. Tomorrow you can relocate him into the house."

Nicole sank back down into her chair. She stared across the table at him. "Are there any other secrets you haven't mentioned?"

"Have you told me all your secrets?" he countered, trying to dodge the question.

She raised her brows. "All my secrets have been publicly disclosed, some of them I didn't even know." She watched him closely. "So how about you? Anything else I should be worried about?"

Max felt incredibly frustrated and part of that dissatisfaction came from his own guilt. He had enough secrets to make Nicole's hair turn red, yet he wasn't about to reveal them to her. Not just yet. So he did the only thing he could: he lied.

"Not at the moment. I'll be sure to let you know, though, when I do have something to hide," he said, hating the fact that he was forced to lie, fearful of what she would say next.

They sat in silence for several moments, each sipping their coffee, listening to the sounds of the night through the open windows. The spirit bottles clanged together, their clinking melody coming through the windows.

"I know you must be anxious to take Paul and move on to the next town you'll be visiting. When do you plan to leave?" she asked, breaking the stillness.

Somehow he knew this question would come up tonight and he dreaded answering, but the time for her to realize he had no intentions of departing faced them.

"Our agreement said that I would receive half the cane crop," he said, knowing that she needed the money and feeling bad for letting her believe he would take half of it "I'm staying until we harvest the crop."

"I don't think so," she said, her voice rising. "Our agreement also stated that our marriage would only be temporary. There's no reason for us to continue as man and wife. Your part is complete, you may go at any time."

He let her sit and wait several moments before he responded, knowing the pause would vex her and also give her a moment to cool down. "I expected to be here until the crop could be delivered to the mill and I received payment. I'm not taking less than half of the money made and I intend to remain here until the job is complete."

"You can't!" she said. "That won't be until sometime in

November."

"Why can't I?" he asked, standing and coming around to her side of the table. "The crop this year is doing better than ever before. Why do you want to risk losing it? You don't have an overseer or anyone who can help you. I'm here, let me do this for you."

"I can run this plantation, I've done so for the last four years," she stated. She took a calming breath. "Look, I know you've worked very hard and I appreciate it. I'll pay you for your time here, but you are free to leave; there's really no reason for you to stay. Sometime in the next few days, you and Paul can pack up and go."

Max felt himself getting desperate, so he pulled all his punches, though he wished she would relent and let him stay.

"No. I'm not departing just yet. When you ran the plantation, how many of those years were profitable?"

"That's not fair. You know that we experienced trouble with insects last year. It takes several years to make a profit, and this year we should do well."

He nodded. "That's right. I intend to make sure that we do well. But until the crop is sold, I'm going to continue living here."

He watched the myriad expressions cross her face, the flash of anger in her blue eyes, and her jaw tense. Finally, a look of resignation showed on her beautiful face.

She took a deep breath and released it slowly. "All right. I made this agreement and I'll stand by it, but the moment we sell the crop, I want you and your son gone."

Silence filled the room with the exception of the tick tock of a grandfather clock in the distance and the sound of crickets chirping in time.

"I promise you, things will work out for the best," he said, somehow not wanting the evening to end on such a bad note, though he refused to agree to her expressed date of departure.

~

Nicole rose early the next morning, determined that if Max were going to stay, Paul would not continue to sleep in the barn. She would not allow the boy to be discriminated against in any way while he stayed at her home. From the time she was old enough to understand, she'd always known she was different from most children. It wasn't until she reached puberty that she'd learned the term "love child" and how that made her unusual.

With a determined step she went down the back stairs, through the kitchen garden, and across the yard to the barn. When she reached the wooden building that housed the horses, she opened the door and went inside. She immediately saw Moses, the man in charge of the horses. He glanced up, his eyes widening at the sight of her.

"Mrs. Viel, can I help you?"

"Yes, I'm looking for the boy, Paul," she said.

The boy stuck his head out of a stall, his dark brown eyes wide, freckles sprinkled across his nose and cheeks. "You're looking for me, ma'am?"

She smiled, trying to put him at ease. It wasn't the boy's fault his father had failed to treat him right. "Yes, I'm Nicole Viel, your father's wife. I want you to gather your things. I'm moving you to a bedroom in the house."

He shook his head. "Nice to meet you, ma'am, but there's no need. I'm very happy here in the barn. This is where Mr. Viel put me."

Nicole bristled at the formal name he'd used for his father. Obviously, the boy seldom saw the man.

"It's all right, Paul, I know that Max is your father." She took a deep breath. "I won't have my husband's son living out in the barn. Consuelo has prepared one of the guest rooms in the house. A nice soft bed and a place to put your things is ready for you."

She walked over to the boy and gazed at the young man who stood taller than she. A skinny lad with dark hair that curled loosely on top of his head, his jaw strong and angular like his father's. The boy needed a haircut and maybe even a new pair of pants.

"Your father should have brought you into the house the very first day you arrived. I'm moving you into the house in a room beside your father. You may continue to work in the barn if you like," she said, determined that Paul would feel accepted in her home while he was here.

If she hadn't feared upsetting the boy, she would have marched out here last night and had him moved into the house immediately. But she'd listened to Max and then worried whether the boy was comfortable sleeping in the straw.

Paul put down the pitchfork he was using, walked over to an empty stall, and pulled out a small knapsack.

"I'm ready," he said, his face somewhat dejected.

"That's all you have?" she asked, looking at him in amazement. "Where are your clothes?"

"This is it," he said, gazing at her with apprehension while she seethed with fury. Most beggars had more possessions than this child.

The boy's father drifted from town to town, never earning a great deal of money, yet he'd paid all her bills. Why couldn't he buy his son some decent clothes? Some of her beaded bags were bigger than the knapsack Paul carried.

"Why hasn't your father bought you more clothes?" she asked, stunned by the sight of his small bag.

"Papa's given me money for clothes," he said, his gaze not meeting hers. "Mother needed the money for the rent."

Nicole closed her mouth, trying not to look shocked at his announcement.

"We were a little short that month, but I understand," he said, and Nicole could see a wealth of knowledge in his twelve-year-old eyes.

She took a calming breath, thinking of all the times she'd wished her father had been in her life, had done things for her, wondering how much pain this child had endured by being illegitimate. How much neglect had he suffered at the hands of his mother and father?

"Come on and we'll get you settled in the house, and then you can come back to the barn if you like," she said, heading toward the door.

As they walked toward the house, Paul meekly followed her, not saying anything. "I apologize that we weren't formally introduced by your father."

"It's all right," the boy said. "Papa told me to stay away from the big house."

Her eyes cut to the boy, feeling the anger she'd kept at bay once again flaming to the surface. Was Max so ashamed of his son he didn't want him seen by the servants that were better dressed? "Why would he tell you such a thing?"

The boy shrugged. "I don't know."

"Well, I certainly don't understand how a parent can disregard their son and I intend to tell him so," she said, her anger still smoldering.

"Don't be mad at him. He always comes around, which is more than some of the other children's fathers do."

She jerked around to look at him. "There are other children?"

"I'm not the only child my mother has," Paul said.

"Oh," Nicole said, wondering about this statement but not asking the boy, as he seemed embarrassed. They couldn't be Max's, could they? He hadn't mentioned more than one.

They reached the house and climbed the stairs together.

"What school do you attend?" Nicole asked, trying to find a subject they could discuss without her becoming angrier with Max.

"When I get to go, I attend the local parish school."

"What would keep you from school?" she asked, not certain that she wanted to know, but her concern for the boy increasing by the minute.

"Sometimes I have to see to the younger kids. If the little ones get sick, I have to stay home and take care of them," he said quietly.

Nicole noticed he suddenly seemed uncomfortable. "What about your mother?"

"She sleeps during the day and doesn't like to be disturbed," he said, not looking at Nicole. "It's all right. I don't mind watching them. Mother should have been a famous singer. She means well and takes care of us the best she can."

Nicole felt such anger burning within her, she didn't dare ask any more questions. How could a mother let her young son take on her responsibilities? And how could a father leave town while his son took care of his siblings to the neglect of attending school?

They entered the house and she watched Paul's eyes widen as he gazed about the main parlor. "This is really nice. You must be rich."

She couldn't contain her laugh. "No, I'm hardly wealthy, but thank you."

They walked through the men's parlor to a bedroom next to Max's.

Nicole frowned, a sudden thought occurring to her. How did he see the boy if he drifted from town to town? "Does your father take you with him when he travels from town to town?"

Paul looked at her, his face full of confusion. "Papa doesn't—"

"So I see you found my son," Max said, stepping into Paul's room, interrupting what the boy had been about to say.

Nicole raised her brows at the man she could happily strangle right now.

"Yes, this is going to be Paul's room, where he should have been all along," she said, still upset with Max for the way he'd treated his son.

Max shrugged. "Son, did you want to sleep in the house?"

"No, Papa, actually I liked it just fine in the barn," the boy said.

"The barn is for animals and not for young men. This way he can dine with us," Nicole said. "But I'm shocked this is all the boy brought with him. Where are his clothes?"

"At his mother's, if he still has any that fit him," Max said.

She shook her head, thinking even her servants had better clothes than this child.

"Then it might behoove you to take him to town and get him outfitted with the things that a young boy requires. That is, if you have the money to pay for them."

"Papa has plenty—"

"I'll take him this morning, if you feel he is lacking," Max said, clearly annoyed.

"It doesn't matter what I think. It's your duty as his father. From my vantage point, you don't appear to be a very good parent," Nicole said. "You've neglected him."

Max's green eyes darkened. His mouth tightened, and she knew she'd finally angered him.

"You know nothing about how I care for my son," he said.

"Papa gives me lots of things," Paul defended.

Nicole didn't say anything else. The boy shouldn't hear

them arguing over him this way and she knew that anything she said at this point would only anger Max further.

"Then take him to town and outfit him properly," she said, gazing at Max.

"Thank you for your suggestion. Would you care to join us?" Max asked, clearly piqued.

The thought of riding into town with the two of them, accompanying them while Max bought his son some decent clothes, was tempting. Her attending would at least ensure that what he bought would be decent for the boy, but the miscarriage had only been three weeks ago and the doctor had told her to refrain from riding on horses or in buggies for a while.

"No, I trust that you can outfit him," she said, not ready to ride in a bouncing buggy over ruts and rocks in the road.

"I don't know, Mrs. Viel. According to you, I haven't taken good care of him yet," Max said, his voice mocking her. She could tell he was still annoyed.

"Well, here is your chance to show me what kind of parent you really are," she said, baiting him.

His emerald eyes widened and then he reached out and slid his fingers along her jawbone in a gentle caress, his touch awakening her body, every nerve tingling with awareness. "I'm a good father and someday you'll have no doubts."

Nicole stared at Max, her breath quickening in her throat. How could he make such a simple sentence seem to have so much hidden meaning, and how could the sound of his voice, deep and resonant, send tremors down her spine?

"Paul, I'll get you settled and then you can go to town with your father," she said, stepping away from Max, yet her gaze remained locked with his. His eyes left her feeling naked, vulnerable, and raw with unmentionable need.

She watched Max smile, the intensity of his upturned lips leaving a trail of heat down her spine. How could she live with him until November and refrain from exploring his kiss one more time?

live with him until November and refrain from exploring his kiss one more time?

## Chapter Ten

Later that day, Consuelo found Nicole in the plantation office going over the accounting books.

"You don't need to let yourself get too tired," the older woman said as she tidied up the small room that sat off the kitchen.

"I'm fine, Consuelo, but thank you," Nicole said, her head still bent over the books. "I let these books get behind and now I'm trying to get caught up." She glanced up. "Did you need me for something?"

"No, Max and Paul have returned. They stopped at the post office and picked up the mail. You have a letter," she said, taking a small white envelope out of the pocket of her apron and handing it to Nicole.

A coughing spell suddenly came upon Consuelo, leaving her breathless.

"That cough sounds terrible. How long have you had it?" Nicole asked, taking the letter from Consuelo.

"Most of my life. Now, I have chores to do," Consuelo said, picking up her cleaning materials.

Nicole glanced at the seal. Marian Cuvier.

Trepidation filled Nicole as she held the letter in her hand and stared at the handwriting on the envelope. What kind of news could she receive from Jean's first wife?

"Thanks, Consuelo," Nicole said, not opening the letter but merely holding it in her hand, fearing the information inside. She couldn't deal with any more bad gossip regarding Jean, and lately all the new knowledge she'd learned about her dead husband had been negative. Deliberately, she'd refrained from buying a newspaper or even having Max bring one back from town. She didn't want to know the status of the investigation of Jean's death or anything about the murder suspect, Layla. She wanted to be as far removed from the scandal as possible and try to put Jean's deception and death behind her.

"You're welcome," the older woman said, walking out the door, leaving Nicole alone with the letter from Jean's wife.

She took a deep breath, steeling herself for the news inside, ripped open the envelope, and pulled out the long sheet of crisp, white paper.

*Dear Nicole,*

*I hope this letter finds you feeling better than the last time I saw you. There are several reasons for my writing, one of which is to tell you, you have been in my thoughts and prayers. I also received your package of Jean's things and wanted to thank you for sending them. My children were delighted to see some of their father's childhood things.*

*I have moved on with my life and tried to put the terrible circumstances surrounding Jean's death behind me by marrying a man I truly love. I married Jean's partner, Louis Fournet, and the two of us are trying to restore Cuvier Shipping and also build a new business together near his family's plantation. We're very happy, and with Louis's help, even my children are doing better dealing with their father's death.*

*As for Layla, I can only tell you that the trial is due to start any day now. I don't know if she's guilty or innocent, and I pray that we will not be called to testify. According to the papers, the prosecution has enough evidence to hang her.*

*How is your pregnancy coming along? I hope you're feeling better and preparing for your new arrival. Tiny babies are so innocent, so sweet, and though I know this is a difficult time, I hope you will enjoy your new arrival.*

*Godspeed, and may your life be much happier in the future.*

*Mrs. Marian Fournet*

Tears welled up in Nicole's eyes as she thought of her poor babe. Never would she see its tiny face and hands, or hear her baby's cry. She laid her head down on her desk, and for the first time in the weeks since the miscarriage, she wept.

She stayed that way for several minutes, sobs from deep inside her welling up, the pain she'd pushed aside at her loss suddenly as fresh as the morning of the miscarriage.

"Nicole?" Max's deep, resonant voice questioned. She glanced up to see him standing in the door of the office looking at her, a concerned expression on his face.

"What's wrong?" he asked, bending down beside her.

"It's nothing," she said, wiping a tear from her face. "I just received this letter from Mrs. Cuvier, or rather, Mrs. Fournet, now."

"Is everything all right?" he asked, staring at her, his dark eyes concerned.

"Yes," she said.

"Then why are you crying?"

Nicole shrugged and her bottom lip began to tremble. "I'm sorry; in the letter she asked me about the baby. I thought I was over losing it, but her letter once again made me realize everything I've lost."

Her eyes filled with fresh tears and all her grief seemed to swell inside her heart. She ached with pain. "I know losing the baby was for the best but I wanted that child so badly."

He took her in his arms and pulled her up out of her chair. Standing in the room, he held her and rubbed her back while she cried.

"I'm sorry, all I seem to do lately is cry," she said softly against his shirt.

"It's all right," he said, his arms firm around her,

protecting her, cradling her. Whenever she needed a gentle touch he seemed to be there.

His hands stroked her back in a comforting gesture; she felt so cosseted, so secure in his arms. She looked up from his shoulder, turned her head to find his lips just inches from her own, his breath whisper-soft on her cheek. Her gaze locked with his and her breath caught in her throat. The pupils of his green eyes darkened and enlarged. His look was not one of friendly compassion. It was more like a sizzling fire shining from his eyes, leaving her wrapped in warmth that had nothing to do with soothing.

She licked her lips, her mouth suddenly dry, her tears all erased. "I..."

His mouth came closer and she knew without a doubt he meant to kiss her, and she wanted him to, though she felt as if an eternity passed before he finally moved toward her. She lifted her mouth to meet his, her conscience screaming no, while her heart urged her on.

His lips covered hers, his mouth storming her defenses, crushing her lips beneath his, demanding and fierce one moment, gentle and tender the next. She moaned, the sound coming from deep within her as he sampled her mouth, tasting her as he locked them in a primal kiss that sent the blood roaring through her ears.

God, this man, her husband, a drifter from nowhere, awakened her sleeping body, making every sense aware of him as a man. A man with little ambition and a big heart who cushioned her fall every time he could.

His hands reached for her hair, tangling in her blonde curls, holding her head captive as desire spiraled through her. The slide of his tongue stroked the inside of her mouth, awakening the sensitive pleasure spots of her lips, lighting a smoldering curl of hunger deep within her.

A harsh, spontaneous sound erupted from deep in his throat as he intensified and lengthened the kiss until her senses staggered in a frenzy of need. Never had her body been so alive, so awakened to the longing he incited.

He positioned her hips between his legs, his hands gripping her buttocks firmly until she could feel him hard and ready between her legs. And her spirit and soul longed to join him in the most primitive way, but her mind revolted, warning her of dangers to her heart that she tried to ignore.

She broke the kiss, gasping for air as his lips followed a searing trail of hot, wet kisses down her neck to the tops of her breasts. With a strangled cry, she tangled her hands in his hair, bringing his mouth back to her lips, wanting his kiss to sear the concerns from her mind. She didn't want to think about the consequences; she only wanted the feelings that Max was giving her to continue.

He placed his hands on her breasts, the pad of his thumb brushing the hard nub of a nipple. Even through her clothes she could feel his long fingers tracing erotic circles over the pebbled kernel that begged for his touch. With one arm around her waist and one hand on her breast, he broke the kiss, his mouth planting hot kisses across her chest, down until he placed his mouth upon her nipple. Through her dress, he suckled her sweet nub until she longed to pull down her dress and give him access to her naked breast A burning sensation began to throb between her legs and grow more potent with each stimulating touch. Her breathing came short and fast as her heart pounded in her ears, her nostrils filled with the scent of him.

Nicole put her hands in his hair and pressed his face to her breast. She wanted to tear the clothes from his body and finish what they'd started.

A door slammed in the kitchen and Paul called out, "Papa, are you in here?"

Nicole froze as Max cursed, "Damn."

He rose from his position at Nicole's breast and slowly

stood, his eyes never leaving hers, the intensity in his gaze a blaze that did not dim. Only moments more and they would have been caught in complete dishevel.

My God, what was she doing? She had just let her foreman, her temporary husband, kiss her until she felt near senseless. But the passion she could feel between them still shimmered in the air like a scent, sweet and intoxicating and rare.

Quickly, she straightened her clothes, her hands shaking as she tried to recover. How could she feel so wanton with Max? How could this man make her forget her heartache with a kiss?

"In here, Paul," Max said, his eyes still watching her as he stared.

The boy walked into the small room. "Hi, what are you doing?"

Silence filled the room and he looked from one to the other, the tense atmosphere choking.

"We were just discussing the plantation, Son," Max said, his gaze still on Nicole.

She gazed at her husband and took a deep calming breath. "If the two of you will excuse me, I think I need to go to my room and rest for a while. I'll see you both at dinner tonight."

Nicole stepped around Max and Paul, and walked toward the main house, her legs shaking. What had just happened between the two of them? Max seemed to know how to attract her, how to mold her like a potter works with clay. But she'd already been scarred once at love and she wasn't willing to risk her heart a second time on a man who would never settle down. Jean had wounded her enough to last a lifetime.

Max Viel needed to leave before the wild hunger he ignited within her overcame them both and led them down a foolish path indeed.

Nicole hurried through the main parlor to her room, eager to put as much distance as possible between her and Max. She desperately needed time to cool her heated body and remind herself of all the reasons she could not become involved with Max.

Never before had any man turned her blood to molten lava, never had her lips seemingly melted beneath the onslaught of such a kiss, and never had she wanted to give herself to a man more than during the space of those few moments. And that frightened her. For to feel such passionate emotions for a man could only lead to heartache.

Max Viel seemed to touch her heart in ways she'd never experienced before. His kind, gentle nature had kept her head whirling and her emotions yearning for him in a passionate sense.

When she reached her room, she lay down on her reclining couch and gazed out the window at a steamer as it rolled down the river, its big wheel pushing the boat toward New Orleans. The vessel had a definite destination, whereas Nicole felt like a steamer out of control, spinning around in circles, unable to determine her destiny or her place in life.

Each course she plotted seemed fraught with sandbars and bad currents. Yet Max appeared like a lifeline thrown to her in a desperate moment, and now their courses seemed plotted in the same direction. Still, she needed to remember that a wanderer's course never stayed in one direction for long.

With a sigh, she picked up the diary. Anything to get her mind off Max. She hoped the woman's journal would remind her why she never wanted to be involved with a man again.

The cruelty of Jean Cuvier should convince her that no man could be trusted ever again, but with Max she didn't feel as though he would betray her, only that they both were two lonely souls searching for their paths in life.

She opened the diary.

*How cruel fate is. Today Jean informed me that our affair has outlasted its usefulness to him. My heart is heavy with sorrow and I can scarce write for the tears that fall from my eyes. In my youthful folly, I followed my heart and eternally alienated myself from the high and noble association of people with whom I could commune. Even my own family disassociated themselves from the embarrassment of my disgrace, some members considering me no better than dirt. Instead, I devoted myself to establishing a sweet haven for Jean to come to, knowing full well that our time would be limited, but well spent, in each other's arms. Yet now his affection has lessened, and I in my estrangement will somehow struggle on to earn a living for our daughter. Our home shall remain in my name until I'm overcome by deaths shadowy presence and lay in my grave.*

*Dear Julianne, our daughter, is now three, and Jean in his infinite wisdom has decided that lama bore who drains too much of his time. Is our daughter, the fruit of our love, to be cast away from him also? I count the days we were all together as a family a blessing, and thank God for my daughter, the light of my life. For without her, the path I am destined to follow would surely have put me in the grave before now. How her father cannot miss seeing her beautiful smile and hearing her laughing voice pains me too much to dwell on. For our sweet child knows nothing of her father's fickle heart, and Julianne and I will go on without him, though it shall not be easy and the way will be lonely. I only pray that somehow he '11 have a change of heart and he '11 remember the happiness we shared.*

Nicole shut the diary, unable to read the woman's story anymore for now. Tears filled her eyes as she thought of the young woman all alone. Anger so intense at the way

Jean had hurt so many lives filled Nicole, and for the first time since his death she knew she no longer loved the bastard. He hadn't loved her—or anyone but himself. Nicole hated him with a fierceness that drove him from her heart.

Now as she looked back at their life together she saw the incongruities, the times he couldn't account for, the times he didn't show up, and she realized she'd known something wasn't right but had pushed her doubts aside, believing his lies. But never again would a man get away with deceiving her. Never again would she love a man blindly.

~

Two weeks passed and Nicole deliberately avoided Max. She took her breakfast after he'd left for the field. She managed to avoid him even for lunch and dinner. Somehow she didn't want to gaze into his dark green eyes and see the passion she knew lurked beneath the shadows. She feared the responses he awakened in her body and the way his scent caused her blood to rush. He invaded her dreams, leaving her restless and waking her in the middle of the night to feverish imaginings of the two of them together. She knew without a doubt that he was a danger to her senses and she refused to fall in love again.

Sun streamed in through the windows of her office, making the little room seem stifling. Nevertheless, Nicole had little difficulty bringing up to date the plantation books that she let fall behind during her illness. Soon she would be resting beneath the fan in her room.

Consuelo appeared at the door, and Nicole glanced up at her to see her dark brown eyes wide with fear. "Come quickly. Mr. Viel is out in the yard speaking with some woman. I think she's Paul's mother." Consuelo rolled her eyes. "I fear that the woman is nothing but white trash."

"Consuelo! You don't normally talk that way," Nicole said, rising from her chair. "I'm surprised at you."

Nicole had confided to Consuelo what she knew of Paul's background.

"Well you won't be after you see this woman. I can't believe that Mr. Viel would associate with such a tramp. But then again, their affair must have been many years ago. Maybe she looked prettier then."

"You're certain this is Paul's mother?" Nicole asked as she followed her servant out the door of the house.

"I don't know but they're out front arguing. He's done told her to leave, she's not welcome here."

Nicole recalled the conversation with Paul regarding his mother, and the details he'd told her of his life came crashing back with a harsh reality. The woman seemed less than the perfect mother, yet Nicole didn't think that Max made a much better parent.

Once outdoors, she saw Max standing in the drive that led to the house, staring at a woman dressed in gaudy finery that made her appear tawdry. A purple dress clung to the curves of her figure and fell in graceful lines to the ground. A red petticoat peeked from beneath special slits that showed the colored lace when she moved. Tinted red curls spilled out from beneath a wide-brim hat that shaded her face from view, and a folded matching parasol hung from her arm. She looked like she belonged in a saloon, not like a mother coming to retrieve her son.

The expression on Max's face appeared hostile yet bored as he stared at her.

"I'm not certain that's her," Nicole said to Consuelo, gazing at the two of them standing in the drive, the woman's voice loud and animated.

Max stood with his arms crossed over his chest, his face like stone, with no muscles moving. Even a hurricane would have a difficult time forcing Max from his rock-solid foundation.

Nicole halted on the verandah, gazing down at the two who stood sideways to her, their every expression in view. She stared, uncertain that she should approach them, yet unable to walk away.

"I think it's best if we leave him to deal with her," Nicole told Consuelo.

"If that ain't white trash, then I'm still twenty- three," Consuelo whispered, nodding her head.

The woman's voice became clear and shrill enough to reach Nicole. "You've been hiding my son from me and I'm going to take him home."

Consuelo and Nicole turned and looked at one another. Yes, this woman was Paul's mother.

"I didn't hide him from you. You took him to my father, after he ran away. Father brought him here to me," Max said calmly, his arms still crossed over his chest, his feet spread apart in a solid stance.

Nicole had never seen him look so unmovable. She glanced at the woman and couldn't help but wonder what he'd seen in her. She didn't appear to be the type of woman a man like Max would care for. Yet they'd had a child together.

"Yes, and then the old bastard wouldn't tell me where you were. How could I know where my baby was if your father wouldn't tell me?" she whined. "I want my son back."

"You obviously found him on your own," Max said, his voice cool as a cold winter's day.

"Only because someone I know saw your wedding announcement and told me you'd recently married." She glanced around at the house and land. "Seems that marriage has certainly paid off for you."

Max didn't respond, just stared at her with the coldest, blankest eyes Nicole had ever seen. A shiver went through her at the expression on his face, his body stance a solid force to be reckoned with as he stood there, and saying nothing. She'd never seen this side of him and the severity of his coldness surprised her. The warm, gentle man she knew now appeared ruthless.

"I want my son to come home now!" the woman said, her voice loud and strident. "He's my boy and you can't take him away from me."

"I'm not trying to take him away from you. You gave him up when you took him to my father. Don't blame me for this situation," Max said coolly, his voice not rising but remaining dead-even. "Your gentleman friend didn't want Paul around, so he ran away. He said he told you and you did nothing."

The woman placed one hand on her hip, leaned forward until she was almost in Max's face. "Paul knew it wasn't permanent. And now that man is no longer seeing me, so I'm here to take my son home."

"He's not ready to go with you," Max said.

"I'm his mother and he'll do as I say. Now get him so that I can take him home before I start searching this place for him," she said, her voice loud enough that Consuelo and Nicole could understand every word.

"Desiree, I'm his father," Max said as though he was speaking to a small child. "When Paul tells me he's ready to return to you, then I'll bring him back. But right now he's happy here and wants to stay."

"I'm sure you've made him very happy," she said. "Bribing the boy, buying him things to keep him with you. But if you really cared about him, you'd send him money to buy those things."

Max said something that Nicole couldn't hear, something that sent Desiree off into a fit of rage.

"If I lived in a big fancy place like this, he'd want to stay with me all the time too. I do the best I can with the money I have and you can't keep him away from me."

Nicole wondered where Paul could be and wanted to protect the boy and keep him from seeing his parents fight like this.

"I'm not leaving until I see my son," Desiree said, folding her arms across her chest with a defiant toss of her head as she raised her chin.

"Fine. If you can find him, then you go right ahead and speak with the boy. But me, I have work to do now, so if you'll excuse me, I must return to my duties," Max said and turned and walked toward the barn, leaving her standing in the dusty drive.

"This is not the end of this discussion," she screamed. "I'll bring the sheriff back. Paul! Paul, you get out here now!"

Max didn't say a word, but continued walking away, his back to the woman. As he passed the house, he glanced up and saw Nicole standing on the verandah.

He nodded an acknowledgment, as though nothing were amiss, and kept on walking.

"Paul!"

"Consuelo, where is Paul?" she asked quietly.

"Paul!"

"He's out in the fields with the rest of the men. His father has been sending him out there each day," she said, her voice barely above a whisper.

"Send Moses to make sure that he keeps the boy away from the house. He's not to tell him anything, just keep him in the field until she's gone," Nicole said, angry that any child should have to deal with this kind of treatment.

Paul's mother stood in the middle of the driveway looking helpless for a moment as Max walked away. She screamed after him, "Damn you, Max Viel, this is not the last you'll hear from me. I want my son back. I need him. Paul! Paul, you come out now!"

Nicole couldn't help but wonder if Desiree, though not the best specimen of motherhood, wouldn't do better if she received the monetary support she needed to raise all of her children.

Nicole's own mother knew from experience how difficult it could be to raise a child alone. She'd been fired from her teaching position and from then on had taken in sewing and lived with her parents in order to survive until she'd finally succumbed to pneumonia.

To this day, Nicole had no idea who her father was or why he'd rejected her mother and her. Not a day went by that she didn't wonder about who he could be and where he lived.

She glanced at Desiree still standing in the driveway, yelling for Paul, and suddenly, Paul seemed so much like herself at this young age without a father.

There had been no money for luxuries, no extras, nothing that they didn't have to work and scrape for. In school, the children tormented Nicole with the knowledge that she had no father.

In her mind, Max took the place of her father and all she could think about was that, once again, a child suffered because of the mistakes of his parents and his father didn't seem to care.

It seemed so unfair, so wrong, that a child endured the pain of his parents' mistakes rather than those who had created him and brought him into the world.

Nicole slammed into the house. Why did people do this to their children? Max, the one man she thought might be decent and kind, had a major flaw; not taking care of his son! Not living up to his responsibilities!

Maybe he wasn't much different from Jean after all.

## Chapter Eleven

**M**ax walked up the stairs and crossed the verandah, going in the back door of the big house. How quickly he'd become accustomed to living here and how the old house felt like he'd come home.

There were so many things he wanted to do around the house, but he waited, knowing that his first priority could only be his union with Nicole. Soon, very soon, he would have to be honest and tell her that he'd knowingly married her for the land, but until then he kept hoping that she would see how wise it would be for them to stay together. Certainly, they could have a good married life; the kiss they experienced the other day showed there was something between them.

Today when Desiree had shown up, he'd been afraid she would reveal too much of his identity, and Nicole would realize that something didn't add up. But he'd managed to scrape through yet another incident and even managed to hang on to his son. Though it was only a matter of time before Desiree would return and begin to hound Paul to come home, unless he worked out something with his lawyers.

He opened the door and stepped into the pantry adjacent to the dining room. As he entered the dining room Nicole stood waiting for him, her hands on her hips. His eyes were drawn to her beautiful mouth. He couldn't help but stare as he recalled the warm touch of her lips against his, the feel of her breasts in his hands. The memory of their last meeting began a hungry ache within him and he wanted to finish what they'd started.

"Where's Paul?" she questioned, her voice stern, her manner cold, not at all welcoming, bringing him back from his reverie.

"Well, hello to you too," he said, aware her greeting was not a glad-to-see-you, welcome home response. "He hasn't returned from the fields yet. Why?"

"I'm worried about him," she said, gazing at Max, her expression wary. "You're not going to send him away with his mother, are you?"

The urge to wrap his arms around her, feel her body next to his and give her a proper hello seized him, but tension radiated from her and she seemed on edge, almost angry, and he knew his embrace would not be welcome.

Max shrugged, trying to appear indifferent, trying to focus on the present He'd love to keep his son with him all the time, but Desiree would make the boy feel guilty for not staying with her. "That is Paul's decision. If he wants to stay with me, he's welcome to, but I'm not going to force him."

Nicole seemed to draw up and he could see her eyes widen with fury, which surprised him. "You'd let him go off with that woman? You wouldn't fight to keep him?"

"She is his mother," Max said, warmed as he realized that Nicole seemed genuinely worried about Paul. "And the boy is old enough to decide where he wants to stay. Why are you so concerned about him?"

She stared at him, the irises of her blue eyes flashing daggers at Max as she walked closer to him and crossed her arms across her chest defiantly.

The smell of lilacs filled his senses, surrounding him, setting his blood to pounding in his veins. Anger stiffened her body and yet he wanted to soothe her, mold her body to his, kiss her senseless until she begged him for more.

"Do you have any idea how hard it is for a woman alone to raise a child without a father?" she asked.

"I think so. Desiree has five children including Paul, but she seems to do all right," Max said, and then hastily added, "only Paul is mine."

"Five children!" Nicole seemed stunned. She began to pace the length of the room. "My God, how does she manage? How does she feed and clothe those children?"

Max gave a little laugh, wishing Nicole would relax and they could discuss anything other than Desiree. "You may not want to know the answer to that question."

Nicole turned on Max, her face red, her blue eyes flashing. Why was she so angry? "You can laugh, because Desiree must have to live a disreputable life just to take care of her children. But her children are the very ones who suffer."

"Desiree was hardly forced into the life she's chosen," Max said, suddenly uncertain as to the turn of this conversation. Nicole seemed to want to pick a fight and he suddenly wondered what they were really arguing about.

Nicole walked around the dining room table, shaking her head. "You have no idea how hard it is on an illegitimate child. The constant harassment from the other children at school because their parents shared your dirty little secrets with their children. The fact that your mother can't afford a new frock for you every time you outgrow yours, so she adds a new hem, but it may not be of the same color or even the same fabric as the original dress. The fact that your mother, who was once one of the schoolteachers in town, is now taking in sewing to support the two of you because the school board thinks she's not of good moral character and should not be teaching the other children."

Max didn't say a word as Nicole spewed forth the ugly things he'd known happened in some towns, and realized suddenly she had experienced the dreadful bias in some fashion.

She took a deep breath. "I have no father. Don't know who he is or why he never married my mother, who paid dearly for her mistake. No one in town ever forgave her or let her forget what she'd done. When I was eighteen, I moved away to escape the horrid stories and whispered stares, only to have Jean put me in the same situation."

At this information, Max felt like someone had slapped him. Why hadn't his lawyers given him these facts? Suddenly he understood why Nicole insisted on marrying right away. So many of her actions suddenly made sense. Her urgent need to belong to the community, yet her shyness at meeting new people.

Nicole was illegitimate.

"Have you tried to find your father?" Max asked gently.

"My mother refused to tell me his name, saying that if he wanted to be involved in my life, he would come to see me," she said, her voice shaking. "I don't know where to begin to find him. And it's obvious he doesn't want to know me or be a part of my life. Yet, I would like to know who he is. Just knowing would ease my curiosity."

"Are you certain that would ease your curiosity?" he asked, repeating her words back to her.

"No, but I'd like to be offered the choice of knowing." She shook her head. "A man gets a woman with child and then doesn't want to marry her and leaves all the responsibilities of raising that child to the woman." She paused for a moment, her full gaze returning to his, her face almost sad. "And now I find out that you're no different than the other men I've known. You have an illegitimate son, whose mother must scrape and beg for her living. No wander. She dresses so brazenly."

Max stiffened, feeling unfairly accused.

"That's not true. You don't know how Paul came into my life or what I've done for him," Max said.

"What you've done for him? It's obvious you're ashamed of the boy. He comes here, you put him in the barn, and the poor kid has only one set of clothes. How does that reflect on a father who cares for his son? You helped create him, you should be taking care of him."

The hair on the back of Max's neck started to rise. He'd always been very involved in Paul's life. He loved his son, regardless of the fact that he had never loved Desiree.

"I do care for him, the best I can," Max said, knowing he had to be careful what he said, but needing to defend his actions as Paul's father. "I know it doesn't look very good, but I give Desiree money and I buy the kid new clothes and I try to help him in any way I can.

"You're right, it doesn't look good," she said.

Max waited, trying to let his anger cool before he set her straight He crossed the room, the dining table between them, his blood pounding in his veins. "I was young when I made a huge mistake with Desiree. We had a very brief affair. Paul is the result of that liaison and I recognize that I'm partly responsible for his being here today."

"So you think you can just pay Desiree some money every so often and that takes care of your obligations?" Nicole asked, her voice rising.

"No! I do the best I can to help Desiree, but I was not about to tie myself to her for the rest of my life just because she'd gotten with child," Max said, his anger rising at the way Nicole seemed determined to make him into someone who didn't care about his son. While Max knew his actions regarding his son were appropriate, he needed Nicole to believe in him.

"For Paul's sake you should be involved in his life. He needs you there, showing him that you care, that he's important to you. It's more than just money and clothes, it's about love and support" Nicole said, coming around the table toward him.

Max took a deep breath, trying to calm the resentment he could feel building within his chest. From the day Paul was born, Max had done everything he could to help the boy, except marry his mother. And he just couldn't bring himself to go that far. Max didn't like Nicole accusing him of not being a good parent, especially when she didn't understand how he'd been involved in Paul's life. And he couldn't explain to her without telling her the truth about himself.

"You know nothing about me and my son," he said, his voice tight

"I know I see a child struggling to survive the best he can, while his parents argue and neglect him."

Nicole took a deep breath and released it slowly. "Paul deserves to be treated better."

"I'm not going to let Desiree control my life. I'll do everything I can to help Paul, but Desiree lives her life the way she wants to," he said, his voice rising. "And whether you believe me or not, I take care of my son. I'm not your father, Nicole. I'm just a man who made a mistake, like your mother, when I was young."

Max turned and walked out the door. He'd never felt so angry and defensive regarding his son. Somehow Nicole had managed to find the one topic that Max was sensitive to, the matter of his son Paul. Before today, no one had ever accused him of being a poor father and he'd prided himself on taking care of his son, but could he be blind to his faults as a father? And Nicole knew from her own experience the pain of being an illegitimate child, but Max wasn't like her unknown father.

~

Nicole watched Max hurry from the dining room, his back stiff. She'd never seen him react to something she said so vividly. The sharp features of his face all but smoldered with fury, his green eyes widened and flashed with barely suppressed rage. But his last words stunned her. Was she being unfair by comparing Max to the man who'd only helped conceive her?

Yes, she'd compared Max to her nonexistent father and found a lot of similarities. Or at least a man who hadn't cared properly for his child.

Her mother had refused to tell her the name of her father, carrying the secret to her grave. For a while Nicole had searched for some clue as to who he could be, rummaging through her mother's things after she died, and still she'd never found a name, a picture, or anything that would give her a clue as to his identity.

Sometimes she felt like a piece of the puzzle was missing. She had given up searching the faces of strangers and even wondered if the man was still alive. Yet she couldn't help but think that even a name wouldn't satisfy the secret longing she still felt.

She'd wanted a father just like all the other children and Paul deserved the same in his life.

Nicole sank down in a chair, knowing that soon it would be time for dinner, though she hardly felt ready to face Max again. Had she been wrong to accuse him of not taking care of Paul?

She only knew that from everything she'd seen he didn't appear to have taken his guardianship of the boy seriously. The only reason she knew about Paul was because she'd seen him wandering about the plantation. And then, when she confronted Max, he'd told her that the boy was sleeping in the barn. She'd hardly qualify a building where the animals slept as the best place for a twelve-year-old child to sleep. Why would he put Paul there unless he was ashamed of his own son?

The poor child had few clothes and it wasn't until she'd confronted Max that he had taken the boy to town and purchased him some new trousers. Then, after witnessing Desiree's emotional hysterics this afternoon, she hardly thought that Max stood up to the woman, let alone defended poor Paul.

Could Max possibly have taken care of Paul and she just didn't know the circumstances?

All she knew was that the man she'd come to think of as a rock solid, dependable person seemed to have a large flaw she couldn't overlook. As a child who grew up with only a mother, with no means of support, she could not stand by and watch another child suffer the same treatment.

Maybe Max did watch after Paul, and maybe he did send them money, and maybe he tried to be a good parent to the boy, but so far everything she'd witnessed screamed neglect.

But Paul had defended his father once before. In all fairness, she should talk to Paul and see what the child would tell her. The last time she'd spoken to him, they'd been interrupted when Max joined them. Maybe this time she could question him at length about his father, find out how a drifter could support a child when he must have trouble supporting himself.

A drifter who no matter what he did, she couldn't seem to quit thinking about who'd entered her world by accident and now seemed such a big part of her life. She wanted him to leave, yet she feared when he left that nothing would ever be the same. And that frightened her most of all.

~

Max went to his room and stretched out on the bed, determined to get away from Nicole before he said something he regretted. She seemed determined to argue over Paul and he couldn't help but think that stemmed from her own experience of being illegitimate.

The news had shocked him, yet the signs had all been there and he'd foolishly overlooked them. If only he'd paid attention to her need to get married so her child would not be considered illegitimate, her need to be accepted by the people in town, and her concern for Paul. Everything put together should have alerted him to the circumstance of her birth.

Yet every time they were together, he couldn't think straight. The smell of lilacs would pervade his senses, sending his thoughts to the fullness of her mouth and the way her lips felt against his own. To the way her breasts felt crushed against his chest and how he wanted to spend an eternity mapping her body. Sometime in the last three months together he had come to enjoy being with Nicole. He liked her determination and spirit. He only hoped all would not be lost when she learned the truth.

Nicole couldn't get past her own experience of being illegitimate, no matter that Max had been the best father he could be. He didn't like her thinking that he wasn't a good father, he didn't like her having sympathy for Desiree, yet how could he blame her when all her life she'd been shadowed by the fact that her father didn't want her? And Max didn't understand how her father could not want to know his daughter. Nicole would have made the man proud, yet he'd chosen not to be in her life—or did he even know she existed?

There were so many variables that could have happened, Max wondered if it were possible to even locate her father. Even if he could find the man, would it be his place to tell him of his daughter? Certainly Nicole could benefit from learning of her father, and she was all he cared about.

Maybe he could have his lawyers search for any information on Nicole's mother. Then if they found her father's name, Max could at least give Nicole the option of locating him.

Max knew in his heart that he wasn't like Nicole's father, that he would always be there for his son. Yet convincing Nicole to trust him to be better than her own father, and believe he would always be there for her and any children they might have together, seemed impossible.

~

A week later, sitting in the main parlor working on some embroidery, Nicole heard Paul come in alone. Usually Max and Paul came in together, but the boy had returned early and Nicole knew this could be her chance to talk with him.

She called to him as he passed the main parlor. "Paul, do you have a moment?"

The boy stopped in the doorway and looked in, his brown eyes wary. "Yes, ma'am?"

"Have a seat. I'd like to speak with you."

"Oh, no, ma'am. I've been out in the fields and I don't want to dirty up your pretty furniture. It's way too nice for me to sit on," he said, leaning against the door frame.

Nicole smiled at him. "Your mother has taught you well."

He shrugged. "I guess. We don't have such pretty things in our house."

"I saw your mother last week when she came to the house. I'm sorry to say I didn't get a chance to meet her," Nicole said, watching the kid's eyes widen. She should never have mentioned seeing his mother.

"Mother was here?" he asked, clearly shocked.

"Yes, she came and spoke with your father. I would have thought that Max would have told you," Nicole said. Why hadn't he told Paul about Desiree's visit? The boy looked worried. "What did she want? She's been wishing for me to come home."

Nicole smiled, trying to reassure the boy. "She spoke with your father, not me, but I don't think you have to worry."

"She'll be back," Paul said, glancing at Nicole worriedly. "I wonder how she found me."

"You mean she didn't know where you were?" Nicole asked, surprised. Why would Max keep Paul's whereabouts a secret?

"No, I asked Grandpa to keep it secret from her," he said. "She knew I was all right; I just didn't want her to know where I was living. I didn't want her to come here."

Nicole found this information stunning. "Why would you do that Paul? She's your mother."

"Yes, but I didn't want her following me out here, because I didn't want to go home. Actually, it's taken her longer than I expected to find me."

Why would the boy feel this way about his mother? "Isn't your mother good to you, Paul?"

"Yes, ma'am, she does the best she can on the money she receives, but there are five of us kids and the other fathers seldom pay her anything. Plus her gentlemen friends don't always give her enough money."

Nicole bit her lip to keep from gasping as Paul acknowledged his mother's behavior.

"My mother likes to use men for their money and sometimes it gets her into trouble," the boy said, shocking Nicole even further. "That's why I wanted to spend some time with my father. He's always taken care of me when I needed something. I wanted to live with him and see what it's like."

With a nod of understanding, Nicole said, "I guess this is your first stable home with your father."

The boy shrugged. "I could have lived with Nana and Grandpa Viel in New Orleans, but they're kind of strict and Nana yells at Grandpa a lot. But Papa always spent time with me, if that's what you mean."

Nicole silently thanked her mother and grandparents who had lovingly taken care of her.

"I don't understand how your father has paid for you all these years. I'm sure he doesn't earn a lot of money in the jobs he does."

"I don't know about that. He's always given my mother money every month for us to live on. It's one of the reasons she doesn't want me to move away. She'd lose that extra money."

Nicole was astonished at the boy's statement. He seemed so pragmatic about his relationship with his mother.

"Don't you think that your mother would miss you? I'm sure she loves you very much, Paul."

He shrugged his shoulders. "She'd miss me taking care of the children, doing the dishes, and she'd miss the money my father gives her. I guess she'd miss me."

Nicole looked down at the embroidery in her lap and then back up at Paul, noticing for the first time the size of his hands and feet. Once his body grew into his frame, he would be a large man, even bigger than his father.

"How about you? Do you miss your mother?"

He nodded his head. "I miss her, but I don't want to go home. Not yet," he said. "I like living here."

"Has your father always been involved in your life?" she questioned, unable to resolve the idea that Max could be different from her own worthless father. Could Max be right, that she compared him to her own experience?

The boy nodded his head. "Papa always comes around to see after me. I feel kind of bad because my brothers' and sisters' fathers never come around to see them or give them things. Just my Papa. I guess I'm lucky to have him."

Nicole wondered once again if she'd been wrong about Max. Could the drifter really care for his son, despite the fact that circumstances were against him? "Yes, Paul. I guess you are lucky to have him."

"I have to go now," he said. They're waiting for me in the barn.

Nicole watched the boy hurry out the door and

scramble down the stairs. She felt a twinge of guilt. Maybe she had overreacted to Desiree and maybe Max had been telling the truth.

~

Max tried one more time to tie the cravat of his tuxedo with no luck. It still looked crooked. He glanced at the clock and realized they should be leaving in the next five minutes. He crossed the main parlor and knocked on the door to Nicole's room.

"Yes," she called.

"It's me. I need some help," he said.

She opened the door, and he felt as if his breath was whisked away. The dress she wore accentuated her sparkling blue eyes, with loose curls framing her delicate face, her hair twisted in a knot on her head. Lace teased the bodice of her low-cut dress, draping from her shoulder to her waist and then secured with a tiny bow to one side, giving an elongated heart- shaped effect that looked enchanting.

"What do you need?" she asked, her voice lilting with excitement "I'm almost ready."

The dress was fitted to her bodice and waist, clinging to her and then falling into a flared skirt. Blue satin that matched the color of her eyes filled the v-shaped insert in the front with a matching train trailing behind her. Puffed sleeves were edged with more lace and the rest of the dress was made of some sort of filmy material with floral bouquets scattered all over it. He stood staring at her, knowing she'd never been more beautiful.

"Uh, sorry, I wondered if you could help me with my cravat," he said, trying to return his focus to the problem at hand. In the six weeks since the miscarriage she'd lost weight, and slowly the smile had returned to her face.

"Of course," she said, and stepped within inches of

him. Immediately, the smell of gardenias surrounded him, penetrating all of his senses. The urge to take her in his arms and kiss her until she was senseless overwhelmed him, but he merely cleared his throat and tried to concentrate on how she tied the knot at his neck, which was a difficult task.

He watched as she tilted her head sideways, her nimble fingers deftly working his cravat until it fitted to her satisfaction.

"There. Now that should work," she said, giving it one last tug and then patting it with her hand. She glanced up at him and their gazes locked; the blue of her eyes darkened until they seemed almost liquid.

Max could feel the tension between them sizzle with sudden awareness. He watched as she flicked her tongue nervously across her sweet, sensual lips and he longed to cover her mouth and sample her until he'd had his fill.

"I think I'd better finish getting ready," she said anxiously. "I don't have any slippers on yet."

He glanced down at her delicate stocking feet and felt his blood pounding in his veins. When had he ever been enamored of a woman's feet before? Good grief, he was beginning to get a little carried away with this whole idea of marriage. But it wasn't the marriage, it was Nicole.

"Yes, I see that," he said, wishing they could stay home and he could slowly undress Nicole layer by layer. "How much longer do you need?"

"I'll meet you at the carriage in ten minutes," she said, stepping away from him and retreating back into her room, closing the door with a decisive click.

Max stood there, breathing in the gardenia-scented air. Sometime in the next few weeks, he needed to sneak off to New Orleans and find his way to the Storyville District, where he could ease this need he seemed to have developed. He would feel this way toward any woman at this point in his life, wouldn't he? There was nothing special about this woman, was there? Yet a part of him couldn't help but refute what his mind kept repeating. Nicole could be happy, she could be joyous, and she could incite his passion quicker than any woman he'd ever met. He turned away, went back to his room, and finished dressing, then hurried down the stairs to make sure the carriage was ready to take them to Ashland Plantation. Tonight the Prudommes were holding a party to announce the engagement of their daughter and the Viels had received an invitation on the advice of his good friend James Francisco, the man he'd met at the crawfish festival.

A few minutes later, Nicole came out on the verandah, and then, with her dress carefully lifted, giving him a quick glance of her trim ankle, she walked down the stairs until she reached his side. God, she was so beautiful, and he was determined they would enjoy themselves this night.

"You look lovely, Madam Viel," he said, deliberately reminding her of their marital status.

"Thank you, sir," she said, not taking his bait. "I think I'm ready."

"Good." He helped her into the enclosed carriage he had rented for tonight's occasion and climbed in beside her. Moses sat in the driver's seat and, as Max closed the door, the servant called to the horses.

"Where did you get this carriage?" she asked, looking around in awe.

"I borrowed it," he said. "I didn't want you to get too hot and dusty before we arrived, and I worried it would rain, so I found this."

"It's nice," she replied, running her hand across the upholstery.

"You know, we could have gone by boat. They're just up the river from us," he said, teasing her.

"No, thank you." She laughed. "I prefer traveling by

carriage. Fewer bugs."

He smiled back at her, thinking how pretty she *appeared* tonight. "I guess I never thought of it that way."

For several moments she said nothing, but gazed out the window at the passing landscape.

"I haven't had a chance to speak with you this last week," she said, turning back to look at him, her face questioning.

"Yes, I've spent more time out in the fields," he replied. He'd deliberately stayed away from the house, trying to give them both time to sort things out after their discussion regarding Paul. He'd needed time to cool but he'd also carefully considered everything she'd said. He wanted to be a good father to his son.

"While we're here like this, I feel the need to tell you that I spoke with Paul at length the other day," she said.

Max tensed, afraid of what his son could have told Nicole, wondering if he'd let anything slip that would alert her to Max's real purpose. Then he relaxed. If so, wouldn't Nicole have been angry?

"He's really proud that you're his father," she said, gazing at him with admiration. "I was shocked to hear him tell about his mother and his brothers and sisters. He said you were one of the few fathers who sends his mother money."

Max nodded, knowing she must wonder how he earned enough money as a drifter. "That's right. I do what I can."

"I didn't know, Max," she said, surprised, her face gazing at him in awe. "I guess you've been trying to tell me, but I just didn't want to believe you. Paul convinced me that you're a good father, and he's very proud of you."

"He's a good kid," Max said. "I just never could have married his mother, no matter that she was expecting my child."

"Do you mind my asking why? I mean, I would think

that a man who is involved sexually with a woman should be at least considering marriage to her," Nicole asked, and Max wanted to laugh at her naiveté.

"At eighteen, young men don't always think with the brain God gave us. Desiree was older and well... let's just say the infatuation soon wore off, but by then she was expecting Paul."

What he didn't tell Nicole was that by then he'd realized he wasn't the only man in her life.

"Did you consider marrying her?" Nicole asked.

"Yes, but my mother talked me out of it and I'm glad she did," he said. "Though I wish the circumstances were different for Paul."

"At least he knows who you are, and you seem to be involved with his life," Nicole said and took a deep breath, then released it slowly.

The sun hung in a precarious balance, caught barely hanging above the horizon, as they turned on to the main river road and headed toward the Ashland plantation.

"You know, sometimes having both of your parents can be just as troubling as not having your father. I mean, my parents have been married forever and they fight all the time; and each of them seems to want to hurt the other as much as possible." He sighed. "It can get very ugly."

She nodded. "I'm sure that it can. Sometimes people make you wonder why you would ever want to chance getting married again." She glanced over at him, her blue eyes inquisitive. "Are your parents the reason you've never married before now?"

He smiled. "No. I've never been in one place long enough and there hasn't been anyone I couldn't live without. After the way my parents fight, I wasn't going to choose just anyone. I didn't want to live with that type of situation, so I determined to make sure I found the right person."

"Until me," she said.

"Until you. And then I knew I needed to help you," he said, feeling like a louse for lying so blatantly to Nicole. He'd married her for Rosewood, and though he'd felt sorry for her plight, he still knew his own selfish interests had led him to her.

"I don't know if I've told you this or not but thanks Max. You've been a big help, even if things didn't turn out right," she said, the blue of her eyes sparkling with faith.

"You're welcome," Max replied, knowing he'd taken advantage of her situation. Yet maybe tonight he'd make progress with Nicole. Maybe tonight he could show her how good they could be together.

~

Nicole felt nervous as she stepped out of the carriage, giving her hand to Max. God, he looked handsome standing there with his hat on, the tails of his suit fashionably long.

"Where did you get the new suit?" she asked as they climbed the curving staircase to the main floor of the mansion. Light streamed through the open windows, the sounds of a waltz drifted on the breeze.

"I borrowed it," he said.

"Who do you know that would let you borrow such a suit?" she asked, staring at him as they reached the top of the stairs.

"You remember James, from the crawfish festival?" Max asked. "I've been visiting him about once a week in town. He helped me find it."

"Why have you been visiting this man every week?" she questioned, feeling uneasy about why he would become friends with a man in town. Why would he make bonds with people when he would not be staying after the harvest?

"We have a lot in common and we've become friends.

He's given me some good tips on how to burn the cane fields when it comes time to harvest them."

Why would a drifter become friends with a planter who had been in this area for many years?

Before Nicole had time to question Max further, they were greeted by their hosts and pointed in the direction of the ballroom, which was actually two parlors joined to become one room. In each room, a large glass chandelier hung from the ceiling, and a white fireplace decorated the main wall. In the largest room, above the fireplace, hung the picture of the lady of the manor, her portrait in a golden frame. Between the rooms, curved arches separated by white columns outlined in plaster frieze joined the two parlors into a ballroom.

"Pretty fancy," Max said as he gazed about the room.

Floor to ceiling windows faced the river and they were open to let in the cool fall breeze. In the corner, a small band played as couples waltzed.

Nicole gazed about the room at the ladies dressed in gorgeous gowns and the men in their dandiest suit or tuxedos. She felt out of place and she held on tightly to Max's arm as they walked about the room, saying hello to people they had met at the crawfish festival.

She held her head high, determined not to run in cowardice from this evening, but to greet the people as if she deserved to be here in this room. As lady of Rosewood Plantation, this was her rightful place.

"Are you all right?" Max asked, gazing at her oddly.

"A little nervous," she admitted. Then smiled at him and lifted her chin. "I'll be fine as soon as I have a chance to dance."

"Then by all means, let me be the first to dance with my wife," he said, his voice a husky whisper that sent shivers down her spine. The way he said those two little words made her hesitate, yet she wanted so badly to feel his arms around her once again. Those words were only for tonight, for this moment in time, and soon they would mean nothing. For once the crop came in, Max would be gone.

He held her in his arms, his hand on her waist as they waltzed in time to the music. He dipped and twirled her as they circled the floor and she couldn't help but stare into the intensity of his green eyes, unable to tear her gaze away. His eyes darkened until a ring of emerald surrounded the darkened pupils, leaving her dazed by the heat she felt in his gaze.

The scent of Max, a tempting blend of soap and aftershave, seemed to envelop her as they waltzed. Never had she felt such intense warmth that seemed to curl and spread through her as they moved to the music of the Viennese waltz. People who stood on the edges of the floor seemed to fade away, and only the two of them existed at this moment, in this room, and she'd never been more aware of Max as a man.

And then abruptly the music ended and Nicole swallowed, trying to calm her erratic heartbeat and break the spell that Max seemed to have woven around her.

He took her hand, brought it to his mouth, and kissed her gloved palm. "That dance, *mon chere,* I will always treasure," he said, his husky voice settling over her, sending tremors through her like small prickles of fire dancing over her skin. "Thank you."

"You're quite welcome, *monsieur.* Shall we join the others?" she asked, knowing there was safety in numbers and feeling the need to mingle and keep these dangerous emotions she felt at bay.

"Of course," he said, and led her off the dance floor. As a waiter passed with glasses of wine, Max handed her a crystal goblet and took one for himself.

He lifted his drink to her, clinked the rims of their glasses together, and said softly, "To the most beautiful woman in the room tonight."

"Thank you." Nicole smiled and tried to make light of his vocal caress, her palms sweating nervously. "I never knew you were such a flirt. I'm going to have to remember this about you."

"There are a lot of things you've yet to learn about me," he said, the deep timbre of his voice soft and musical, playing along her spine.

She sighed, luxuriating in the moment as she sipped from the crystal glass. Max made her feel like a cosseted woman and no man had ever made her feel so special before.

Nicole glanced up to see Mr. Francisco, a short Italian man, hurrying toward them. "There you two are. I've been looking everywhere for you and you're over in the corner acting like a couple of newlyweds. There's plenty of time for that later; come along, I want to introduce you to some people I know," he said as he took Nicole by the arm. "You're looking lovely, Mrs. Viel."

"Thank you," she replied as she glanced back to see Max following, a smile on his face.

The man hurried them over to a group of men and women standing in a circle talking.

"Hello everyone. If you haven't met the Viels, let me introduce them. This is Maxim Viel and his lovely wife Nicole," he said, releasing Nicole's arm.

The group included Anna DeChoskey, one of the women from the mercantile. She sneered at Nicole, who merely returned the woman's smile, thinking that tonight no one could upset her.

An older man in the group frowned at Max. "You know, there used to be a family who owned one of the local plantations and the daughter married a man named Charles Viel. Are you any relation to them?"

"I don't know, I'll have to ask my parents the next time

I see them," he said.

"The young girl's parents owned the house, but the mother was dead, so just her father lived there with the daughter. The father probably would have been your grandfather's age," the old man said.

"Max, do you know about your grandfather?" Nicole asked.

"Very little. He passed away when I was quite young," he said. "Besides, there are so few Viels in this country. Most of them reside in France."

She glanced at Max. Could he have had family in this area before and never known? Nicole turned toward the man, curious about this tale. This was the second time someone had mentioned the Viel name being in this community before. "What happened to these Viels?"

"I think they were forced to sell. Seems they never recovered after the war and when sugar prices dropped they had no choice but to auction off their plantation."

"How sad," Nicole said. "Max, dear, this is the second person who has mentioned the name Viel. Maybe you should check into this further."

"You're right, honey. I'll ask my parents the next time I visit them and see what they can tell me," he said, looking at the older man and not at Nicole. "I guess it wasn't uncommon back in those days for people to lose their homes."

"No, not many of the original owners survived the war, and then we had several years where the price of sugar became so low, you could make more money raising earthworms. And then in 1881 winter arrived before we'd harvested the cane and most of us lost over half of our crops," the older gentleman continued on, obviously enjoying reminiscing.

Nicole caught Anna staring at her waist and smiled at the woman.

"You look like you've lost a little weight," the woman said, her look more condescending than friendly.

"Yes, I have," Nicole said with a smile she hoped convinced the woman of her sincerity. She glanced briefly at Max and then returned her gaze to Mrs. DeChoskey. "With my husband home all the time, I stay busy."

Before Anna could respond, Nicole heard her name being called.

"Mrs. Viel," one of the older women called.

Nicole turned around at the sound of her name and noticed Mrs. Francisco approaching her with an older, fashionably dressed lady. The woman wore a tailored dress trimmed with ecru lace that also lined the high neckline that covered her throat. She carried an antique pearl fan in her right hand that she flicked open as she halted beside Nicole.

"Yes?" Nicole said.

"I'd like you to meet Mrs. Reuss. She is in charge of the Women's Society Club here in town, which raises money for the Willowbend Orphanage in New Orleans," Mrs. Francisco said.

"How nice to meet you," Nicole said.

"We're having a tea next Friday at my home and we're going to be discussing this year's fund-raising activities. We'd love for you to join us, Mrs. Viel," the older woman said. "Usually we plan a fund-raiser at each one of the homes along the river. I don't think we've ever held one at Rosewood, and if you and Mr. Viel are interested, we would love to add your home to our schedule."

"Of course I'll be at tea," Nicole said, her heart pounding with excitement. They were asking her to tea. Her stomach did a flip-flop and she tried not to appear overly excited. Maybe Max's being friends with Mr. Francisco wasn't such a bad idea after all. "And I know my husband and I would love to host one of the annual fund-raisers."

"Wonderful! It's good to see you and Mr. Viel becoming involved with the community," she said as she walked away.

A sense of elation spiraled through Nicole, making her almost giddy. Max said he'd become friends with Mr. Francisco, and apparently whatever he and this man did during their visits seemed to be working. They were definitely being accepted. But as soon as the cane was harvested and Max received his share of the proceeds from the crop, he would be leaving and then she'd be alone once more.

"Could I interest you in another dance?" Max asked, slipping up behind her and putting his hand on her waist, his breath whispery-soft against her hair.

She turned to face him and couldn't help but feel her heart begin to accelerate at the sight of those green eyes darkening, becoming heavy-lidded behind his jet-black lashes.

"Yes, that would be nice," she said, placing her hand in his.

"I saw you speaking with Mrs. Reuss. Do you know who she is?" Max asked, his voice husky and low as he glided her across the room to the strains of the "Bird Waltz."

"I'm not sure, but she invited me to tea and asked us to host one of the annual fund-raisers for the Women's Society Club here in town," Nicole said excitedly.

Max smiled.

"How did you do it?" she asked. "I know you talked about being involved in the community, but how did we suddenly start receiving all these invitations?"

He shrugged. "Making friends with some of the men seems to have been worthwhile."

"Max, thank you. You've done so much while you're

here. I can't thank you enough," she said.

He didn't say anything, but a frown appeared between his brows. "Come on, everyone's gathering in the main room. I think they're about to announce their daughter's engagement and offer champagne. We could both use a taste of that champagne."

"I don't know if I need much more wine or champagne."

Max twirled her off the dance floor and she giggled, feeling light-headed. She didn't know if the feelings rushing through her were from the alcohol, Max, or a little bit of both. But she was having a marvelous time.

~

"Good-bye," Nicole called to their hosts as Max helped her into the carriage and then climbed in behind her.

"Goodness, that was the most wonderful evening," she said, leaning against Max in the carriage.

"I'm glad you enjoyed it," he said, wondering if they should have indulged in that last glass of champagne.

"Are you feeling all right[5]" he asked.

"I feel fabulous," she said. "You know, I think we were quite the toast of the party. I think people actually enjoyed speaking with us and want us to come to their parties," she said, leaning against the back of the seat.

"You were the most beautiful woman there," he said, turning his face until his mouth was next to her ear. He breathed deeply, the scent of Nicole filling him.

"No, I think your becoming friends with the Franciscos helped get us noticed. Especially when you made that toast to the newly engaged couple. I didn't know you had such a way with words."

He laughed. "I've had lots of practice, watching my friends marry."

She turned her head to look at him. Their faces were

mere inches from each other in the darkened carriage. "You've hardly lived the kind of life that I expect from a man who wanders from town to town."

Max tensed, realizing his actions were so unlike any drifter he'd ever known. Nicole had picked up on little idiosyncrasies of his tale and one day she would put them all together and realize he'd lied to her. "I make friends easily."

They rode along in silence for a few moments. She shivered in the carriage. "Fall is almost here, the night air has become cooler."

"Are you cold?" he asked, unable to resist thinking of how he could warm her.

"Just a little," she said with a deep sigh. "Max, when the fund-raiser is at our house, we could hold it outside under the oak trees and put torches around the verandah for the people who don't want to dance, but sit on the porch."

He wrapped his arm around her and she looked at him in question. "I'm trying to warm you up, you're trembling."

"Oh, yes, that does feel good," she said, her voice suddenly becoming lower. She leaned her head back away from him and gazed at him in the darkness. "But if it's after the harvest, you won't be here. How can I do this party without you?"

"Don't worry about the party now, Nicole," he said, and he kissed her on her neck, causing her to shudder.

"What are you doing?" she asked, her voice quivering.

"What does it feel like? I'm kissing your neck," he said. She lay her head over to the side, giving him more access to the tender area around her ear.

"Um, why?" she asked, her voice becoming breathy as he continued his path along her neck. Her eyes were closed and a soft smile curved her full lips.

"Because I love the way you taste and I like to hear the little sighs of pleasure that escape your lips," he said, and his mouth suddenly reached hers. He stopped and glanced at her wide-open eyes in the darkness. Her mouth seemed to be trembling with anticipation. "And unless you stop me, I'm going to kiss you."

He waited for just an instant and when there were no signs of protest, he placed his lips upon hers and felt a hot, melting sensation seize him. He cupped her face with his hands, molding her lips against his until he thought he would expire from the sheer pleasure. He moved his hands up her face to cradle her head and then he laid her back against the corner of the carriage, until he lay on top of her.

She felt so good beneath him, her breasts crushed against his chest, her mouth soft and pliant as he greedily plundered her lips. She moaned a sound deep and urgent as his tongue stroked the inside of her mouth, igniting all the emotions he'd tried to resist.

Nicole depended on Max, leaving her vulnerable and free to him, and he loved this part of her that needed him. Yet she had a will of iron and would fight for what she believed in and stand up to anyone who got in her way.

She pulled away from his lips, her breathing heavy. "What are we doing?"

"Kissing," he said, his mouth barely above hers, his voice rough and thick. "And it feels so nice."

"I don't think we should be doing this," she said as her hands brushed back a lock of his hair. Her fingers caressed his face tenderly. He could see the desire so clearly in her eyes and hear it in her voice.

"There is something between us. Something that I think is worth exploring," he said against her mouth. "Tell me no and I will not pursue this any further. But if you feel as hungry for me as I am for you, then let me kiss you."

"Oh, Max," she said and pulled his mouth down to hers, her lips parting willingly, their breaths mating as he reveled in the feel of her so soft and pliant in his arms, the delicate little cooing noises coming from deep in her throat.

The need for this woman, in his arms, trusting him, suddenly seemed more important than any piece of land or family needs. Only Nicole mattered and he needed her desperately as he succumbed to the hot, melting sensation that overpowered him as he tasted the honey sweetness of her lips.

The carriage suddenly came to a halt, and he wanted to curse as he heard their driver call out, "Mr. Viel, we're back at Rosewood, sir."

He broke the kiss and sat up, fearful that the driver would open the door. "Thanks, Moses."

She sat up and suddenly started to giggle and he knew the champagne must still be affecting her. "I feel so young," she said with a laugh. "Come on, I want to show you something."

Max wanted to curse as she jumped up, her skirts in hand, and swung open the door to the carriage. She leaped out like a fairy in flight, laughing as she went, and disappeared in the darkness. The soft tinkling of her mirth haunting him.

"Oh, hell," he said as he jumped up and ran after her

## Chapter Thirteen

**N**icole couldn't remember a time when she'd felt so carefree, so happy. She ran along the path she knew from memory, through the trees, the moonlight shining brightly to show her the way.

She heard footsteps behind her and turned to see Max hurrying to catch up with her. She giggled and lifted her skirts higher to run like a young girl through the moonlit shadows. Moss snagged at her hair from the low-hanging branches. Then suddenly the trail widened and she came out into the garden area she'd found hidden away one day. She crossed the Roman bridge made of stone to a small island surrounded by a reflecting pond. On the island, she hurried into the gazebo, laughing softly.

"Nicole?" Max called in the moonlight She didn't answer him as she waited quietly inside, looking out at the overgrown gardens, the remnants of a Chinese pagoda toppled in a flower bed. Max stepped into the lattice building, his entry soundless, though she felt his presence.

He moved behind her and wrapped his arms around her, resting his chin on her shoulder. The strength of him, warm and strong against her back, felt too good to tell him no. He was right; whatever this thing was between them, it tempted her to throw away her fears, her convictions, and give in to her desires. Though the memory of Jean's betrayal still remained, Max seemed different. He'd cared for her when she'd been so ill. He seemed genuine, honest, and caring. And more alluring than any man she'd ever known.

"Are you looking for me?" she said, her voice husky as she leaned into his body, the feel of his might seeping into her bones, spreading a heat through her.

The moon cast shadows through the lattice of the open

building as he pulled her tight against him, the solidness of his chest a comforting shelter. She felt protected and cared for, feelings she hadn't experienced since childhood.

"I didn't know where you were going. I was beginning to worry," he said, his voice sending shivers down her spine.

Max placed his lips against her ear, the warmth of his breath stirring the tendrils of her hair. "Is this part of Rosewood?"

His low husky voice touched her in places she knew sound could not reach. She must concentrate and refuse to let the beams of the moonlight weave a seductive spell over her and Max. Yet images filled her mind, of the two of them entwined in each other's arms, naked and wanting.

*Concentrate!*

"Yes, the last owner of Rosewood built this, but he died before he finished it," she said, her voice quivering with desire and longing.

She swallowed as she felt Max's hand move up and touch her breast through her dress. The pad of his thumb rubbed against the hard kernel of her nipple, and she drew a sharp intake of air. Her breathing quickened and she tried to resist the feelings of arousal his stroke created. Though his touch could melt her into a puddle, she couldn't let him dissolve her will. "I've only been able to have the gazebo redone and start..."

His lips trailed down her neck, pushing the lace aside, touching the spot that caused a shiver to ripple through her. "... the work on ..."

He kissed the top of her shoulder. She tilted her neck over to the side to give him easier access, unable to resist the sensations his lips created. "...the garden ..."

"You really love this place, don't you?" he said, lifting her breasts in his hands, the pads of his thumbs continuing the erotic circles on her nipples through her dress. He pressed himself against her buttocks, letting her feel the fullness of his erection through her skirt, and she gasped, the sound deep and husky in the night.

"Yes...I do," she, said her mind unable to concentrate or even form coherent sentences.

As he turned her to face him, his lips came crushing down on hers, hard and demanding.

Part of her wanted to run and hide from the fierce, insistent emotions that Max incited, while another part of her wanted to succumb to those same feelings, explore this inexplicable yearning, and see if her experience with Max could be different.

All rational thought fled as she quit fighting her internal struggle and opened herself up to the full experience of Max's kiss. She was incapable of denying herself the pure sensation she felt in his embrace. She wound her arms around his neck, her knees feeling weak as his sensuous tongue invaded her mouth, arousing places of pleasure not even near her lips.

She opened her mouth fully, giving herself completely over to the mindless stimulus that the hot press of his lips commanded.

He reached behind her, his fingers deftly unbuttoning her dress. He broke the kiss and pulled the front of her dress down, his lips following the path of the material until he reached the tops of her breasts. His lips fastened around the kernel of her nipple, suckling her breast until Nicole thought the heat from his mouth would sear her in two. Passion emanated from her center, causing a moan to spill from between her lips.

He grasped her breasts in his hands, his palms radiating with warmth as he kneaded her, his lips caressing her until she thought she would scream from the pleasure. She'd sworn to never again give herself to any man, but she wanted Max more than anything she'd ever craved in her life.

His hand lifted her skirts, bunching them up until the frothy whiteness of her petticoat glistened in the moonlight, his fingers urgently seeking the slit in her drawers. When his fingers found her center, she arched her back, a sigh of surrender escaping her lips.

Never before had Nicole felt so feminine, so completely woman to a man. There would be no denying her body this pleasure, or denying her soul this need. There would be no denying the joining of their bodies.

"This is what we've been destined for since the day we met," Max whispered against her mouth.

"Max," she said, her breathing harsh, her voice husky with need. "I want you."

"I've waited so long for you," he said, his voice rough and deep.

With a yank, his suit coat came off and he laid it down on the bench. In the darkness, she could hear him removing his clothes until the moonlight danced across his gleaming muscular profile. Like a moon god he stood before her, proud and strong.

His hands moved to remove her dress from her waist, sliding the silk down her body. He held her hand as she stepped out of the full dress and tossed it to the side. Next he untied her petticoats and released them from her body, dropping them to the floor. Slowly he undid her corset, loosening the strings enough to pull the garment off her body.

He kissed the back of her neck and down her collarbone until his lips found her chemise. When he started to pull off the filmy garment she halted his hand.

"Wait," she said, feeling suddenly shy to be naked in front of this man.

Max sat down on the bench and pulled her onto his lap, his lips covering hers with a kiss that seared the questions quickly forming in her mind.

She didn't want to think, because if she thought about what they were doing, she'd stop him. All she wanted was to continue feeling this passion that only Max created.

With one hand he tenderly cupped her chin as he slanted his mouth over hers, the damp heat of his lips engulfing hers, singeing her to the tips of her toes. She leaned against the rock hardness of his chest, his body absorbing her weight. He lay down on the bench, taking her with him, and rolled her to the inside. They lay side by side, with just her chemise, drawers, and stockings between them.

Max made her feel alive, he gave her hope with his gentle touch and kind words.

He untied the top part of the filmy garment and pushed the material aside to find the tip of her breast He drew the nub into his heated mouth, and laved the pebbled kernel of her nipple, his tongue drawing erotic circles. His fingers searched and found the slit in her lacy white drawers and delved into the center of her being, teasing her mercilessly. She gasped and arched her back toward his hand, needing to feel the magic his touch created once more.

Every sense in her body craved Max, wanted him, and needed him as he awakened each nerve. Wherever their skin touched and every place his lips stroked, all burned with sensuous warmth that pooled in a flood of liquid heat between her legs.

But still he lingered, the heat of his mouth caressing her breasts, while his hand tortured her with pleasure. She reached down and touched his manhood, needing to feel him with her hands.

Nicole grasped him and heard Max's swift intake of breath. "Nicole!"

She ran her hand up and down the length of him, feeling the strength of him beneath her hands. In the shadow of the moonlight she watched the pleasure on his face with each stroke as she touched him.

Suddenly he rolled her beneath him on the bench and yanked off her chemise and drawers, leaving only her stockings and garters. He parted her thighs and pushed his own legs between hers, his naked skin sensuous against the nylon.

Nicole lifted her hips to meet his thrust as he entered her swiftly. A sigh of completion escaped her lips as she felt the fullness of his arousal, her mind numb with the pleasure.

He felt so natural, so complete, as she clutched at his back, her hands gripping him tightly. With each slide and twist the tension built, her mind dizzy from champagne and gratification. Her sighs of pleasure changed into feverish moans with each primal stroke until Nicole felt they were as one.

As he slid within her body, she welcomed him into her heart. With each stroke Max replaced Nicole's memories with new, better ones of their own.

She felt numb, her passion spiraling higher and higher until in a moment of shattering release she tumbled out of control, crying out his name. The world seemed to splinter into a thousand strands of silvery light as she came crashing back to earth, all thoughts of how lovemaking should be replaced by thoughts of Max.

He swelled within her and clutched her to him one last time as he cried out her name, his voice rough and husky, his body tense, and then he relaxed.

She lay in his arms, stunned, trying to catch her breath, amazed at what she'd just experienced with Max. The soft pitter-patter of rain splattered against the roof of the gazebo seeping into her passion-numbed mind. The damp, cleansing breeze blew into the little building, bringing a sense of renewal.

Never in her life had she experienced such a night of ardor that left her so complete. Never had she felt so loved.

She gazed at Max, who lay breathing hard, his dark eyes watching her in the moonlight. He reached out and stroked her cheek with his fingers.

A chill began to seep into her bones and she shivered in his arms. What would they do now?

"Cold?" he asked, kissing her cheek as he slid down beside her on the bench.

"Yes," she said, reaching for her dress to cover herself, a feeling of awkwardness overcoming her. Her heart pounded with fear as she realized suddenly the vulnerable position in which she'd just placed her healed emotions.

Max wrapped his arms around her, pulling her in close and covering her with his body, then pulled her dress over the two of them like a coverlet. "Better?"

"Yes, thank you," she said, trying to resist the urge to jump up and run to the house, away from the feelings Max evoked.

"I always thought our first time would be in a bed, but I must say, this is so much more memorable," he said, kissing her temple. "This thing between us is so different from anything I've ever experienced."

"I never thought there would be a first time," she said, her voice quivering with fear.

The doubts began to assail her as she lay there by his side, all her misgivings overwhelming her. "How long will the physical pleasure between us last? Especially when you leave after the crop comes in."

~

The next morning, Nicole woke to the sound of birds screeching their noisy cackles at one another. She opened her eyes, feeling like something was different and the memories from the night before swamped her.

She sat up in bed, instantly regretting her quick motion. "Oh, my God."

Not only did her head pound this morning from the champagne, but the memory of her impulsive actions from the night before made her moan. How could she have been so stupid as to make love with Max? Had she lost all common sense?

Thank goodness he hadn't argued with her once they reached the house and had gone to his own room, giving her time to wonder how to face this awkward situation. She needed to adjust to the thought of having marital relations with her husband. Relations she'd never intended on fulfilling. She needed to consider how this would affect their business relationship.

Yet even now at the thought of him, her body seemed to thrum with awareness. She flung back the quilt, unable to lie in bed a moment more.

Hurriedly she dressed and splashed cold water over her face before walking the short distance to the dining room. She felt so confused. She wanted to see him, yet she knew she needed to resist these feelings. Hadn't she learned they only led to heartache? Why would she want to let herself be hurt yet again? Eventually he would leave and she would be alone.

As she walked across the parlor to the dining room, she almost ran smack into Max. She felt irritable and stupid for letting the champagne and the moonlight go to her head and making love to her husband. For a moment they stared at one another. She watched the expression on his face, trying to decipher how he felt about her this morning.

"Good morning," he said, his green eyes watching her. "I hope you slept well."

"Not really," she lied, knowing it'd been ages since she'd slept so deeply, so soundly. "I tossed and turned all night, and then this morning I woke with a throbbing headache."

He smiled. "Drink some coffee. It'll make you feel better."

"I don't want coffee," she snapped as she pushed past him into the dining room. "I don't know what I want this morning."

Patiently, he followed her. He wrapped his arms around her and leaned in close to her ear, his breath brushing against her lobe, sending shivers through her. "I slept very well last night, dreaming of you." Part of her thrilled at his words, while yet another part reacted with fear. Would Max become another Jean and betray her also?

She tried to pull out of his arms, but he only let her turn until she faced him, wearing a frown. "I'm glad to hear you slept well, but dreams are only illusions. They never last, just like yesterday is gone forever." He shook his head. "No, last night will live on in my memories until I depart this earth."

Nicole pulled out of his arms and walked across the room, trying to put distance between them so she could clear her mind of the dangerous emotions his touch ignited. His words frightened her. They sounded so promising and final. Between his touch and his words, her thoughts became scrambled and whatever control she possessed over her body seemed to melt away. She couldn't let this happen a second time. She just couldn't face him again.

She walked around the table and picked up a plate before going to the sideboard where breakfast waited. Food didn't interest her, but she needed something to occupy her hands, needed the space between them, needed to control her drumming heart.

"From your silence am I to gather that last night doesn't hold special memories for you?" he asked, his voice questioning and uncertain.

How should she respond? If she said yes, then things

would become so much more complicated than they already were. But if she said no, she'd lie. She turned her back to him and took a deep breath, not knowing how to react, afraid of her honest response, not wanting to face him and let him see that the night had affected her in ways that frightened her.

She kept her back to him. "I don't know what to say. Last night should never have happened. You and I both know this is impossible. You're leaving. And I'm never involving myself with a man again."

Max approached her, and spun her around to face him. Nicole felt an incredible ache to put down her plate and slide her arms around him, letting him hold her and soothe away her fears. She resisted. Succumbing to her impulses again would not make the situation any easier.

He lifted her chin with his hand until their gazes locked. "We're married. What happened between us last night most couples do several times a week. Why do you still refuse to accept this feeling between us? You can't deny that there is something there. We both feel it."

"You know why," she said, frustrated, pulling her face from his hand, though her chin tingled from his touch. "I never want to let a man get close enough to hurt me ever again. Don't you see that every man I've ever known has only brought me grief? Why would I want to risk that pain all over again?"

"I'm not your father, Nicole, and I'm not Jean."

"No, you're not. But if I let you get close to me, then I give you the opportunity to wound me just like the others. I've already let you way too close."

Max stood there gazing at her, his emerald eyes shadowy. "So what are you going to do? Spend the rest of your life hiding away? Never risking or receiving love ever again? Do you want to be alone all your life?"

Nicole shook her head. "I don't know what I want right

now. All I know is that the simple arrangement I made with you to be the father of my child has turned into something I never expected."

"Do you think I thought this would happen?" he asked, calmly walking up beside her, his hand lightly touching her arm. "We're married. We could have a good life together you and I," he said. "Maybe even have a couple of children."

She squeezed her eyes shut, trying to block out the pain of his words. She'd wanted children so badly, and he was giving her the opportunity, but she was so afraid to trust in him, to give him her heart. Could she put the past behind her and trust her heart to a drifter? "This is not what I planned."

"No, it's better," he said, more determined.

She opened her eyes, held up her hand, and walked away from him. "I can't talk about this right now. I need some time to think, to sort things out." She took a deep breath. "You'll be here through the harvest. Let's just try to keep things as they were until after the harvest. Then we'll talk again. Please, give me this time. I have to be certain."

He crossed the room to her side. Placing his hand on her jaw, he lifted her chin to meet his gaze. "I'll give you your time. But I'm not giving up pursuing you. I want you as my wife, Nicole. I want our marriage to last."

~

Max fairly skipped down the front stairs on his way to the barn. There was a bounce in his step this morning that hadn't been there in previous days. A warmth lingered from the night before when he thought of Nicole, his wife.

Last night had been exquisite. And even this morning though Nicole at first seemed insolent and difficult, in the end she appeared to listen to his reasoning. Hopefully, during the next few weeks before the harvest, he could prove to her that their marriage could work. That they could be happy together.

Yet part of him worried over what her reaction would be to the news that his family had once lived at Rosewood. If possible, he would keep the information that he'd wed her for the land with him and take it to his grave. He didn't want to hurt her and that knowledge could only cause her more heartache.

Her distrust of men would only become worse if she discovered his reasons for agreeing to their arrangement. He didn't want to inflict her with any more anguish.

Jean's deception had scarred her worse than her father's rejection, and now Max's taking advantage of the situation would be construed as a form of trickery if she ever learned the truth. And if he were honest with himself, he should have been upfront with her from the very beginning.

But he'd come into this marriage only to obtain the land and it had turned into so much more. He pulled open the barn door and strode in to find his horse and saddle. Lifting the saddle, he slung it up on the back of the roan.

How could he have known that he would come to care for Nicole? How could he have known that her previous husband and father had hurt her so badly?

Yes, he cared about Nicole. He didn't want to hurt her now that he knew her well. And after last night, he felt very good about their marriage. Good enough in fact that he wanted to do something special for his wife.

Max pulled the cinch on his saddle, making it tight Nicole needed to know who her father was. Without that information, she would always wonder about the man who sired her. Perhaps she could learn the reason her parents had never married, learn her father hadn't actually rejected her. And Max felt compelled to show Nicole that he wanted their marriage to be happy and prosper. He had the resources to find Nicole's father. He would contact his lawyers and have them begin the search for her father.

Then, someday soon, he could give her the information she so badly wanted. Until then, he would do his best to show her he could be trusted, though he would have to live with the knowledge that he'd lied his way into her life.

~

After breakfast, Nicole met with Consuelo and the two of them went over the meals for the next week along with the supplies list, preparing for the coming weeks of the harvest.

Later, after she'd taken care of her correspondence, she picked up the diary of Jean's lover. She glanced at the worn leather of the book, wishing she knew the date the writer penned these words or at least the woman's name. Nicole wanted to tell her that she wasn't the only victim of Jean's deception, that there were others just like her, and that somehow she would live through the disgrace and the humiliation.

Nicole suddenly realized her thoughts and smiled. Even though her marriage to Jean could only be described as a sham, even though she'd lost the baby, she'd survived. She would be all right. And no matter what happened with Max she would continue to exist.

She thought of Max's words that morning and wondered about making a life with him. Could she give her heart to him and live her life as his wife?

It surprised her that the drifter wanted a future with her, yet he would prosper more from their marriage than she would. So did he want her, or did he long for the land and the value of the crop more.

Would he someday suddenly be taken by the urge to travel once again, and leave her behind? And was she willing to take that chance? As the wife of a drifter she couldn't count on him to stay long in one place.

Quickly, she brushed the thoughts away; she couldn't think about them anymore. What happened last night had been beautiful, special, and more than she'd ever dreamed possible. But she still couldn't give her heart away again to another man.

She opened the diary and began to read the daily entries. After several pages, they stopped abruptly. It looked as if a huge gap in time elapsed before the next account Nicole shivered as she read the opening words.

*Today I buried my baby girl. After struggling for two weeks to fight off yellow fever, she finally succumbed to the dreaded disease late two nights ago. My precious child went with only her dear uncle and myself at her bedside, though I begged God to take me and not my dear, sweet daughter. But my prayers were not answered and now the pain of losing that sweet child torments me more than I can bear.*

*When we buried her today, I included her favorite doll and a stuffed toy that she treasured. A part of my own soul went into that grave with her, for everything that I truly loved has been taken from me. I have nothing to live for now. Jean has abandoned me and death has snatched away my only child. What reason is there for me to continue on living with this pain?*

*Her father did not even come to see his daughter buried. Though I let him know the day and time of her funeral, he chose not to acknowledge her. There were only a few close friends, myself, and my dear brother at her eulogy. Oh, how I shall, miss her sweet laughter and joy. The cuddles of her child's body, her sweet childish kisses. My memories are not enough to sustain me through this lonely life. Only death could release me from this torment, this loneliness I feel.*

*Charles worries about me and I fear in the end my decision will hurt him even more than my previous behavior. If only I'd listened to him in my youthful exuberance, then my life would not be in shambles. For dear Charles warned me that Jean was married, but I foolishly believed that he would leave his wife and follow his heart. How gullible my young girl's heart to believe the vows of matrimony could be so easily discarded.*

*And even when Charles tried to caution me that there were other women and begged me to forget Jean and marry another, I foolishly clung to the hope that someday our love would unite us. But now I see how improvident my love for Jean made me and believe my life is beyond repair.*

*I have nothing to live for. No love, no dear child. There is nothing but pain and I can't bear it anymore. Oh, that God would grant me peace in the hereafter with those I love and have gone before me. And that my dear brother will forgive me for my cowardice, for I seek relief from the pain of my life.*

Blank pages followed the last entry and for a moment, Nicole sat there, stunned. Tears streamed down her cheeks for the woman and her child. She wiped her eyes with her handkerchief and flipped to the last page of the journal, hoping there would be something to indicate who the woman had been, but there was nothing. No name, no dates, nothing that could tell her the woman's identity or give her any indication of what happened to her.

As she sat there wanting so desperately to help the woman, her mind raced with all kinds of thoughts. Anger boiled inside her at how Jean had destroyed this young woman's life, just like he'd scarred all the Cuvier widows' lives.

She thought of everything that she knew about the woman: a brother named Charles and a daughter named Julianne who she'd lost to yellow fever. She lived in a house in New Orleans on a street that overlooked a park. Was there any way to locate her?

Rage roiled through her at the thought of Jean not attending his own daughter's funeral. No wonder someone wanted him dead. How many other women had he ruined or played falsely?

Nicole slapped the leather volume in her hand, wishing she could hit Jean with the book, when the thought struck her.

Could Jean's death have somehow been related to the diary? But if she didn't know the identity of the woman in the diary, then how would it be possible to trace and find her?

Nicole gazed at the diary wondering if it held the secrets to Jean's death. Why wasn't the diary with the person who wrote the journal? How had Jean obtained this book?

She thought of Layla, on trial for murdering Jean, and suddenly she knew she couldn't keep this information all to herself. Even if the diary led nowhere, she must tell Drew Soulier so that he could investigate and find out if this book held any clues to Jean's death. And hopefully find the woman in the diary.

Nicole stood and walked to the plantation office. She pulled out the secret compartment in her desk drawer and placed the journal there to keep the book safe. Then she sat down and composed a letter to Drew Soulier, Layla's attorney.

## Chapter Fourteen

**A** week later Max received a note from the bartender at the Gator Bar that someone wanted to see him. He hurried to the local bar, afraid of what he would find. When he walked in the door, he saw his father sitting at the counter, a bottle of whiskey in front of him.

He approached his father, wishing things could be different "Papa, what are you doing here? I asked you not to come until I sent for you."

Charles Viel turned, his reddened eyes on his son, and for a moment Max wondered how much longer his father could continue drinking like this.

"Don't be getting all upset. I came to give you a warning," his father said, gulping down a shot of whiskey. "And to celebrate your aunt's birthday."

Max frowned, realizing his father was here to get drunk. "So what's the warning?"

"I don't know how much longer I can keep your mother from coming to Rosewood," his father said.

His mother *couldn't* come, at least not yet. Not known for her tact, Audra Viel would reveal the fact his family had once owned the plantation and ruin everything he'd carefully built with Nicole. He wasn't ready for Nicole to learn the truth; they'd made so much progress since the party.

"I thought she threw you out of the house?" Max questioned.

"As long as I'm not drinking at the house, I have been readmitted to my own damn home. So that's why I'm here drinking," his father said, his speech slurred. "In fact, why don't you join me?"

"It's not even lunchtime and you're already drunk," Max said with disgust, disappointed that once again his father's drinking appeared out of control.

"Come on, Son. Join your old man in a toast to your Aunt Blanche. After all, part of your wealth came from the inheritance you received from her," he said, picking up the bottle and pouring Max a finger of whiskey into a clean glass. He lifted his own glass. "May she be singing with the choirs of angels in heaven today."

Max picked up the glass, clinked it against his father's, and drank the fiery liquid. "Okay, Papa, you've had your toast, now come on and I'll put you up in a hotel in town where you can sleep it off."

"I'm not sleepy and I'm not through drinking," he said, his voice getting louder. He picked up the bottle and poured another shot. "I'm not through celebrating your aunt's birthday."

His father's lips had a tendency to become quite loose once he'd been drinking and Max didn't need him divulging anything regarding his family and Rosewood to the bartender.

"Have another one, Son. We can observe her birthday together," he said, swaying in his chair.

Max glanced around the small bar, thankful few people frequented at this time of day. "No thanks, Papa. I'm not going to sit here and get drunk with you. I don't think Aunt Blanche would have wanted you to drink on her birthday."

The older man shrugged. "No, but then we didn't see eye to eye on a lot of things."

The old man stared up at Max, his eyes so much like his own, only his appeared old and beaten. Life had been hard on his father, but so many things he'd brought on himself.

"You know, I used to feel sorry for the fact that your mother and I never had more children after you. But maybe you were lucky not to have any brothers or sisters. They never disappointed or hurt you till you nearly bled to death."

Max didn't say anything but simply gazed at his father, not understanding most of his ramblings.

"Your mother didn't want any more babies. Afraid her figure would be completely ruined by her expanding waistline." He glanced at Max. "Hell, your grandfather practically raised you since your mother didn't have time. The old man wanted to make sure that you knew your destiny. I guess he did all right, since you've done everything he asked of you."

Max felt uneasy. With the thought of his grandfather came bittersweet memories. All his grandfather had wanted him to do in life was get Rosewood back in the family. Now Max couldn't help but feel a sense of guilt when it came to obtaining Rosewood. Nicole loved the plantation so much and he felt guilty for marrying her to acquire the land his family wanted back. Yet now his familial obligation was fulfilled, so they should be happy.

"You married Nicole. Now the land is as good as yours," his father said. "A woman's property becomes a man's once she's married. Hell, why does a man leave a woman property? You know your mother and grandfather at least, up until he died, have been just waiting for you to acquire their precious Rosewood back."

"What about you, Papa?" Max asked. "Did you want me to acquire the land back?"

"Hell, I don't care about that piece of ground. I couldn't save it for them, so I became useless to your mother and grandfather," he said. "I even tried to buy it back not too long ago before you became involved, but Jean wouldn't sell."

"You never mentioned you'd tried to buy back Rosewood."

Charles shrugged and took a swig of whiskey. "No point. The bastard wouldn't sell it to me."

Max frowned, surprised at this knowledge. "Come on,

Papa. Let me take you to a hotel."

"No!" he shouted. "I'm celebrating." He took another long swig. "By the way, that woman Desiree is looking for you. She wants her son back."

"Yes, I know. She found me."

"Did she take the boy back?" he questioned, his eyelids barely open.

"Not yet. I'm hoping Paul will decide to stay with me permanently."

His father shook his head and swayed in his chair; Max feared he would fall out. "Then demand that he live with you. You're his father, just tell him, you're living with me."

"Papa, he's almost thirteen years old. It's time he started making his own decisions in his life."

"Decisions? He can make resolutions when he's on his own, but until then you're his father and he needs to mind you." The old man gulped down his drink.

Max realized there was no sense in talking to a drunk. He watched his father's eyelids try to close over his tired, weary eyes.

"Maybe you can protect your family better than me ..." he said as his head hit the bar.

The bartender walked back up to the counter and glanced at Max. "You know him?"

"Yes, he's my father," Max replied, thinking of how Nicole didn't know her own father and he wondered if she spent time with his, if she'd still want to meet hers.

"He's been here drinking since we opened up this morning. I think he's pretty soused," the bartender told Max.

Max looked at the man. "I'll take care of him." He shook his father's shoulder. "Come on, Papa. Help me get you on your horse."

~

Later that day, Max found his son working alongside the field hands, repairing a wagon that would haul the cane to the mill. The crews were busy preparing for the harvest that would take place in just a few weeks.

"Paul," he called from his horse as he sat, watching the workers.

The boy glanced up from where he stood holding a wooden slate in place.

"Yes, sir?" he replied.

"I brought you some lunch," Max said. Paul had joined in with the workers and Max felt proud of how hard he'd worked alongside the men.

Paul and the other workers dropped their hammers and the side rails they were hammering to the frame of the wagon.

Max swung his leg over the saddle of his horse and dropped to the grassy field. He ground tethered his horse and then reached inside his saddlebags for the sandwiches Marie had prepared for him to bring to the boy, who looked more like a man every day. He walked to a large oak tree and sat down in the shade.

Paul came running up to him, the remnants of a cap on his head, and dropped at Max's feet. "Hello, sir."

"Hello, boy. How are you?"

"I'm all right. Why did you bring me lunch? I could have eaten with the men," the boy said, looking worried.

"Well, since you've been working so hard, we haven't had a chance to talk, and I wanted to see you, spend some time talking," Max replied. "Seems you're gone from sunup to sundown."

He frowned. "Mother's come back again, hasn't she? You're sending me home."

Max shook his head. "No, though I expect her just about any day now, and I'm not sending you home. I thought maybe we could eat a bite of lunch together and discuss your mother. You could tell me what you want. School started a week ago and you're going to have to make a decision."

A wrinkle appeared on Paul's brow as he gazed at Max. "A decision?"

Max handed the boy a sandwich. "Yes. I hope by now you realize that I would like for you to stay here and live with Nicole and me. I would take you to New Orleans to visit your mother occasionally, but you would live here and go to school here."

Paul's eyes widened. "You'd let me stay?"

"Yes. I worry that at your mother's home you don't attend school on a regular basis. I fear that you look after your brothers and sisters instead of your studies."

"Sometimes," Paul admitted, his voice subdued. "What about my mother? Have you told her that you want me to stay?"

"No, I'm waiting until you make your decision. It's your life, Paul. You're my son, I love you, and I'd like you to live with me. But regardless of whether you decide to stay here or return to your mother, I want to be involved in your life."

Max watched as his son swallowed and he could see that his eyes were watery. "I miss my brothers and sisters, but I like being here with you and working on the plantation. If I stayed and worked real hard, could I maybe get a horse?"

Max laughed, pleased that Paul was beginning to sound more like a young boy than the miniature adult he'd been all his life. "Well, I was going to give you the same pay that the laborers receive for working the harvest. We'll see how much you've earned and then we'll talk again about buying a horse after the crop comes in."

The boy frowned. "Mother's never going to let me stay here with you. She'll be back soon and I'll have to go back with her or she will—"

"Wait!" Max held up his hand. "Let's decide first if you want to stay or not. Then, if you do, I'll handle your mother."

Paul glanced at his father. "I want to stay. I like it here. I want to be with you, Papa."

Max smiled, and almost sighed with relief. "Good. Don't worry about your mother. I'll arrange things with her. But first we need to get you enrolled in school. You can't miss any more schooling."

~

Two days later, Max rode his horse into town to take care of some things and to mail his lawyer a letter regarding his son. He wanted to arrange a trust fund for Desiree with the stipulation that if she harassed Paul or came to Rosewood, the money would revert back to Max. Hopefully this money would be used to take care of her other children and convince her to leave him and his son alone.

Max wanted to restrict her from coming out to Rosewood and making a scene. All she would accomplish would be to upset Paul and make him feel bad for leaving her if she got the chance.

While in town, he wanted to run down to the parish tax office and check to make sure that the taxes on Rosewood had been paid. If Nicole owed money to the shop owners, it suddenly occurred to him she could owe taxes on the plantation.

Life would be way too cruel for Max to come this far and then lose the plantation to back taxes. If they were paid, she need never know that he'd verified her payment history. But if they weren't, he'd take care of them today.

After going to the post office, he pulled up his roan in front of the Iberville Parish Courthouse where the county records were kept. He threw his leg over the saddle and stepped to the ground. After tying his horse to a post he crossed the front lawn and hurried up the steps.

Inside the courthouse, several windows that resembled bank tellers' stations occupied a corner of the room. As Max walked across the wooden floor, his boots rapped in a staccato rhythm. The sound echoed in the small room and several people standing around glanced at him; he smiled back and nodded in their direction.

He walked up to the window.

"How may I help you?" the man behind the counter asked.

"I would like to verify that my wife has paid the taxes on our land and property."

"Where do you live, sir?"

"I live at Rosewood Plantation," he said. "My wife is Nicole Rosseau Viel."

A frown soon formed on the man's forehead. "Just a minute, sir. There's been a recent transaction, I know, but let me verify what the status is."

He hurried behind the counter to a big ledger that lay open on a desk in the back. As he flipped the pages, the little man put his spectacles on and ran his index finger down the page.

"Oh, yes, here it is. Back on May twenty-sixth of this year, Miss Rosseau signed the deed over to a Miss Consuelo Salvador. We have since recorded a new deed to Miss Salvador."

*What? Max* felt as if someone had just slammed him into the ground. He couldn't have heard that correctly. "I'm sorry, I don't think I understood you. Could you repeat that information?"

"Miss Rosseau signed the deed to Rosewood Plantation over to Miss Consuelo Salvador on May twenty-sixth of this year," the man repeated.

Max stared, stunned. Nicole no longer owned the plantation. Consuelo, her servant, now held the deed to Rosewood. Why? Could Nicole owe money to Consuelo? Could there be some complication to Jean's death that caused Nicole to give the plantation to Consuelo?

Or since the date was a day before their wedding, could Nicole have signed over Rosewood to Consuelo to keep him from gaining control of the land that she so dearly loved?

She'd outsmarted him plain and simple. She'd made sure that he would not gain control or even own a portion of Rosewood.

Max felt ill. He'd married her for Rosewood and the day before the ceremony she'd given it all to Consuelo.

"Sir..."

Damn, how could this be happening!

"Sir...Are you all right, sir?"

Jerked back to the present, he stared at the clerk who looked at him anxiously. "I'm all right. Have the taxes on the land been paid?"

"Yes, sir, everything has been taken care of. Rosewood's new owner is current on her taxes," the little man said, looking at him nervously.

"Thank you," Max said, walking out the door. He felt as if he could strangle the next person he saw. All this time, he thought that the plantation was his, when instead she'd given it to Consuelo.

He fumed on the way home, wondering how he could speak to Nicole without alerting her to the fact that he'd married her for the plantation. Whatever he said, he needed to be careful or she would know immediately his reason for making her his wife. Nicole was not dimwitted by any means. If this action was an attempt to keep him from taking the plantation from her, it showed her total lack of trust in men and her obvious endeavor at protecting what she considered hers.

He rode slowly back to Rosewood, needing time to collect his thoughts and cool his anger. At first he'd been completely stunned, and then he wanted to go back to Rosewood, pack his bags, and ride out, taking his son with him. But finally, on the last half of the ride home, his common sense began to prevail over his temper.

Leaving now, when he was closer than ever to getting everything that he wanted, would be foolish. After all, Consuelo was his wife's trusted servant and Max had every intention of keeping his marriage to Nicole intact.

There was still a chance he could get the land back. It might take a little longer, but he would overcome this obstacle just like he'd surmounted everything else to get Rosewood back for his family. He would win Nicole's trust and then she would get the plantation back from Consuelo and he'd still end up with the land.

Max kicked his horse and hurried on to Rosewood.

~

Nicole sat in the office, her head bent over the desk, her pencil scratching figures on a piece of paper. As he entered, she glanced up at him, her blue eyes widening at the sight of him, her mouth turning up in a smile.

God, she looked beautiful, and behind that smile was a calculating woman with a head for business unlike anyone he'd ever met before. She'd outsmarted him plain and simple, and now he had to make her aware he knew—and see her reaction.

"I've been doing some calculating on how much profit we could make off the crop this year. We may do all right, after all," she said. "After I give you half, I should have enough left to plant next year's cane tubers."

She stopped when he didn't appear excited at her news. Her brows drew together in a frown. "What's wrong?" she asked. "Is Paul all right?"

The fact she feared for his son left him with a warm feeling. He shook his head. "Nothing is wrong. I happened to be at the courthouse today and I thought I would check to make sure that the taxes on the plantation had been paid."

"Oh," she said, gazing at him with interest. "I thought I asked you not to concern yourself with plantation business."

"You did, but I don't take orders very well. Though it appears I didn't need to worry about the taxes. Consuelo has already paid them for this year," he said, watching the way her eyes grew wide as she realized he knew her name was no longer on the property title. She picked up her pencil and tapped it on the desk. "Yes, she's very thorough."

"Is there something you need to tell me?" he asked, unable to prevent the caustic tone from slipping out. "Such as why Consuelo's name is listed on the tax rolls and not yours?"

"There's nothing special about it. We have a temporary business arrangement, similar to the agreement between you and me. The land is mine and eventually I'll have it back. But until that time, the plantation is in Consuelo's name."

Nicole gazed at him defiantly, her eyes daring him to say out loud that he knew the reason she'd put Consuelo's name on the property deed. But he wouldn't give her that satisfaction. Instead, he'd tackle it from another angle.

Max leaned against the desk, his arms folded in front of him, and crossed his legs at the ankles. He took a deep breath and released it slowly to control his anger and make her wait just a little longer for his response.

"Why did you want to know?" she questioned.

"I was concerned that if you didn't own the land, it

could affect my portion of the crop money."

She blinked in surprise and gazed at him with a quizzical expression on her face. "How could Consuelo owning the land possibly affect the crop?"

"Well, if you don't own the land, you could be forced to pay a portion of your earnings to Consuelo. I just want to make sure I'm still going to receive half the payment for the crop."

The tension that previously held her body tightly seemed to dissipate and she relaxed. "Don't worry about Consuelo," Nicole said. "This is just a temporary arrangement that has nothing to do with the crop. You'll receive your money," she said, gazing up at him, scanning his face as if searching for any sign that she'd caught him in his lies.

She had indeed signed over the land to Consuelo to keep him from getting the plantation. He reminded himself that he'd come this far and was so close to getting what he wanted; he couldn't ruin everything now with his temper. He took a deep breath and released it slowly.

No one could say that Nicole Viel was an addle-brained twit; she knew exactly how she'd protected her land from him. Yet could he really blame her for her actions? Now Max felt even more compelled to make sure their marriage lasted.

Somehow he had to up his side of the stakes and make them even; but how? What could he do to hang on to the plantation and ensure his place here? What besides convincing Nicole that their marriage could last would keep her from sending him away? What could possibly tie them together forever? The idea hit him and he couldn't help but smile at her.

A baby. He needed to get Nicole with child.

Max smiled at Nicole, remembering the night in the gazebo. He didn't mind a bit trying to impregnate Nicole. It would be downright fun.

"As long as you and Consuelo are all right with this deal, then it won't bother me," he said, suddenly feeling cheerful.

He turned and walked through the plantation kitchen and then across the verandah into the main house. If he could get his wife pregnant, there'd be no question of his staying and no doubt that the land would be returned to Nicole and Max.

Now the question would be how to breach Nicole's guard and tempt his wife back into his bed.

## Chapter Fifteen

**N**icole sat in her bedroom parlor. Her embroidery lay in her lap. She'd started this piece months ago and laid it down when she'd realized she was with child. Now once again she'd picked up the wall hanging, hoping to complete it before they held the harvest dance at their home.

She'd met with Mrs. Reuss and they decided on a date that was less than a month away. Though it wasn't much time, the Thanksgiving holidays would soon be upon them and Nicole wanted the party held before Max left.

Nicole pulled her needle through the linen cloth, the tiny stitches making a delicate pattern, her hands shaking at the thought of her husband.

She took a deep breath and sighed. Max confused her in so many ways. When he'd found out about Rosewood she'd expected him to be angry, but instead he'd seemed more concerned about the money he anticipated making from the crop than not owning the land through marriage. Now, she didn't know what to think. By ensuring the plantation remained hers, could she have overreacted somehow? Could he truly not be interested in the land, but only in the crop? Yet how could she have risked the plantation she loved and how could she have known Max would be trustworthy when they'd very first married?

Part of her wanted to give in to Max's suggestion that their marriage be real in every way, while another part refused to trust him with her heart. Jean's deception had scarred her and left her cautious, fearful of trusting any man completely ever again. Yet she could not deny that she cared about Max. A strong man, gentle and caring, he'd been good to her. So why couldn't she accept their marriage and embrace Max as her husband for the rest of their days?

Because she still couldn't trust him.

How could she learn to put her faith in an honest, upstanding man like Max, and give him her heart? After everything that Max had done for her, didn't he deserve to receive her faith?

He knew the truth regarding the land and he hadn't seemed particularly bothered by the fact that Consuelo owned Rosewood. Maybe Consuelo was right, that Max was a good man, and maybe Nicole needed to put the past behind her and give him a chance.

Consuelo walked into the parlor; her dark complexion seemed pallid.

"Are you feeling all right, Consuelo?" Nicole asked, looking up at her. "You look pale today."

"It's nothing. I didn't sleep well last night. I'll be fine once I get a good night's rest."

"Why don't you lie down and rest this afternoon? Maybe you're coming down with something," Nicole warned.

"If I get a moment. Right now, there's a Mr. Drew Soulier here to see you. He came to the gentlemen's door, but he wants to speak with you. Do you want me to put him in the main parlor?"

Nicole remembered the letter she'd written several weeks ago to Drew regarding the diary and knew that must be the reason for his visit.

"Yes, please do, and if you don't mind, bring us some tea, Consuelo," she said, rising and laying her stitching aside. She followed the older woman into the main parlor and then waited until Consuelo showed Drew in.

Drew Soulier looked the same as she'd seen him at the reading of Jean's will, though his face appeared more drawn, with lines around his eyes that weren't there before. He wore a worried frown.

"Mrs. Viel, how good to see you again," he said, walking into the main parlor. "You're looking much happier than the last time we met I was pleasantly surprised when I read you'd remarried."

She smiled. "Yes. Shortly after Jean's death, I married Mr. Viel. Please have a seat."

Drew took a seat on a settee and Nicole sat down in a rocking chair close by. "So how is Layla's trial going? I read in the papers that you are her lawyer."

"Yes, I am. Unfortunately, the prosecution has quite a case against her," he said, his brows drawing together in a frown. "It hasn't been easy."

"Do you think she killed Jean?" Nicole asked.

"I don't know. I took this case to defend her and that's what I intend to do," he said, his green eyes serious. "Your letter mentioned you'd found something of Jean's that I might want to see."

Nicole nodded. "Have you ever wondered if Jean married or was involved with more women than just the three of us? It's obvious the man was a womanizer, but what if there was a fourth woman? Or even a fifth?"

"I'd say with that many women in his life, Jean should have died of natural causes," Drew said. "Why? Do you have reason to believe there's another woman?"

"I have a diary that indicates so," Nicole said with a smile. "When Consuelo and I went through Jean's things, we found the journal. But who the woman is, I don't know. Someone ripped out the page that likely showed her name and there are no dates. In the diary she mentions a child she bore by Jean before he ended their affair."

Drew frowned. "He never mentioned another child to me. Of course, even as his lawyer, I'm learning things about Jean that shock me. Do you know the child's name?"

"Julianne, but she died of yellow fever. There's nothing to indicate what happened to the woman. Her diary ends on a very ominous note, almost as if she were contemplating suicide."

"May I see this diary?" Drew asked.

Nicole smiled. "Why don't you take it with you? You might find something that I missed. I only ask that when you find this mystery woman, please tell her she's not alone. That Jean hurt many women, including the three of us considered to be 'The Cuvier Widows.'"

"It may take me a while to find out who she is, but once I know, I'll be sure to tell you," he said. "What other information did the diary give you?"

"She met Jean when she was just a young debutante and he convinced her he would leave his wife and marry her. From her writings I gathered that she had an older brother who disliked Jean."

"Is his name in the diary?" Drew asked. "Maybe we can track her down through him."

"There were no surnames mentioned at all. Though she calls him by his first name, I can't remember what it was exactly. She mentions him on the last page. Let me get the diary for you."

"Here you go," she said, handing him the journal and then returning to the rocker. "I've read the entire book and I think it helped me resolve some lingering feelings. For Jean to have so many women, it wouldn't have mattered what I did. I couldn't have prevented his roaming any more than any of his other wives, and I can't be held responsible for Jean's cheating."

"Of course you couldn't stop Jean. You were a victim, just like the other women, Mrs. Viel." He took a deep breath. "Jean was my client and I never knew that he led this triple life. Frankly, I don't know how he could juggle so many wives, and I've seen the destruction his lies caused."

Drew took a deep breath and stood. "Thank you for writing and telling me about the journal. If you should find anything else, please let me know. Layla will hang if she's convicted and right now I'm not winning this trial."

"Just promise me that when you find out who the woman is that wrote this journal, you'll tell me. I think she needs to understand that she's not alone," Nicole said.

"I will. Thanks again, Mrs. Viel. I must get back to New Orleans today and be in court tomorrow. You still may be called as a witness."

"Of course. Good-bye, Mr. Soulier," she said, and walked him to the door on the men's side of the house.

With a click, she closed the door and leaned against the portal, thinking of Layla. At first she'd hated the woman for killing her husband, but now she wondered if someone else could have murdered Jean. But who? Who could have wanted him dead?

Marie came running into the men's parlor. "Mrs. Viel! Mrs. Viel! Come quickly, Consuelo has collapsed!"

Nicole felt her heart skip a beat and then pound hard in her chest as she hurried after Marie into the kitchen out back. "What happened?"

"I don't know. She was standing beside me making the tea you requested and then she made a moaning noise and fell to the floor," the petite black lady said, wringing her hands.

Consuelo lay on the kitchen floor not moving when Nicole saw her. She knelt down beside the woman she loved and grabbed her shoulder, shaking her. "Consuelo, Consuelo. Wake up, Consuelo!" She turned to Marie, panic in her voice. "Get me some smelling salts, quick."

Nicole placed her hand on the older woman's wrist, trying to find a pulse, but felt nothing. She patted her cheek. Her mind was unable to comprehend that this could be happening. "Consuelo!"

Only silence greeted her.

Marie came running back with the vial of smelling salts. "Here, ma'am. Try this."

Nicole held it under Consuelo's nose, but nothing happened. Not a flutter of her eyes, not a moan, nothing. "Oh! Oh, God! I think she's dead, Marie. I can't find a pulse."

Just then the kitchen door opened and Max walked in.

"Max, come help me!" she cried in alarm.

He hurried over, a worried expression on his face. "What's wrong?"

"Consuelo collapsed and I can't seem to get her to come to. Not even smelling salts are working." She sobbed. "Do something. I can't find a pulse."

Max knelt beside the older woman and picked up her wrist, placing his thumb on the underside. He shook his head and laid his ear on her chest then put his hand on her mouth. Finally he looked up at Nicole. "I can't find a pulse or a heartbeat either, and she's not breathing. I think she's gone."

Nicole looked down at the servant who had been with her since she was a young girl. Her body felt numb and she felt as if this couldn't be real. "Oh, Consuelo. No!"

She sobbed as Max wrapped his arms around her, holding her while she cried at the loss of her friend.

~

They held a small funeral for Consuelo the next day with Father Jonathan coming from town for the graveside service. There were no family members present, as her kin in Spain had disowned her years ago. Only Max and Nicole and the people who worked with her gathered around to say good-bye.

Nicole couldn't help but feel that she'd lost her best friend as she watched them entomb the woman who had been with her since childhood. The doctor had come late the previous evening and said it seemed as though her heart gave out. He told them her death had been immediate and she'd felt little pain, though Nicole wondered how he knew.

Clouds billowed across a gray, overcast sky, like a pall over the mourners gathered for the simple service. Nicole felt lonely as the day ended and the evening gloom came upon the house. Marie tried to cheer her, but she couldn't help missing her friend.

"Would you like for me to fix you some fresh tea?" Marie asked when they got back to the house.

"No, thank you. I'm going to my room. If anyone needs me, I'll be there," Nicole said, walking through the door that led into her room and adjoining parlor. She missed Consuelo so badly and felt bereft at the loss.

Max watched the workers seal the aboveground tomb, mourning the woman he'd barely known. Nicole had insisted her old servant and friend be entombed in the small family cemetery, which sat a short distance from the river.

After the workers departed, Max made his way back to the house just as the sun was setting. A cold drizzle had begun to fall, and he prayed the cold weather would hold off just a little longer for the crop.

Once inside the house, he walked to the woman's side and stood in front of Nicole's closed door. He almost changed his mind, and passed her door by, but then decided to check on her. All day she'd looked stunned by Consuelo's death, and he was worried about her. He knocked on her door.

"Who is it?" she called softly.

"It's me, may I come in?" Max asked.

"Yes," she said, her voice flat.

Inside he found her lounging in bed reading, her long blonde hair pulled back and braided, accentuating her pale cheekbones. "I wanted to check on you. Make sure you're all right."

"I'm tired, but I don't feel sleepy, so I thought I would read," she replied.

He pulled a chair over and sat down, wishing he could crawl into her bed and hold her. He couldn't help but notice the dark circles under her eyes. She'd lost so much in the months since he'd known her.

"Consuelo had been with you for many years," he said, thinking that her blue eyes seemed kind of lost.

"Yes, since I was ten. Actually we were together more years than my mother and me. In many ways, she became my second mother," Nicole said with a sad smile. She sighed. "One of my fondest memories is when she tried to talk me out of marrying Jean."

"I always knew she was a smart lady." Max smiled and reached out and grabbed Nicole's hand, needing to touch her and give her comfort. "She always watched me like a hawk. Like she was waiting for me to rob the silver or do something she could catch me at."

Nicole nodded and her blue eyes warmed. "She felt very protective of me. But actually she liked you. She thought you were a good man and told me I'd be foolish to let you go."

Max felt taken aback by this statement "Really. She warned me not to hurt you."

Nicole chuckled. "I'm not surprised. I think if someone else hadn't already killed Jean, she would have taken care of him when she found out about the other wives."

"It's nice to have someone care about you. I know I always felt like I could depend on my grandfather. No matter what, he would always be there for me," Max said, wondering why he was telling Nicole things he told very few people. But it felt good to be talking so openly with her.

"After the rest of my family died, Consuelo took their place. She wasn't just a servant; she was a close friend." Nicole sighed. "I'm going to miss her. She saw things about people that I missed. After Jean, I listened to her more than ever."

"Yes," Max said, "I can just hear Consuelo telling you what she thought of Jean."

Nicole gave a sad little laugh. "I'll never forget, I attended a party with my grandfather who once worked in the shipping business and Jean was there as a guest. When we met I thought him very handsome and quite good with the ladies." She laughed, the sound ironic. "Then a year later, we met again, and by then all of my family had died. We started courting and he came to my grandparents' house for the first time."

She smiled, her gaze distant, remembering. "When Consuelo met him, she told me he would never be faithful. He would only hurt me. But I thought she believed that of all men, since a man hurt her years ago. I didn't listen to her. Soon we married in a quiet little ceremony by a preacher he knew. After that she only referred to him as 'that man who comes home occasionally.'"

She sighed. "Jean knew I longed for some place to put down roots, so he bought me this house as a wedding gift and put the plantation in my name. I thought his gesture so sweet; now I realize he didn't want his first wife to find out. But I'm grateful he put Rosewood in my name or I would have lost it upon his death."

"You never had any indication of other women or other wives?" Max asked, amazed that the man had the gall to carry out such lies.

Nicole shook her head. "No, I never suspected other wives. Toward the end, I wondered if there could be another woman, a mistress perhaps. Though Jean treated me as well as a man like him treats any woman. Consuelo never liked him. She never said anything bad about him, but her opinion was obvious just the same. Later I realized how right about him she'd been."

"So were you happy with Jean?" Max asked.

"When I look back, I seem so naive. Our life together was one big lie. I wasn't unhappy, but I..." She stopped, and gazed at Max in the evening light. "You're the first man who has treated me with kindness and respect, who has comforted me in times of sorrow and in good times. You're the only man who has come close to what I expected of a husband. And when I married you, I had no intention of staying married."

Max felt stunned for a moment. Her words moved him and he lifted her hand to his lips and placed his warm mouth against her skin. "Thank you, that means a lot to me, to hear you say that."

Max wanted to do more than just kiss the back of her hand. He wanted to hold her, kiss her rosy full lips that beckoned him. She'd just made him feel ten feet tall and all he could do was sit there and hold her hand.

Nicole believed in him, and Max hated the fact he would do as all the other men in her life had done and betray her.

The thought filled him with guilt and he wanted to protect her from himself. Yet he knew to get what he wanted he needed to press his suit and try his best to get her with child. Why couldn't he just pretend he'd never lied to her? Why did she have to find out the truth? If she did, then everything they were building together would be ruined.

When he married her, he hadn't planned on concerning himself with Nicole. He'd been doing her a favor to marry her and give her baby a name. Yet he'd never taken into consideration her feelings and how he could be hurting her, only that he would be regaining the house and the land for his family. Now, he couldn't help but think of Nicole and he didn't want to hurt her. But he couldn't give up his quest. He'd promised his grandfather and he couldn't walk away.

Did he dare hope that she could be considering their marriage would last, or should he even press that issue here? Her brilliant blue eyes were tired as they gazed at him. He wanted so much to stay, but somehow he feared being with her. Somehow he was frightened of the emotions she evoked in him. He cared about her more than he'd ever thought possible, and yet he couldn't fall in love with her, because he worried she would hate him when she learned the truth. The honorable side of him bade him say good night and walk away.

"I think I should go now and let you rest," he said, unable to sit here in this room a moment longer with her, while he thought of the things he'd like to do to her body, knowing everything he did was all for his gain.

He stood to go and she grabbed his hand, her blue eyes beseeching. "Don't go. I... I want you to stay."

She pulled back the sheets, revealing the outline of her long limbs beneath her soft, clinging nightgown. He swallowed and tried to resist the sight of her shapely curves shadowed by the supple material. Her blue eyes gazed up at him, insistent with a magnetic intensity that left him spellbound. She tugged on his hand.

"Hold me like you did one other night when I felt lonely and sick with grief. Hold me and comfort me and make me believe everything is going to be all right," she beseeched him, her voice a husky tone that traveled down his spine like a gentle touch.

He swallowed, knowing that he would love to join her in that bed, knowing that once he wrapped his arms around her there would be no holding back his passion. He ached to feel Nicole in his embrace once again, as much as she wanted him there.

She glanced up at him, the blue of her eyes sparkling with something that looked like desire. And then she wet her lips with the tip of her tongue, and he all but groaned. She tugged on his hand and slid over, inviting him into her bed.

Passion swirled in the air around them like a fragrant perfume. She might want him to hold her for comfort, but he knew once he touched her there would be more than just solace he would offer her.

"Come and show me how you would console me if our marriage was going to last. Come and prove to me that you want to be my husband," she said softly, her blue eyes insistent.

Max groaned. He had held out and even considered walking through the door until she gave him that last challenge. How could he walk away from her, when he wanted to get her with child? Yet his principles prodded him to leave, until those last words.

*Prove to me that you want to be my husband.*

God, did he ever want to be her husband, but he also was trying so hard to listen to his conscience. He didn't want to hurt her anymore, yet he desired her like no other woman.

He shed his coat and cravat, and yanked off his boots which dropped to the floor with a thud. His pants followed next then he crawled under the sheet with Nicole. She turned her back to him and he wrapped his arms around her womanly body, pulling her tight against him. She felt like heaven snug against him.

"That feels nice," she said. 'That night you held me and comforted me after I lost the baby, that was the kindest thing anyone could have done for me." She turned in his arms to face him. "Thank you."

How could he resist her as she leaned into him, the soft weight of her breasts pressed against him? His body hardened in a hungry craving that left him rigid and wanting. Their gazes locked, neither one backing away, and for a moment Max was stunned by the intensity. A sparkle of iridescent blue shone from the depth of her eyes. Dark lashes lay against her pale cheek, with wisps of blonde curls escaping the braid she'd woven.

He reached out and ran his finger down her velvety smooth skin, igniting a spark of longing within him that awakened all his senses.

"Nicole, I don't think I can lie here beside you and just hold you," he said, his voice thick with need.

"I don't want you to," she whispered huskily as she ran her fingers lightly down his chest. Her touch left trails of fire that traveled way past where her fingers halted.

Max sucked in a lungful of air only to inhale the sweet scent of Nicole. Her brows rose slightly. "Do I continue?" she asked. "Or do you want me to stop?"

His hand reached out, grasping her head, and pulled her mouth down to his, hard; his lips covered hers, sampling her, tasting her moist mouth. His tongue teased and tantalized her, branding her with his fierceness as his hands cradled her head, holding her captive.

"Nicole," he crooned softly against her lips, his hands releasing her only to mold her against him, letting her feel him rigid and hard.

He rolled her onto her back and moved his mouth down, his hands untying the tiny drawstring at the top of her nightgown and then brushing the material down past her breasts until they were exposed to his gaze.

The creamy mounds with their rose-colored areola beckoned him and he leaned down and brushed his lips against a puckered nipple. He closed his mouth over her breast and gently suckled her, his tongue drawing erotic circles around the pebbled nub. Her hands grabbed him by the hair and she held him pressed against her breast, low moans escaping her throat.

He glanced up and watched the vulnerable expression on her face and realized in that instant, she trusted him or she would never have initiated tonight. The power of her faith filled him and he wanted to make this night special.

Max sat up and grabbed the hem of her nightgown and helped her remove the silky garment, lifting it over her head. For a moment he sat stunned at her loveliness, her curves exposed to his gaze. The gas lamp cast a golden glow to the soft pearliness of her skin. She was breathtaking, and he reached out a tentative fingertip to trace a path from her breasts, past the flat of her abdomen to the downy skin between her thighs.

She trusted him and now he longed to see the ruddiness of passion leave its telltale flush across her body. He wanted to watch as her body burst with pleasure and carried her away. He wanted to see her expression when he brought her to her peak.

His nimble fingers delved in between her thighs, teasing the sensitive bud between her legs, and she arched her back in response. His fingers were moist with the evidence of her desire as her lips brushed the side of his face, her breath warm against his ear tormenting him.

His breathing was ragged and uneven and still he waited. Waited for the sign of her ultimate surrender to him. His fingers continued the rhythmic skimming of the sensitive bud between her legs. As he watched her face, her eyes met and held his gaze, her lashes fluttered, and she released a guttural cry as she tensed around his hand, crying out his name. Her body clenched in a violent response to the shudders that racked her.

Max covered her face with kisses, his lips brushing her eyelids, her nose, and finally her lips, lingering as his mouth conveyed the passion that held him in its grip. Nicole returned his kiss, her hands clutching him to her, her breathing harsh.

He broke the kiss and quickly finished undressing, tossing the last of his clothes to the floor, his body roused and hungry for her touch. His skin felt like it was on fire as she put her hands around him. His own breathing became ragged and uneven as she touched him, leaving behind a scorching trail of heat that gathered within him.

Her fingers gently squeezed as they pulsed around the tip of him until he thought he would lose his self- control.

"Enough," he said as he gripped her thighs and plunged into her body.

She met his thrust, welcoming him.

She groaned, the sound echoing in the room as he covered her mouth with his own in a punishing kiss that fanned his arousal even more.

No woman in his life had ever wound her way so tightly into his heart quite so quickly, and it frightened him. He wanted to spend his days with Nicole and his nights in her arms. Now she was truly his wife in every sense of the word and he wanted her to wear his ring from now until death parted them. He wanted children, he wanted grandchildren, and he wanted forever after with Nicole. Their union could be happy if only she never learned of his deception.

He released her mouth, her eyelids fluttered open, and he stared into the depths of her blue-eyed gaze, feeling her searing touch all the way to his heart. He needed her, he wanted her, and somehow he would find a way to keep them together.

Nicole slid her palms down the length of his back, her fingernails digging into his taut muscles as he pounded into her body, the rhythm moving them to sharper peaks of ecstasy. He lost himself in the depths of her ocean-blue gaze and together they came crashing back to shore as wave after wave of pleasure rocked them.

With one last shudder, Max collapsed next to Nicole, his breathing ragged and rough, her own sounding loud in the small room. Somehow he found the strength to wrap his arm around her and pull her close to him.

She curled around him, wrapping her legs with his and

her arm around his waist as she lay her head on his shoulder. Skin to skin they lay together, sated for the moment. Max couldn't help but enjoy the warmth of her silken body next to his own, while he tried to keep thoughts of the future at bay.

For several minutes they lay there, letting their breathing return to normal, their heartbeats slow their sensual dance.

Finally Nicole raised her head to gaze into his eyes, her own wide with wonder. "Please, Max, stay with me tonight Stay and comfort me and make love to me." He brushed his lips against hers, a soft, tender touch. "You couldn't chase me from your bed tonight." He murmured the words against her lips. "I'm here as long as you'll have me."

She lay her head back down on his chest and he pulled the sheet up around them, cradling her in his arms.

Nothing felt more right at this moment than being here in her arms. It felt perfect and precious, and suddenly, he feared the future.

# Chapter Sixteen

**N**icole woke the next morning to an empty bed, and she stretched, feeling lazy and satisfied. They'd made love long into the night and later she'd fallen asleep in his arms.

They hadn't talked, only made love, and somehow she'd pushed aside thoughts of whether Max would stay or go after the harvest. She didn't want to think of that time, but rather get through these next few weeks.

Last night as she'd fallen asleep in his arms, she'd never felt so close to a human being as she did with Max. She'd thought when she married Jean, that she loved him, but though she'd fought long and hard to keep from falling in love again, she now realized she loved Max. Loved him more than she'd loved any man before him. The thought both frightened and thrilled her. But she had to get over her fear of living and give her scarred emotions a second chance.

For she'd realized yesterday at Consuelo's funeral that life was fleeting and time didn't wait forever. And she knew she loved Max, and with time, hopefully he would help heal the scars that Jean had given her.

Since the first time they made love, they'd never spoken again about making their marriage real. She wanted to believe in Max, she wanted to trust him and let him be the husband she dreamed of, but she felt so unsure. And even though she knew she loved him, she was still so afraid.

Yet last night she'd boldly invited him into her bed, something she'd never done in her entire life. Yes, they were married, but for their vows to become permanent and lasting didn't seem possible. Would he want to continue roaming the countryside while she remained here at Rosewood?

And if their marriage ended, why would she want to

stay behind, with no chance of a family, no one to share the beauty of the land with?

The original owner had built Rosewood for a family with roots and heritage, to create a legacy. Yet somehow, her dreams of giving her children everything she'd never had, had paled. The tradition she'd dreamed of building around friends and family would never happen, not unless she accepted Max as her husband.

And could that be so bad? In his arms she felt safe and secure, as if she were meant to be there. She thought back to her marriage with Jean. Never had she felt so close to a man as she did with Max. Jean popped in and out of her bed more like a drifter than Max ever appeared.

With Max she felt almost as if they breathed in unison. And there was this "thing," as he called it, between them. This sense that no matter where she could be in a room, when he walked in she knew he was there. A sense of looking at Max and feeling an inexplicable yearning that left her breathless and heady. Just the thought of him caused her breath to quicken and the feeling of safety and security to overcome her.

Never had she experienced such unrestrained physical attraction to a man. Not with Jean, not with anyone.

She brushed her braid back and sat on the edge of the bed. Consuelo would be bringing...

No, Consuelo would never bring her coffee again. Pain rocked her for a moment at the loss of her friend. Nicole felt truly alone in the world—no family, no one at her side any longer. The memory of Max comforting her filled her with warmth and brought a sad smile to her face.

How many men would marry a woman to give her unborn child that wasn't his a name? And how many times had Max comforted her during their marriage? He'd taken care of her when she'd been sick during her pregnancy. He consoled her when she lost the baby. He calmed her when she'd been grieving over the loss of the child, and he'd mourned with her when Consuelo died.

No other person had helped her through happy and sad times as much as her husband, and yet she held back a small part of herself from him. The time had come to put the past behind her and give him her heart.

Yes, there were many unanswered questions, but did they matter when it seemed evident from Max's past behavior that he cared for her? What would happen if she gave all of herself to this marriage?

She could give her heart to Max and give their marriage a chance, or she could shrivel away a lonely woman who let a man's deception scare her away from life and love. And then Jean would still be controlling her—from the grave.

The thought of Max leaving frightened her. Unlike her earlier declarations of wanting him to leave, suddenly she didn't want him to go. She didn't want him to leave Rosewood. For her heart knew what her mind had refused to accept for many weeks now: she loved Max. Had loved him almost from the moment he'd married her to give her unborn child a name. A kind and decent man, Max had slowly slipped into her heart with his kind deeds and gentle soul. She'd never met a man so loving, so kind and so tender. Now she must put the past behind her and give their marriage—and hopefully her love—a chance to grow.

In time, she would give her marriage everything that she'd never given her life with Jean. Not only would Max receive her love, he would receive the gift of her faith in their future.

~

Max walked into the house from the fields, pleased that the crop would be ready to burn in the next few days. Everything was going so well—even Nicole seemed to have accepted their marriage, and soon he would tell her the truth regarding his past and his reasons for marrying her. Last night, she'd surprised him with her invitation to spend the night by her side.

This morning he'd wakened at dawn and gently slid out from beneath the mosquito netting that covered her bed. He'd been loath to leave her, but the cane was in the process of being cut and then they would burn the fields. They were so close that he worried about every little detail. Including Consuelo's recent death.

If Consuelo's name remained on the deed of Rosewood, who owned the plantation now that she was gone? He knew this would be a delicate subject with Nicole, but he needed answers to feel reassured. He didn't need a relative of Consuelo's to realize the opportunity and suddenly take advantage of Nicole's attempt to keep him from owning the plantation.

Yet he had to phrase his questions to Nicole delicately, so as not to put her on the defensive. Things were going so well between them that he didn't want to undo all the progress he'd made.

He went through the dining room to the plantation office, where Nicole sat going through a trunk.

"Hello," he said, noticing the way she'd swept her blonde hair up off her neck, longing to kiss the spot on the top of her shoulder. The place that made her shudder.

She smiled up at him. "Hello. You're back early from the fields. Is everything all right?"

"Yes. We started cutting the cane today," he said, wondering how to bring up the subject of Consuelo's will. "How are you this morning?"

Her blue eyes rose to his, dark and poignant. "I'm fine, though every time I hear footsteps I look up and expect to see Consuelo coming through the door, and then I'm sad because I realize I won't see her again." She paused and glanced down into the trunk. "It's hard to believe that this is all that's left of her life. I'm searching for her will. She told me she recently updated it, but I haven't found the document yet."

Max felt a sense of relief. If she'd updated the will a short time ago, hopefully they'd put something in about the plantation, yet he wanted to be sure. "I know you had a business arrangement with Consuelo regarding Rosewood, but I couldn't help but worry about who owns the land now. I only ask, Nicole, because I know how much you love this place and I want to make sure you don't lose it."

Nicole frowned, her brows drawing into a furrow on her forehead. She glanced up at Max, her eyes searching his. "I own the land." She swallowed, the realization evident on her face. "And as my husband, you own it too."

A sense of satisfaction and relief swept over Max, yet he couldn't appear too eager. He smiled at her and shrugged as though it were no big deal. "I'm just concerned about the payment of the crop."

She watched him, her eyes gazing at him worriedly. And then she sighed. "That's not going to be a problem, Max, I promise you." Then her eyes narrowed and she stared at him. "I have a confession to make. The reason that Consuelo's name was on the deed to Rosewood was to keep you from trying to claim the land as my husband. After all, the plantation was mine before I married you and at the time we wed, our vows were only temporary. I never intended to fall in love with you."

He blinked, and stared at her. "You love me?"

She smiled and nodded her head. "Yes, no matter how hard I've tried to keep from loving you, you managed to find your way into my heart."

He walked to where she sat and pulled her up from the chair. He brushed her lips with his own and then held her in his arms. The moment dragged on, feeling awkward when he didn't confess his love to her. But he didn't believe in love and if he whispered words of affection, wouldn't she hate him even more when she found out the truth?

God, how he wanted to confess to her, tell her the truth, but he was enjoying their time together. He didn't want to end the closeness he felt with Nicole, not yet. Just give himself more time to enjoy the feel of her in his arms, the love she surrounded him with. Then he'd be honest with her.

She pulled back and gazed at him, waiting expectantly. "What did I do before you were in my life? You're so kind and considerate."

Max kissed her nose, guilt riding him hard. He'd only taken care of her the way she deserved to be treated. "Tell me that after we have our first disagreement."

She laughed. "Don't make that anytime soon, please. I'm enjoying being with you way too much." He pressed her head against his chest and held her close, afraid of her slipping away. God, if there were only some way he could keep the truth from her, he would. She deserved never to know his faults. She'd shown him how it felt to be loved and he would repay her with his lies. Guilt overwhelmed him. Nicole deserved better.

~

Two days later Max stood under the shade of an oak tree watching the field hands burn the cane. Everything was going so well, even Nicole seemed to have accepted their marriage and soon he would tell her the truth regarding his past and his reasons for marrying her. Her declaration of love had shocked him. He'd been so intent on working to make their union a reality, he'd never considered love.

Love had always seemed such a superfluous emotion and one that he'd honestly never experienced much of in his life. He loved his son and his grandfather had always shown his affection, but Max couldn't say that he'd ever loved Desiree, and his parents' relationship never was one that made him seek out love.

Max felt confused by her declaration of love. All his life he'd strived to do what his family wanted to regain the family home. Yet since he'd married Nicole, he'd experienced everything that a family should feel like. She'd made Rosewood into a home, and for the first time in his life he felt the warmth and tenderness of how a marriage could be between a man and a woman. He'd experienced her love and never been happier, except for the feelings of guilt that persisted in reminding him of how he'd tricked her.

He had to tell her the truth sometime, and then all the love she felt for him would turn into hate, just like the way she felt about Jean. If only she would understand his reasons why he'd married her then maybe they had a chance. Surely she could appreciate him wanting to get back his birthright?

He couldn't lie to her about being in love though, because he wasn't sure he believed in the emotion. His parents were certainly not shining examples of love that made a man want to spend his lifetime with one woman. Though with Nicole, he felt he knew her, he understood her thinking and wanted to share her joys, her heartaches, and her happiness. But love?

Would she repeat those three little words once she found out that he'd married her for the plantation?

The sound of a boat whistle shocked him out of his reverie and he turned toward the river. He watched the big steamer dock at the landing and feared who it could be. He untied his roan and stepped into the stirrup. With a kick to the horse's flanks he rode toward the house, hoping to intercept the wagon that traveled down the lane to Rosewood.

He worried he already knew who was riding beside Joseph and had expected her arrival days before. He rode his horse to the front steps and saw that Nicole stood waiting on the verandah to greet their guest. He glanced up at her standing in the shade.

"Who is it, Max?" she asked.

"I don't know," he lied as he swung his leg over the saddle and stepped down from his horse. He led the animal to a post in the yard, looping the reins securely around the piece of wood beneath a large oak tree that shaded the animal from the fall sunshine. Max felt uneasy as he watched the wagon pull up into the yard with none other than Desiree.

Max positioned himself between her and the house.

In her hand, she held an envelope. She saw him and she frowned, her painted brows drawing together. As soon as the wagon came to a halt, she climbed down and approached Max, her hips swaying.

Desiree hurried up the walk to the wooden stairs where Max stood waiting for her, knowing he would never let her enter the house.

She halted before the bottom step, looking up at him as he stood there with his arms folded. She shook the envelope at him. "What is this? If you think you and your fancy lawyers are going to keep me from my son, you're crazy."

"There are provisions for you to visit with Paul whenever he wants to see you, or at least once a month," Max said calmly, hoping that Nicole didn't pick up on the "fancy lawyers" or would assume that Desiree had misused the term.

"Once a month! Never! I've come to take Paul home with me today. That boy should never have left and I want him back, now!" she said, her chest heaving beneath her tight purple dress.

Max took a deep breath and kept his voice at an even tone. "Paul is not here, so you're unable to visit him today. Plus, if you thoroughly read that document you're holding, you will see a clause in there that states if you come around threatening or making a scene in front of Paul, you jeopardize the money you receive from me each month. I don't have to pay you and in fact I won't send you money if you harass us." Her face flushed red and her eyes widened in disbelief. "I can live without—"

"Desiree, be very certain of what you're about to say. I don't have to pay you. I'm only giving you money so that Paul doesn't worry about his brothers and sisters. God knows, those children deserve a better life, but if you make my son feel guilty for wanting to live with me, or you continually come here and throw your temper tantrums, then you won't get a dime. Do you understand me?"

"He's my son, too!" she shouted.

The spirit bottles clanged noisily together as the breeze shook the limbs of the oak tree. The sound seemed loud in the tense atmosphere, but Max refused to back down. Paul's future was at stake and Desiree wasn't a shining example of motherhood.

"And you'll see him. But you and I both know that I can give him so many more opportunities that you're unable to offer him. You had him the first twelve years, now let me turn him into a man," Max said gently, trying to reason with her.

She stopped for a moment, pulled a handkerchief out of her sleeve, and dabbed at her eyes. "But I need Paul. He's..."

The woman should have been an actress. Exasperated, Max shook his head. "Turn off the tears, Desiree. They are not going to work. You'll need to find someone else to watch your children because Paul will be spending his time getting an education."

Her dark brown eyes flashed at him, her red painted lips turned into a grimace that would frighten most people. "Fine! You can keep the boy, but if so much as one check stops coming to me, then I swear I'll be out here hounding you day and night I might even bring the other bunch of brats to live with you." Max smiled at her. "That's more like the Desiree I'm accustomed to seeing. Now get back in the wagon. The steamboat is waiting for you and I don't want to see you again until I bring Paul in to visit you next month. Do not come out here again, Desiree." She whirled around, the red ruffles of her petticoat flouncing through carefully cut slits in her skirt as she strode off to the wagon, her feet almost stomping. She climbed up onto the bench seat and then Joseph slapped the horses' backs with the reins, and the wagon lurched.

Max stood there and watched her leave, feeling somewhat successful. He still had his son, and hopefully the money would be enough to keep her from intruding too much in their lives. Though he loved Paul, he wished that somehow he'd never met Desiree. Never given in to his foolish romance with her.

He turned to go up the stairs and saw Nicole standing on the verandah. She'd witnessed everything. A frown furrowed her brow and he could see that she stood contemplating everything she'd seen and heard. After the first five minutes, he'd forgotten all about her standing there. And now she gazed at him as if she'd never seen him before.

"So," she said, her voice dragging the word out. "How does a man who drifts from town to town afford 'fancy lawyers' and manage to pay someone a monthly fee?"

Max cringed at his own slip about the payments. For a man who hated lying, he felt as if he was drowning in his own lies.

"That's where some of the money from the crop is

going to go," he replied without hesitation.

He watched her puzzle his response and finally, after several moments, her lips came up in a smile. "You always have the right answer, don't you?"

Max shook his head. "No, not always. If I always had the right answer, I would never have gotten involved with Desiree."

Nicole laughed. "Maybe your luck doesn't apply to women."

"That could be," he said, walking up the stairs, his eyes never leaving hers. When he reached the last step he placed his lips in the curve of her neck. "The men are working in the fields. Paul is away at school. We could slip off to the bedroom for a while."

She leaned back and smiled down at him. "You are so naughty. It's daylight."

"I know," he said. "I've never seen the way the sunlight looks on your naked body."

She hesitated just a moment, then smiled coyly at him and tugged on his hand. "I doubt that you'll pay much attention to the sunlight today either."

Max followed her eagerly into the house.

~

The sound of the steamboat whistle woke Nicole. She stretched in the bed, her arm coming into contact with Max's naked back. She curled around him, his warm bare flesh awakening her body once again. She couldn't seem to get enough of him, and that surprised her.

The whistle blew again and Nicole heard footsteps outside her bedroom door. A soft knock sounded.

"Mrs. Viel, Joseph has gone with the wagon to pick up more visitors."

"Thanks, Marie," she said. A second set of visitors in one day? Or could Desiree have decided to return once again?

Max rolled over, his face coming within inches of hers. "Did I fall asleep?" he asked.

"I think so," she said. "We both did. How sinful of us to take an afternoon nap."

He reached up and pulled her mouth down to his, giving her a kiss that heated her all the way to her toes. She longed to give in to his kiss and spend the rest of the afternoon here in his arms. But they had guests arriving.

She pulled back in his arms, her lips inches from his. "Didn't you hear the steamer whistle blow? We have more guests arriving."

Max frowned. "If that's Desiree, she's going to see what living without my checks is like."

"Come on, they're probably already on their way up the drive and we're still in bed," she said, giving his lips better access to her neck.

"All right," he said, pulling away. "But I'd rather stay right here."

She giggled. "Me, too. But we've got tonight."

He rolled on top of her, pinning her to the bed. She gazed up at his dark green eyes and wondered how she'd ever lived without him.

"Until tonight," he said, and brushed his lips against hers.

Max rolled off her and pulled her up with him on the bed. He rose naked and began to pick his clothes up off the floor where he'd hurriedly tossed them earlier.

Nicole slipped her undergarments on and then turned to him for help with her corset He laced her up and then she slipped on her stockings.

She had just put her dress on when she heard the wagon coming down the lane through the open windows. She ran a comb through her loose curls, not having time to pin her hair back up.

Max had finished dressing and the two of them hurried out the door of her bedroom parlor onto the verandah, laughing.

She glanced down, eager to see who their visitors were, and saw a man and woman sitting beside Joseph. She didn't recognize them, but then suddenly she noticed how quiet Max had become.

One look at him and she became worried. All the color seemed to have drained from his face. "Who is it, Max?"

He groaned. "It's my parents."

Nicole looked down at the approaching wagon and stared at the older couple as they pulled up to the big house. They appeared an odd twosome from the distance. She looked stylish, a large hat tilted to the side of her head, shading her face from the sun, and a fan in her right hand cooled her. But Max's father didn't have the same finesse about him and looked out of place beside Mrs. Viel, a surly air about him.

Max slowly went down to meet them and Nicole followed, wondering how Max's parents had located their son. The closer she came to the couple, the more she realized as she looked at them that they weren't exactly the kind of people she expected to have birthed Max.

His mother's dress looked like a picture from a magazine, with a matching parasol. When the wagon came to a halt, she waited for Max to help her out "Maxim Reginald, darling, you look superb," she said as he lifted her from the wagon. When he set her on the ground, she kissed his cheek.

"Hello, Mother," he said, not at all friendly. "I thought I asked you to wait."

She glanced at Nicole, her eyes giving her a quick once over, a smile on her carefully made-up face. "You did, dear, but I couldn't stand it any longer. I wanted to see you and I wanted to see Rosewood. And of course, I wanted to meet your lovely new wife."

The older woman, whose eyes were just like her son's, assessed Nicole. "She doesn't appear a country bumpkin. Of course your hair, dear, would be much prettier put up."

"No, Mrs. Viel, I'm not a country bumpkin, and if we'd known to expect company, we'd have been better prepared," Nicole said defiantly.

"Oh, she has spirit, too. Very good," his mother said with a nod of her head.

"Mother!" Max said, his tone completely exasperated. "This is Nicole Viel, the owner of Rosewood Plantation. Nicole, my mother, Audra Viel."

"Nice to meet you, dear. Has my son told you anything about his family?"

"Very little, ma'am," Nicole said, feeling completely shocked by the woman.

"Shame on you, Maxim," she said, turning once again toward her son, and tapping him lightly with her fan.

"I still need to introduce you to my father, Nicole," Max said, ignoring his mother.

He pulled her toward his father and introduced them. "This is my father, Charles Viel."

"Nice to meet you, Mr. Viel," she said, shaking the gentleman's hand.

"Same here," he said, eyeing her with a frown.

Nicole took notice of them as they stood outside the wagon and she couldn't help but observe that this couple didn't look like your average older married couple. They obviously had money and Nicole could see right away that Max's mother ran this clan and was accustomed to getting her way.

She glanced at Max, her fears coming back with a vengeance, and took a deep breath. "Leave your trunks behind and I'll have Joseph bring them in for you. Come along and I'll show you to your rooms." "Goodness, the place still looks grand, doesn't it Charles?" Max's mother said.

Nicole turned around and looked at her questions running through her head. "Have you been here before?"

She caught Max giving his mother a warning look and wondered at the exchange.

"Oh, no," she said, frowning at her son.

With trembling knees, Nicole led the group up the stairs to the women's side, through the parlor of her bedroom, and into the main parlor of the house. "If you'll follow me, I'll take you to your rooms. You can freshen up a bit and then I'll tell Marie we'll be having two more for dinner."

Nicole felt so uncomfortable with Max's parents that she suffered a touch of guilt She disliked his mother almost immediately, yet she was trying to remember that this was Max's mother, her mother-in-law.

"I'll take Papa over to the men's side of the house," Max volunteered. He gave his mother a last glance. "Behave yourself, Mother."

His mother gave him an elegant glare. "Why are you telling me to behave myself when it is you I'm worried about?" She turned to Nicole. "Wait until you have sons who treat you this way. It's such a shame."

Nicole led the way to a room next to her own bedroom, hoping to get away as quickly as possible. She opened the door to the guest room. "Here you go, Mrs. Viel. If you should need anything at all, please let me know and I'll be sure to get it for you."

"Thank you, dear." She stepped into the room. "Oh, how quaint you've made this room. I like what you've done in here.

Thank you," Nicole said, wary that she would add another comment that would ruin her compliment "My maid will be arriving tomorrow; which room should we put her in?" Audra asked.

Nicole swallowed. The woman had her own personal maid?

"The servants' quarters are located behind the kitchen. I'll find a place for her out there," Nicole said, not feeling very calm at the moment.

Mrs. Viel turned her attention to Nicole, her eyes staring at her as if she could see all the way into her soul.

"So tell me about you and my son," she demanded. "I know why he married you, but why did you agree to marry Maxim?"

A shiver went through Nicole. "Mrs. Viel, that's a subject I really don't want to discuss. I will say that I think meeting your son has been one of the luckiest days of my life. I just hope he's through roaming and will settle down and stay here with me."

"Roaming? What do you mean by that term?" the older woman asked, looking stunned. "Why wouldn't he settle down here? This is his home."

Nicole felt prickles along her spine at the woman's assumption. "When we met, he said he wandered from town to town," Nicole said, feeling anxious. "He came to my rescue one day while I was in town."

Mrs. Viel looked at Nicole, a frown appearing on her forehead. Then she laughed. "There's been some kind of mistake. My son runs one of the biggest financial firms in New Orleans, where he has lived almost his entire life." She started to laugh. "I don't know what he's been telling you. A man with more stable roots you'll never find."

Nicole stood there, stunned for a moment, taking deep breaths. She turned her back on the woman, needing to get away to think about what his mother had just revealed. "If you need anything, please be sure to let me know, Mrs. Viel."

She shut the door and walked away, not giving the woman a chance to respond, then hurried to her bedroom, feeling the questions building inside her as she closed the door with a resounding thud.

How could Max be in financing if he was a drifter? She thought back over every time she'd doubted his word and he'd always had a ready excuse. So why would he lie? Why would he tell her he was a drifter if he ran a financial firm in New Orleans? And why would he work as a planter instead of doing his job at the firm?

All the signs had been there, but she'd refused to believe them, hoping that somehow Max would either be who he said he was or he'd tell her the truth. But just like all the other men in her life, he'd lied. Max was no drifter and she didn't know if she should be cautious or glad.

# Chapter Seventeen

**N**icole went to the men's side of the house, looking for Max. She needed an explanation and she wanted the details from him *now*. Charles stood in the doorway of his room, watching her.

"Where's Max?" she asked, walking up to him, feeling odd being alone with her father-in-law.

He walked into the men's parlor, taking his time, and poured himself another drink. Slowly he turned to face her, his eyes studying her, and she wanted to scream at his leisurely pace. "Max was called to the servants' quarters."

"Thank you," she said, and headed back through the dining room and out the door that led to the servants' quarters. She hurried across the outdoor covered porch, down the stairs to the kitchen, situated a ways from the house.

She opened the door and Marie looked up expectantly. "Yes, Mrs. Viel?"

"Have you seen Mr. Viel?" she asked.

"Yes, ma'am. Joseph came in and asked him to come to the field right away. Noah, one of the field hands, was bitten by a snake," she said.

Nicole shuddered. Snakes liked to hide in the cane and the workers wore high boots to protect their feet and legs, though sometimes they were still bitten. Max would be gone for at least a couple of hours, and even if she went to the fields to find him, they wouldn't have a chance to talk.

"Thanks, Marie. Delay dinner as long as possible," she told the older woman, not wanting to dine alone with her in-laws. Her mother-in-law would be putting on airs, while her father-in-law would sit like a semiconscious stump. The tension would make eating impossible, unless Max was there to ease the atmosphere.

She walked back up the stairs, her mind racing with the information that Max's mother had given her. As she went into the house, she crossed the dining room to the door to the women's side of the house. She shut the door to her bedroom and leaned against the wooden portal, her mind reeling from the fact that Max was not a drifter as she'd believed.

Why? Why would he misrepresent himself about his profession if he ran a financial firm in New Orleans?

What would cause him to take on the disguise of a drifter and marry her? She put her head in her hands and felt the tears welling within her. Just when she'd decided to give her heart to Max, she found out he'd perjured himself to her, but she didn't understand why. Could there be a rational explanation? A reason he didn't want to tell her he owned a financial brokerage firm?

She thought back over the last few months, trying to remember their conversations, but nothing stood out that would help her to understand exactly why he'd kept the truth from her.

Could Max be just like Jean in that he'd deceived her? Was he no better than her previous husband? She lay down on the bed and let the tears fall.

This could not happen a second time. She wouldn't let a man make a mockery out of her once again. The first time she'd been naive, but this time, this time her heart was more involved than even the first time love betrayed her. If Max deceived her, then she needed to know the reason why.

She lay there for over an hour, her mind swirling with thousands of questions, trying to figure out why he would tell her he was a drifter when in reality he was a broker. A financial broker with money. No wonder he'd paid her bills at the shops in town.

The times he'd paid off her loans, the way he'd bought things for the plantation, and the way he'd agreed to pay

Desiree came rushing back. So many things now made sense. Every time she'd asked him how a drifter could pay for these items, he'd always said he had money saved or that he was going to use his share from the cane profits.

The sound of the spirit bottles tinkled on the breeze blowing through the open window, their musical notes soothing.

Max was a broker. Max had money. Max had her heart.

Marie knocked on the door. "Mrs. Viel, dinner will be served in ten minutes."

"Thank you, Marie," she called. She rose from the bed determined to face her husband and her new in-laws and learn the truth. Right now, she had the advantage. Max didn't know she knew about his deception and she intended to use that to her benefit. She went to the basin and poured water, splashing the tears from her face. Quickly she put her hair up and changed into a dress of blue satin brocade, determined to look her best when she faced her husband and confronted him with his dishonesty.

~

Max looked at the man laid out on the stretcher. "How's he doing, Doctor?"

"He's sick, but I think he's going to survive. Keeping him calm and opening the wound probably saved him," the doctor said. "I'd like to take him back to town, to my hospital, and keep him overnight just as a precaution."

"We'll load him in the wagon and then Joseph can drive him into town," Max said, feeling anxious. He needed to get back to the house. Of all the bad luck for one of his men to be snake bitten this afternoon when his mother and father arrived.

The thought of his mother alone with Nicole left him unnerved. He'd repeatedly asked his mother to wait before she came to the house, but his time had run out and still

Nicole didn't know the truth.

He needed to warn his mother not to say anything, yet he feared her telling Nicole everything while he spent the afternoon caring for Noah.

At last they loaded Noah into the wagon and Joseph pulled away, heading toward town. The doctor stepped into the stirrup and swung his leg up and over the saddle on his horse.

"Don't worry about Noah. I think he's going to be fine," he said, and with a wave he rode off.

By now the sun sat low in the sky and the men looked anxious and tired. "Why don't we call it a day and start fresh in the morning," Max said to the men. "See you at sunup."

No one complained and they all hurried to the wagons, eager to reach their cabins. Max climbed up on his horse and rode for the house, impatient to arrive back at Rosewood and somehow speak with his mother alone. He pulled his horse to a halt in front of the house and quickly handed the reins to a stable boy.

"Take care of my horse," he told him.

Racing up the stairs, he flung open the door to the men's side of the house and entered his bedroom.

A knock sounded on the door. "Mr. Viel, dinner will be served in ten minutes."

Hurriedly, he changed clothes, wanting to spend a few minutes alone with his mother before they went to dinner, determined to warn her not to say anything in front of his wife. He should have told Nicole before now, but he'd selfishly wanted their happiness to continue.

He rushed out the door, his hair still wet, and went to his mother's room. He knocked on her door feeling a sense of relief that he'd caught her before dinner.

"Mother, it's me," he said quietly so as not to alert Nicole.

The door to Nicole's bedroom opened and Max turned to face his wife. Dread seized him and he knew his chance of speaking to his mother alone would not be now.

"Back from the fields, I see," she said, her tone cool, yet she bestowed her smile upon him.

Something about her seemed different.

"Yes, the doctor came and he thinks Noah's going to be all right," Max said, watching Nicole carefully. "I thought I'd spend a few moments with Mother."

Nicole shook her head at him. "Sorry, dear, there's no time for that. Maybe after dinner."

His mother opened her bedroom door and smiled at him. Then she glanced at Nicole and raised her brows. "I see we're all here for dinner."

"Yes, Max, why don't you escort your mother to the dining room?" Nicole said with a smile, her gaze somewhat reserved. Maybe she felt nervous with his parents here. God knew, he certainly felt anxious.

How could he possibly keep his mother from saying anything during dinner that would alert Nicole to the fact that this had once been her home? His mother didn't know why he'd asked her not to come, nor that Nicole knew nothing of his family owning Rosewood.

He took his mother's arm and wanted to whisper something to her, but Nicole stayed right behind them, following closely.

When they arrived in the dining room, he pulled out a chair and seated his mother at the table. His father walked into the dining room, carrying a glass of some kind of alcohol.

"Well, if it isn't just like old times," his father said, clearly under the influence of alcohol as he gazed at Audra.

Oh, God, Max thought. He glimpsed at Nicole, but she was staring at his father. He should have told her before now. He should never have kept this from her, but been honest from the very beginning. Apprehension seized him and he tried to think of any excuse to end this evening, but came up blank.

Max took Nicole by the arm; she barely glanced at him as he seated her at the end of the table.

His mother smiled. "Yes, it is; we're with our son, his new wife, and we're at Rosewood." She frowned and then scolded, "Sit down, Charles, before you fall down. I'd hoped your drinking wouldn't ruin our first night here."

Max watched his father raise a brow at his mother and then nod at her as he saluted her with his glass. "Whatever you say, Princess."

Often, his father called his mother Princess, usually when he was drunk or he wanted to irritate her. Obviously his parents intended to show Nicole their worst behavior the first night they were here. Unease trickled through Max and he feared it could be a dreadfully long evening. Why did they have to come today? If only they'd given him until the end of the harvest. But his mother knew the end of the harvest signaled the beginning of the party season and she wanted to be back among the people who lived along the River Road. She wanted to show that her family occupied their rightful place once again.

He should have told Nicole long before now. But their last few weeks together had been so idyllic that he hadn't wanted to ruin them.

"Where's Paul?" Nicole asked Max.

"He's in the barn helping Moses take care of the horses. He'll join us later." Max knew Paul had deliberately found an excuse not to dine with the family tonight. His grandmother had a bad habit of trying to teach Paul the art of table manners in front of everyone.

Marie came through the door bringing in the platters of food, set them down on the table, and then departed the room.

Max glanced at Nicole. She seemed so solemn, so quiet this evening, and he couldn't tell if her quietness was because of his parents or something much worse.

After Marie left, Audra looked at Nicole. "Are we to fill our own plates?"

"Since it's usually only the three of us, we've never been formal. If you'd like I could call Marie back and ask her to fill your plate," Nicole said, her tone almost sarcastic.

Max cringed. His mother must feel that her status had been restored and intended to play the role of the high society matron to the hilt. She seemed to have forgotten those lean years after the sale of Rosewood. The years of living modestly on little money until Max's brokerage had made them quite wealthy.

"No, thank you. I can help myself," Audra said. "It's just that when—"

"How was the weather when you left New Orleans?" Max asked, interrupting his mother.

She glanced at him oddly and frowned. "You're not that far away from there to know that the weather has turned cooler and is very nice this time of year." She tilted her head at him. "You have been acting very odd, Maxim. Are you feeling well?"

He chuckled nervously, thinking if only she knew that right now he sat on pins and needles, wishing he were anywhere but here. "I'm fine, just worried about one of our field hands. He was snake bitten this afternoon."

Audra held up her hand. "Don't discuss it, please. I hate snakes."

Max glanced at Nicole. She seemed withdrawn and remote, as though her mind dwelled some other place. For a moment silence filled the room as they sat eating. She probably felt nervous meeting his family for the first time.

"Maxim, tell us how you met, Nicole." his mother said.

She turned to Nicole. "She was very secretive when we spoke of your marriage this afternoon. For years I've tried to get him to settle down and marry, but he's refused. Then suddenly he comes home to Rosewood and he marries."

"Mother, if you would let me speak, I would tell you," he replied tartly, feeling like a noose hung around his neck.

"Well?" she said, waiting.

Nicole had been quiet all through dinner. He glanced at her and she looked at him, her brows raised. "I thought your mother would rather hear *you* tell her how we met."

Max swallowed, feeling like a condemned man. "We met in town at the mercantile. Nicole needed some help and I offered to assist her. From there it was just a matter of time until we married."

"Dear, you left out the most interesting part," Nicole said in a quiet voice.

One glance at Nicole confirmed that his world was crumbling beneath him. "What part is that?"

"The part where you told me you were a drifter," she said, staring at him, her blue eyes burning with anger.

His mother laughed. "Why would you tell this poor girl that you were a drifter, Maxim?" his mother asked as she dabbed her mouth with her napkin. "I'm sorry, Nicole, for laughing, but that is so funny. Whatever made you say such a thing, Maxim?"

Max felt his insides turn cold. The food he'd been pushing around his plate stared back at him. He lifted his gaze to see Nicole staring at him, all the hurt he'd never wanted to put in her eyes glaring at him.

Oh, God, she knew the truth.

"Mother, stop it!" he said, wishing there was some way he could end this debacle.

She put down her napkin and frowned at him. "Whatever is wrong with you? Did you really tell her that you were a drifter?"

Nicole said nothing and he glanced at her anxiously. Her gaze met his with an intense stare that burned him all the way to his heart. She knew. She'd known since this afternoon. That's why she'd been so cool to him. But did she know about the plantation?

"Mother, Nicole assumed I was a drifter and I never told her any different. I should have told her the truth before now. I didn't think you would arrive so soon."

"What do you mean, 'so soon'? I've been waiting now for several months to come visit the home I loved. I'd have been here sooner if it hadn't been for your father and your curt note."

Max glanced at Nicole quickly. He had to tell her now. He stood. "Excuse us; I need to speak with Nicole in private."

His mother gasped. "Well I never would have thought that my son would leave the dinner table on our first night here."

Max ignored her and walked around to Nicole's chair. "Nicole, please come with me. There's something I need to say to you in private."

She gazed up at him and he could see the fear and anger sparkling in the blue depths of her eyes and it chilled him.

Nicole stood her back rigid and straight as he took her elbow and led her outside on the verandah. Her body was stiff and as soon as they were outside alone, she turned upon him.

"Twice now your mother has referred to Rosewood like she's been here before. What besides the fact that you're not a drifter have you not told me?" she said, anger spilling from her.

He took a deep breath and rubbed his face with his hand. A cool breeze blew across the field from the river, clanking the spirit bottles together. By now he'd grown accustomed to the sound and he welcomed their clatter.

"What's going on that you have not told me?"

Max cleared his throat, his mouth feeling dry and cottony. There was no way he could get out of telling her any longer, and he wished to God he'd been honest before now. He sighed. "My family once owned Rosewood."

Nicole blinked and then she turned her back to him and gripped the railing around the verandah with both of her hands. "When?"

"My great-great-grandfather built Rosewood. My grandfather lost it after the Civil War. My mother grew up here," he said, wishing he could ease the pain he saw in the tense, rigid stance of her body.

For a moment she said nothing, then she whirled around to face him, the realization of everything showing upon her face. She glanced at him, blinking as if blinders had been removed from her eyes. "Why would you lie to me about being a drifter? Unless...you didn't want me to realize you wanted Rosewood back." She stared at him, her blue eyes wide with incredulity. "You married me for the plantation, didn't you!"

"I had no choice," he said. "It was my family obligation. I'd tried several times to buy the plantation from you, but you refused."

Her eyes grew wide. "You were the one who sent me those letters requesting to buy Rosewood? But your name wasn't listed on the letters."

"I had my lawyers contact you," he said quietly.

She clenched her fists, her blue eyes furious. "Damn you, Maxim Viel! Damn you to hell! I didn't want to sell!" She said, her voice rising angrily. "You're no better than Jean!"

She lifted her skirts and hurried down the stairs, running through the kitchen garden down the moonlit path.

The spirit bottles clanged in the breeze, the sound haunting and eerie.

For a moment he watched her go, thinking that maybe she needed a little time. But he couldn't stand the thought of her all alone, hurting this way. He rushed down the stairs, running after her. With a fleeting look in the darkness, he caught a brief glance of her running through the woods. The gazebo.

He ran after her, hastening along the path to the garden tucked away behind some trees. Racing across the bridge, he wanted to call her name, but feared she wouldn't stop if she thought he followed her.

When he reached the little building he found her sitting in the dark crying.

"Nicole," he said, wanting to hold her but knowing she wouldn't welcome his touch.

"You bastard! How could you marry me knowing how much I was hurting from Jean's deception? Did you think that I'm such easy prey that you could take advantage of me too?"

Max cringed inwardly at the pain in her voice. He deserved her hatred and more.

"No, nothing like that at all. I tried to buy the plantation from you, but you refused to work with my lawyers."

"I didn't want to sell!" she cried. "Did you just not understand that Rosewood belonged to me now?"

He took a deep breath. "I know, but since the time I was a young boy, I was raised with the purpose of getting Rosewood back in my family. When you wouldn't talk to my lawyers, I came to town to try to speak with you. And then you got sick that day in town and I helped you. And then later, you asked me to marry you and I couldn't turn away from the chance of getting Rosewood back for my family."

She sobbed in the darkness. "Did you ever consider my feelings, what I wanted?"

"You needed a father for the baby and I saw the chance

to get Rosewood for my family. It seemed like the perfect solution at the time," he said, sitting down on the bench across from her. He wanted to touch her, to help her understand. "I was going to be a better husband to you than Jean."

"If you were going to be a better husband than Jean, then you should have been honest with me. Did you even once think of telling me the truth?" she asked, her blue eyes staring at him, her face tear- streaked.

He ran his hand through his hair. "I was afraid you wouldn't marry me."

She wiped the tears from her eyes. "Of course I would never have married you, because I would fear that you would never end—" She stopped and stared at him. "You never had any intention of ending this marriage, did you? You planned on convincing me to let you stay. You lying bastard."

He couldn't answer. If he did he knew it would be a lie and he'd already lied way too much.

Nicole stood, her body trembling, her eyes large and furious as she stared at him. "You've lied to me about everything. Who you are, your intentions, everything. You're no better than Jean except you didn't involve other women. Take your family and get out now! I want you off my property."

"No, Nicole. I can't leave you like this."

"I don't want to see you ever again. I fell in love with you and you betrayed me just like Jean. Get out! Get out now!"

She ran from the gazebo.

"Nicole," he called after her. "Wait!"

"No, leave me alone," she cried and hurried through the woods toward the house. "I don't want to see you."

Max's shoulders slumped. How could it have ended so disastrously?

~

A week passed with Nicole spending much of her time in her room or out at the gazebo. She took her meals in her room, she refused to speak with Max's mother and father, and she never conversed with Max.

The only people she communicated with were the servants, and Marie stared at her worriedly. She'd also come to Nicole several times upset about the orders that Audra had given the servants. Audra, it seemed, wanted to return the plantation to the ways of her childhood and Nicole remained determined that Rosewood would continue to be hers.

Nicole always managed to soothe Marie and tell her to ignore the woman's requests. Soon she would be gone, or so Nicole hoped.

Every night Max would knock on her door and try to coax her into coming out to speak with him. Once he'd even tried to push the door open, but Nicole had locked him out.

She didn't know what to do. Her love for Max still lived within her heart, but she felt so deceived and foolish. She felt as if everything she'd believed about Max was one giant lie. She missed Consuelo fiercely and wished she were here to talk over her choices.

Yet every time she thought of Consuelo, she couldn't help but remember that Max now owned the plantation. That no matter how she'd tried to circumvent this from happening, he'd still managed to get ownership of the land. And he'd never intended to end their marriage. That thought alone left her furious at his obvious deception.

She felt like such a fool. Twice people had mentioned his family living in the area and each time she'd brushed off their memories as nothing of consequence. Yet their recollections should have warned her.

So what did she do now? How could she continue to live here with Max? With his family?

Nicole sighed. If only he'd been honest with her.

No, if he'd been candid with her she would never have married him. If she'd known that he wanted Rosewood, she would have let her child be born illegitimate. She felt so sad, even her reasons for marrying Max were no longer important. Nothing had worked out as planned.

Part of her wanted to curl up in a ball and just give up on keeping Rosewood, to let Max have the plantation she loved. But the stubborn part of her said he didn't deserve the land. He didn't deserve to have her home. He didn't deserve her love.

No matter what happened between the two of them, she wouldn't give him Rosewood.

The party that signaled the end of the harvest season was four days away and she'd done little to prepare for the event. Eventually she would be forced to come out of her room and kick off the first social gathering of the season here at Rosewood.

She would put on a festive face and show the towns-people that she could be an excellent hostess, while her husband would remain an ornamental object at her side. She may have to live with him, but she didn't have to let him break her heart again. And she didn't have to share her love with him again.

~

Max watched the men picking up the burned cane and loading the stalks into the wagons, his thoughts on Nicole. He didn't know what to do. She'd spent the last week in her room, not speaking to him, refusing to come out. He'd tried to force his way into her room, but she'd locked the door against him.

He missed her. He missed her smile, her laughter, and

the way her blue eyes twinkled with happiness. He missed the smell of her in the morning and the way she'd cared about his happiness. Paul kept asking for her, and Max didn't know what to tell him. How could he tell his child that he'd just ruined his bond with a woman he discovered he wanted to keep as his wife?

All his life he'd been charged with the duty of growing up to replenish the familial finances and reclaiming the ancestral home. Everyone from his mother to his grandfather had given him this responsibility. And, though he'd obtained both, he couldn't help but wonder if his sacrifices were worth the pain he saw in Nicole's eyes. Did retaining the family land mean hurting anyone who got in his way?

For the first time he questioned the motives that had convinced him to lie to Nicole. If murder were necessary to retrieve the land, would he also have killed to obtain his goal? No. And he should never have hurt Nicole this way. He was an idiot.

He loved Rosewood, but the plantation belonged to Nicole and his family's time had long since passed.

And his grandfather, who preached to him from the time he was a small boy about his familial commitments, no longer lived. No matter how much his mother could wish it otherwise, she had to leave Rosewood. They all did.

The memory of the simple wedding ceremony where he and Nicole pledged their lives to one another came to mind. All his life had been spent in the pursuit of acquiring this land, yet now that he had the land in his grasp, could attaining Rosewood be worth the hurt that Nicole would suffer? Enduring the hate she would feel for him forever?

He'd missed her so badly this last week. He'd done everything he could to see her. He wanted to speak with her, tell her he was sorry, but she'd shut him out completely. And could he blame her?

The words she'd slung at him as she left him that night in the gazebo distressed him. He didn't want to be compared to Jean, yet his actions, though not similar, were still abhorrent.

In the end, he'd wounded Nicole just as Jean had.

Max missed her, he wanted her, and the world didn't seem like a good place without her. Could he have fallen in love with Nicole? Could he have married her for the land and then she'd taken his heart captive? Nicole was a good woman with a strong spirit that survived life's hardships. A gentle person who somehow showed him the important things in life, like his son and a family home. He wanted her by his side, having his children. He wanted her as his wife, the one person who he could turn to whenever he needed someone to comfort him. He wanted Nicole for her strong spirit and giving ways.

He thought of her constantly, her image always close to his heart. This must be love, for he'd never experienced anything quite like it before.

But how could he convince her of his love? How did he prove his love when she had so many reasons to doubt him?

His father walked up beside him, pulling Max out of his thoughts. "Looks like you're going to have a good harvest this year."

Max shrugged, not really caring one way or the other. He gazed at his father, feeling miffed at the man, yet it wasn't his fault he couldn't control his mother.

"I know you're angry at me for allowing your mother to come, but I couldn't stop her. You know how she can be," Charles said.

"Yes, she reminded me the other night of just how the two of you can be a son's worst nightmare," Max said angrily, though he realized everything that happened could have been prevented if only he'd been honest with Nicole from the beginning.

"I came out here to talk to you," Charles told him. "We were wrong to come barging into your life like this and now we've made a mess of things."

Max frowned at his father, the red puffiness of his face accentuated by the alcohol. The man was slowly killing himself and Max didn't know how to stop him.

"You can certainly say that again," he said.

Charles looked hard at his son. "You know, the two of you appeared so happy the day we arrived that I was sorry we'd come to interrupt this time. All your life you've been pushed to acquire Rosewood for the family, but maybe that's not what's best for you. Maybe you should think about your happiness and tell your mother to stay out of your life. I know I've never been a strong enough husband for her, but if you don't stop her now, she'll always interfere."

"Nicole and I were happy, Papa. And even now, Rosewood belongs to Nicole, not to me. I intend to give it all back to her." Max stopped, a sudden thought occurring to him. "In fact, I need your help. The harvest should be finished late this afternoon and I want the three of us to pack up and move out of Rosewood."

Charles laughed. "That's a good start, Son. I can tell you right now, your mother is at the house moving furniture around the way she wants it. Your wife hasn't come out of her room, but I know the servants move things back after your mother goes to bed."

Max shook his head. "She just doesn't understand Rosewood no longer belongs to her, does she?"

"No. Her father spoiled her and then I was always such a disappointment to her when I couldn't pay the debt to get Rosewood back. Your mother is a very unhappy woman."

Max nodded. "Then, when I tell her we're leaving this afternoon, she will likely hate me for not fulfilling my obligation."

His father nodded. "Probably for a little while. But I think you're right. Our time at Rosewood has come to an end."

"Yes, it has. Nicole owns the plantation now and it will remain hers no matter what happens to our marriage," Max said, his plan giving him a huge sense of relief. "I can only hope that someday she'll forgive me."

~

"Mother, why have you moved the furniture?" Max asked when he came into the house later.

"Dear, it looks so much better this way. When I lived here, we always had the chest over here. Now we just need to get new curtains and then the room will be back to its former grandeur," she said with a smile. "I knew you would like what I've done."

"I didn't say I liked anything. I asked you why you moved the furniture. This is Nicole's home, not yours any longer," he said, trying to be frank with his mother.

"Of course it's Nicole's home, but I certainly thought she would appreciate my decorating expertise. After all, I have so much more experience living here than she does," she said, moving a vase of flowers just so.

Max shook his head; she didn't want to hear him. "Well, it's not going to matter any longer anyway. Because we're packing up our things this afternoon and leaving."

"Leaving?"

"Yes, the four of us are departing Rosewood for good."

His mother's mouth dropped open and her eyes widened.

"I absolutely will not!" she replied. "I've waited over twenty years to see my home again and I'm not ready to return to New Orleans."

Max stood and calmly gazed at his mother. "I don't care

what you want. You're departing with me this afternoon; if that means I have to carry you kicking and screaming out to the wagon, then so be it. But I suggest that you have your maid pack your belongings or you can arrange for Nicole to have them sent to you."

Her face appeared flushed and her green eyes were wide. "Do you know how insulting this is, to have my own son discharge me from the family home?"

"Spare me the hysterics, Mother. Our time at Rosewood ended years ago. This home now belongs to Nicole and we're going to go peacefully after disrupting her life here," he said calmly.

"You're going to let that—that woman you married just keep everything you've worked for all your life?" she asked, her eyes tearing up. "I'm sure your grandfather must be pounding on his tomb right now, wanting out to set you straight."

"Grandfather is dead. You have one hour and then we're leaving," he said and whirled away, walking out of the room before she could say anything else.

Next he stopped at Paul's room, where he pulled out the boy's meager belongings and packed them in a small trunk. They would pick him up at school on the way into town. There was no need for him to witness the destruction of his father's marriage, especially since the boy cared about Nicole.

Max went to his own room and pulled out his trunk and began to pack his belongings. Though most of his things were still in New Orleans, he had accumulated quite a few items and he quickly packed them in the trunk. With one last glance he looked around the room. He would miss this place, but he had only himself to blame.

As the servants loaded the wagon, he went to Nicole's door and knocked.

"Who is it?" she called.

"It's me, Max," he said. "We're moving out as you requested. I've come to say good-bye."

She opened the door and frowned at him. "Is this some kind of trick?"

"No, everything is packed. Mother is finishing up and Father is supervising the servants loading the wagon. We're leaving," he said, staring at the fullness of her lips, wishing he could taste them one last time.

"Why?"

"I think it's for the best," he said, aching to touch her. "I'm sorry for the hurt I've caused you, Nicole. I let the ambition of my family lead me most of my life, not thinking of how it could harm others. You made me see how destructive my pursuit has been. All I can say is I'm sorry. You don't deserve to be lied to."

She stood, staring in shock at him.

"Where will you go?" Nicole asked as she wiped a tear from her eye.

He shrugged. "Eventually, I'll go back to New Orleans, but tonight I just thought we would go into town and let you have some well-deserved peace."

She stared at him, the look in her blue eyes disbelieving.

"I also wanted to give you this." He handed her an envelope.

"It came yesterday from my team of lawyers. It's your original birth certificate showing who your father was. I can tell you that he knew of you and even included you in his will. His lawyers on the East Coast have been searching for you and will be contacting you soon regarding your inheritance. You'll never need to worry about finances again."

She put her hand to her mouth and stumbled back inside her bedroom until she found a chair. There she sank down, trying to understand everything he'd said.

"You found my father?" She gazed up at him in amazement. "Why?"

"I knew that you've always wondered about him, and decided to do my best to find him for you. This way, you can be relieved about who you are," he said.

She sat there, staring into the distance, shaking her head. "This is too much to comprehend at once."

"Yes," he said. "I wanted to tell you sooner, but didn't have all the information yet."

"Oh, my God, my father," she said, and then she looked up at him. She shook her head. "I can't say anything right now. I don't know what to say. I'm overwhelmed." And then she gazed at him, her face suddenly looking suspicious.

"What about Rosewood?"

He shook his head. "Rosewood is not mine, it's yours."

Nicole raised her brows, but didn't say anything.

"When I get back to New Orleans, I'll put in the necessary paperwork to have our marriage annulled. Though we've been intimate, I may be able to get us some sort of annulment. If not, we can live in separate cities and I'll never bother you again."

Her brows drew together in a frown.

"I won't make any claims against the land and I won't allow any of my family to make any petitions against Rosewood either," he said, watching her eyes grow wide. "It's all yours, Nicole."

She stood there, her mouth open. "Why are you doing this? I don't understand. You married me for the land."

He took a deep breath, knowing that this was his one chance to salvage their marriage. That he had to deliver the biggest speech of his entire life or spend the rest of his years missing his wife.

"This week I realized that I'd spent almost my entire life trying to obtain Rosewood. After I acquired Rosewood through marriage to you, I, too, didn't count on falling in love with you. Until I met you, I'd never been in love and didn't believe in the emotion."

He took a deep breath. "But last week when you said you loved me, I was so afraid that you would find out the truth. I didn't know how to undo all the lies and deceptions to keep both you and Rosewood. In the end, I decided that you are by far more important than any piece of land, and that maybe the time had come for my family to let Rosewood go. So I'm leaving and taking my family with me. The crop is in at the mill and I'll release any holds against Rosewood. I want you to be happy, Nicole. I want you to have this land you love so much. I want to thank you for your love; it's something I'll always treasure."

Nicole stood there staring at him, her mouth open, not saying anything. A pain seized his heart and he felt his insides quiver as she stood silent. She exhibited no response to his words of love. He'd truly lost her and she must not feel that there was even a chance of their marriage ever working.

A wave of pain and sadness so intense went through him, he felt his knees quiver.

"You said you loved me," she said hesitantly. "But how do I know it's true?"

"You don't. I don't have any proof. I can only leave Rosewood and wish you the best," he said, hoping she would realize he had given up his life quest just for her.

Nicole stared at him, looking uncertain.

He swallowed back the lump that formed in his throat.

Her eyes searched his, her gaze somehow still uneasy. "Thank you, Max. This means a lot to me."

He took a deep breath, wishing she would run into his arms, but knowing he'd truly ruined his marriage. "You're welcome." Somehow he had to make a dignified exit. "If you need me I'll be in a hotel in town until the day after tomorrow, and then I'm returning to New Orleans."

"Of course," she said. She opened her mouth to speak and then halted.

"Good-bye," he said, and walked out the door to the waiting wagon below, feeling like he'd left his heart here with Nicole.

## Chapter Eighteen

 $F$or the next three days, Nicole jumped every time she heard footsteps, certain that Max would walk around the corner. Yet every time she'd been disappointed. By now he should have returned to New Orleans and his previous life, leaving her to face alone the party they'd planned together.

Originally, tonight after the party, she'd intended to tell him that she wanted their marriage to last, forever. But now she would greet her guests alone, and when it was over retreat to the house that echoed with loneliness and memories.

She sighed, not really in a festive mood, even if Rosewood was decked out in all its finery. At the first sign of darkness, a pyre of wood stood ready to be lit next to the drive leading to Rosewood. A makeshift dance floor had been constructed under the trees, where the guests would dance under the canopy of stars. A cool fall breeze blew from the river neither too hot nor too cold. The harvest was complete and the totals for the cane staggered Nicole. By far this year's crop was exceptional and she couldn't help but feel that Max deserved the credit for making it bountiful.

Though this party would truly spotlight Rosewood and induct them into the River Road society, she had since lost the urgency to belong. She knew the name of her father, but somehow the need to fit in didn't seem quite as important as before. She would have no children, no family, and no legacy to leave behind. Most of all, there would be no Max at her side.

God, how she missed him and wanted to call him back, but her pride refused to let her go after him. She would not follow a man who lied and misrepresented himself. He was gone and she must learn to get on with her life.

Yet a tiny voice kept insisting he'd apologized. He'd said he was sorry and he'd given her Rosewood when he could have kept the plantation.

And somehow the thought of facing all these people alone seemed frightening. Yet this was what she'd worked toward all these years and tonight was her opportunity to belong to a community, as she'd always dreamed.

But somehow the thought no longer appealed to her.

Max wouldn't be by her side, greeting the guests, showing them about the house. She'd be alone, years of her life ahead of her, to live inside this house she'd wanted, with no one to share the heritage.

Nicole loved Max, had known she loved him for a while, yet she'd let him walk out the other day only because she'd felt so confused when he'd told her he loved her and given her the name of her father.

How could she let him stay, unless she felt certain of his love? But how could she just watch him go, when she knew she loved him? Instead, she'd lost Max, and now she waited to greet her guests, feeling alone and uncertain about her future, missing the one man who could make her feel alive.

She should never have watched him drive down that long dusty road with his family in tow. He'd said he loved her, but the lies were so fresh and the scars from Jean's betrayal were barely healed. She needed to make sure that she understood that he meant to give her the entire plantation, keeping no part for himself or anyone in his family.

She needed to remind herself that he'd taken his mother and father and moved them out of Rosewood to a hotel in town—clearly giving them no quarter when it became obvious that Audra meant to change everything back to the way the house looked when she'd lived there as a girl.

Max had sacrificed everything to restore the house to

her. But more importantly, he'd said he loved her. That he wanted their marriage vows to last forever, and would be willing to get it annulled if she wanted. She didn't want their marriage annulled. She wanted their union to last forever, but first she must get through tonight.

She could let her pride win and say she'd never follow Max, living out the rest of her life alone, or she could go to New Orleans and see Max. Tell him of her love and how she wanted their marriage to work. Tell him that Rosewood felt empty and lonely without him and needed him at the helm.

She could either learn to sleep alone with only her pride, or she could forgive Max and take another chance at happiness. The choice was hers alone to make.

Since the party was mostly outdoors in the cool fall weather, Nicole stood at the bottom of the stairs and greeted her guests as they arrived in their carriages. Tables and chairs lined the verandah where the guests could watch the dancers on the dance floor or simply enjoy the view of the river. A lively band played next to the dance floor and paper lanterns swung from the trees, lighting the area, casting dancing shadows among the trees.

A cool breeze blew in from the river, a full moon graced the darkened sky, and the stars twinkled in time with the music. Nicole stood feeling anxious, a frozen smile on her face. She only wanted the night to be over. A carriage pulled up and Mr. and Mrs. Reuss alighted.

"Welcome to Rosewood," Nicole said, greeting them with a stiff smile.

"Everything looks so lovely, dear," Mrs. Reuss said. "Where is your husband, Mr. Viel?"

Nicole swallowed her nerves and gave her prepared answer. "He's been detained in the fields and hopes to join us later."

The older woman frowned, but nodded her head. "We'll

see him later, then."

"Of course," said Nicole, wishing they would just move on and let her greet the next carriage that arrived.

The couple slowly climbed the wooden stairs as Nicole prepared for the next guests. The sound of a horse's hooves caused Nicole to glance up. She couldn't believe her eyes.

Max came riding up on his roan, dressed to the hilt in his nicest suit. Her heart almost stopped at the sight of him so strong and masculine astride his horse. He swung his leg over the horse, slid to the ground, and then handed the reins to a waiting servant.

She felt his gaze on her as he walked toward her and her hands began to tremble. She felt so afraid.

When he reached her he simply stared at her, his eyes sweeping over her.

"Why are you here?" she whispered, her voice cracking from the strain.

He took her hands in his and leaned close to her ear. "Won't your guests expect your husband to be here?"

"Yes, but..."

The Reusses halted on the stairs, watching them. He kissed her cheek, the feel of his lips warm against her skin. "Sorry I'm late sweetheart, please forgive me."

Tears threatened and quickly she swallowed them back. She looked directly in his eyes. "You're forgiven. I told everyone you'd been called to the fields for some minor emergency, but that you hoped to return soon."

He smiled at her, his eyes intense, and she wondered at their message. "I wouldn't have missed our first party for any reason."

Mrs. Reuss, who stood halfway up the stairs, turned around and walked down to speak with Max. "There you are, Mr. Viel. Rosewood looks lovely tonight."

"Thank you, Mrs. Reuss. I can't take any of the credit, it all belongs to my wife. She's done a great job," he said, placing his arm around Nicole's waist, drawing her against him.

Nicole sighed, the feel of his hand warm and comforting. What could his return mean? Was it only for tonight?

"Well, the old place is looking better than it has in years," she said, and moved on up the stairs.

Nicole gazed into his eyes and saw the warmth there. "You came back."

"I couldn't leave you alone for our first party. I had to come back," he said, his voice soft for her ears only.

"I'm glad you did," she said, trying to convey with her eyes all the words pent up in her heart.

He took her hand and squeezed her fingers.

"I've missed you," he whispered.

She smiled. "Me, too." A carriage pulled up just then and she glanced into his emerald eyes, wishing they had more time alone. "Please stay after the party and let's talk."

He nodded. "All right."

For the next while, they greeted carriage after carriage of guests as they arrived. The servants set up the banquet table on the verandah and their guests went through the food line and then dined on the verandah, where the tinkling of the spirit bottles could be heard in the night air.

After dinner, the band began the next set, and Max and Nicole led their guests in the first dance of the night. As Max whirled Nicole around the dance floor, she couldn't help but wonder if this would be the first dance of a new life together or their last waltz.

She wanted their life together, yet there could be no lies between them. The feel of his arms around her felt so safe and secure, but if their life was built on fabrications and untruths, that security would be fleeting, and she'd already experienced that once. She wasn't willing to settle for that a second time.

Later in the evening, she went to check with the servants that the wine from the basement still flowed and that there were plenty of other beverages for those who didn't want to partake of the wine that Rosewood imported.

As she passed by the dining room she heard loud voices coming from the men's parlor.

"I heard you were looking for a new overseer?"

"Yes, I fired our previous one," she heard Max tell the unknown voice.

"I know a man who is looking for an overseer position. He comes with a very high recommendation and I wondered if I could send him out your way?"

She didn't recognize the voice, but his question made her halt. Who could that be in there talking about the plantation?

Then she heard Max's voice. "Nicole handles the affairs of the plantation. Send him out and tell him to speak with my wife, Mrs. Viel."

Nicole smiled to herself and continued on to the kitchen. Could Max have accepted the fact that Rosewood belonged to her?

She checked with Marie and the servants had everything under control. Nicole hurried back outside to her guests and ran into Mrs. Reuss.

"Mrs. Viel, I wanted to warn you about a nasty rumor that I heard regarding your parentage. I don't know if it's true, but you should be aware it's being spread."

"I see, Mrs. Reuss. What kind of rumor are you talking about and I'll clarify the information for you."

"Well, I didn't want to tell you, but they say you don't know who your father is," she said in a whisper.

Nicole smiled, thinking of how her husband had helped her conquer her doubts regarding her identity. "Don't worry Mrs. Reuss, I know exactly who my father was. William Wing Loring. I'm very proud of him."

The woman gasped. "The major general of the Confederate Army?"

"That's right. So you can assure the other ladies I know exactly who my father was," she said.

"Oh, my! He was such a hero," the woman gasped.

Nicole nodded, thinking how different this all felt, knowing the truth about her parentage. Yet she couldn't help but wish she could have gotten to know her father before he died. Just to have spoken with him would have been nice.

The information from Max's lawyers told her that her mother met General Loring after the war, while she was visiting in Washington. They had a brief love affair and when she left Washington, he went off to Egypt. Unable to locate him, he didn't find out about Nicole until he returned to the States ten years later and her mother had already passed away.

The older woman put her arm around her. "Don't worry about those ladies talking about your heritage. Once they find out that your father was the great General Loring, why, they'll be ashamed of the way they were speaking about you."

"Thanks, Mrs. Reuss, but you know, it doesn't matter anymore. I know who I am and that's all that matters."

Nicole felt shocked as she said the words and suddenly she realized it was true. She did know who she was and what she wanted out of life.

She glanced around the older woman. "Excuse me, but I think I need to find my husband."

The woman smiled. "Of course, dear. I think I'm going to go set that Mrs. DeChoskey straight. The gall of that woman spreading more gossip."

Nicole smiled and hurried off to find Max, suddenly needing to see him. She glanced across the yard and found him talking to a group of men. He looked up, his gaze meeting hers, and he smiled.

God, when would all these people go home?

A little after midnight the last guest stepped up into their carriage and pulled away. Nicole wanted to sink down onto the steps and collapse, she felt so drained.

Max stood beside her, gazing at her. "Tired?"

"Exhausted," she said, and glanced up at him, worried. He seemed tense suddenly and she couldn't help but wonder what could be going through his mind.

Giving way to her tiredness, she did sink down onto the steps, her dress billowing around her. She reached up and pulled him down beside her.

He sat down with a plop. The spirit bottles clanked in the breeze, their melody soft in the moonlight. The band had already packed up and gone home and the servants were scurrying around cleaning up so they could get to bed.

"I guess I should be going," he said, gazing at her, his eyes dark in the moonlight.

"You know, after you left the other night, I was so stunned that you admitted you loved me," she said. "Didn't you wonder why I didn't respond?"

He shrugged. "I thought I had ruined everything between us."

She laid her head back on the stairs. "The funny thing is that I've loved you almost since the day you married me, but was so afraid to commit my heart to you totally for fear you'd betray me just like Jean. And then I found out the truth."

"I destroyed everything with my lies."

Max leaned back against the stairs and gazed up into the sky. "If I could do it all over again, Nicole, I would still marry you, but this time I'd be honest. I'd tell you the truth, but I'd want to marry you all over again."

"If you'd been straightforward, I would never have married you," Nicole said, gazing up at the stars, knowing the truth deep in her heart.

"Probably not," he said.

"I would never condone lying," she said. "But if you hadn't, we wouldn't be together and I would never have fallen in love with you." She knew the words were a certainty. Jean's deception would never have let her take a second chance on love if not for needing a husband for her baby. And she would never have married Max if she'd known he wanted Rosewood.

"So do you forgive me for lying?" he asked.

She paused for just a moment, wanting him to sweat just a little. "Yes, if you'll promise never to lie to me again. That we'll always be honest with one another from this day forward."

He turned toward her, shifting on the wooden steps. "That's an easy promise to give," he said. "I promise to always be honest with you from this day forward. To never knowingly betray you and to love only you and our children until the end of my days."

Nicole felt her heart swell with love. "That almost sounds like we're saying our vows all over again. Do you mean them this time?"

"I meant them the last time when we married," he told her.

She stared up at him. "Were you in the men's parlor tonight speaking with a gentleman about Rosewood?"

"Yes, he told me he knew a man looking for an overseer position. I directed him to tell the man to come see you."

She turned to face Max, her hand reaching out to touch his face. "Thank you! Without meaning to, you proved to me that your love is real. In all the months we've been together, you've always been there for me. When you left the other day, I realized that even though you married me under false pretenses, you've always been there to help me and protect me. I love you, Max Viel, and want to be your wife, bear your children, and create a legacy here at Rosewood with you."

Max sat up and moved closer to Nicole, his arms encircling her, cradling her there on the steps. "My love for you is real, Nicole. I didn't marry you for the right reasons, but you changed my life and made me into a better man. All my life I've been trying to obtain Rosewood back for my family. But you showed me the true meaning of hearth and home. You've taught me the real meaning of being part of a family and I want that with you. Promise me that nothing will ever come between us again. Not land or family or even our children. You'll always be my guiding light, my wife, my love."

Nicole touched her hand to his cheek and pulled his mouth to hers, feeling the strength of her husband as she lay cushioned in his arms. This man had freed her from the chains of her past and taught to love once again. And this time she intended for that love to last a lifetime.

She broke their kiss. "So you and Paul are going to move back to Rosewood?"

"If you'll have us, I'll gladly return home to you."

"I love you, Max Viel. Your home is here with me," she said. He gave her a quick kiss on the lips. "There is one other thing we need to discuss."

"What, love?"

"Your mother," she said, feeling anxious.

He laughed, his mouth finding her neck and kissing her gently. "That's an ongoing problem I promise I will not let come between us. Can we talk about her in the morning?"

He kissed along her neck until he found that special spot.

"Only if you'll take me to where it all began," she whispered huskily. "To our gazebo in the moonlight."

He chuckled. "My pleasure, my love."

The breeze blew across the river, stirring the spirit bottles in the trees, making a soft, joyful noise as Nicole and Max ran to the gazebo where they'd first shared their love.

# <u>Thank you for reading!</u>

Dear Reader,

Thank you so much for reading *Betrayed*.

Whether you loved the book or hated it, I would appreciate it if you let everyone know by leaving a few words on your favorite vendor's website.

If you enjoy western historical authors, please join the Pioneer Hearts group on Facebook. This is a fabulous group of readers and authors who enjoy westerns.

Sign up for my newsletter at sylviamcdaniel.com if you'd like to learn about my new releases as soon as possible.

Reading one of my books is like spending time with me, and I just want to say thank you from the bottom of my heart.

Yours in Drama, Divas, Bad Boys, and Romance!
Sincerely,
*Sylvia McDaniel*

# Books by Sylvia McDaniel

## *Contemporary Romance*

### *Standalones*
The Reluctant Santa
My Sister's Boyfriend
The Wanted Bride
The Relationship Coach
Her Christmas Lie
Secrets, Lies, and Online Dating
Paying for the Past
Cupid's Revenge

### *Anthologies*
Kisses, Laughter & Love
Christmas with you

### *Collaborative Series*

### *Magic, New Mexico*
Touch of Decadence

## *Western Historicals*

### *Standalones*
A Hero's Heart
A Scarlet Bride
Second Chance Cowboy

### *The Cuvier Women*
Wronged
Betrayed
Beguiled

### *Lipstick and Lead*
Desperate
Deadly
Dangerous
Daring
Determined
Deceived

### *Scandalous Suffragettes*
Abigail
Bella
Callie
Faith

### *The Burnett Brides*
The Rancher Takes a Bride
The Outlaw Takes a Bride
The Marshal Takes a Bride
The Christmas Bride

### *Anthologies*
Wild Western Women
Courting the West
Wild Western Women Ride Again

### *Collaborative Series*

### *The Surprise Brides*
Ethan

### *American Mail Order Brides*
Katie

# About the Author

Sylvia McDaniel is a best-selling, award-winning author of historical romance and contemporary romance novels. Known for her sweet, funny, family-oriented romances, Sylvia is the author of The Burnett Brides, a western historical western series, The Cuvier Widows, a Louisiana historical series, and several short contemporary romances.

She is the former President of the Dallas Area Romance Authors, a member of the Romance Writers of America®, and a member of Novelists Inc. Her novel, A Hero's Heart, was a 1996 Golden Heart Finalist. Several other books have placed or won in the San Antonio Romance Authors Contest and the LERA Contest, and she was a Golden Network Finalist.

Married for nearly twenty years to her best friend, they have two dachshunds that are beyond spoiled and a good-looking, grown son who thinks there's no place like home. She loves gardening, shopping, knitting, and football (Cowboys and Bronco's fan), but not necessarily in that order.

Look for her the first Tuesday of every month at the Plotting Princesses blogspot, and be sure to sign up for her newsletter to learn about new releases and contests. Every month a new subscriber is entered into a drawing for a free book!

She can be found online at: www.sylviamcdaniel.com or on Facebook. You can write to Sylvia at P.O. Box 2542, Coppell, TX 7501

Looking for a new book to read?
**Check out Beguiled!**

Recently married Layla Cuvier is awakened to the shocking news that her husband is murdered and that she is not his only widow. It's true, she hated Jean Cuvier who forced Layla's father to sell his shipping company and sanctioned their marriage. There may be three Cuvier widows, but Layla is the most likely suspect to his murder.

Forced to turn to the man she blames for the sale of her father's shipping company, she must trust Drew Soulier, the best attorney in New Orleans. Layla knows that Drew doubts her innocence and is only using her trial to further his political ambitions, yet she can't seem to deny his allure and finds herself struggling to resist her desires. Is Drew the man to find the truth that saves Layla from hanging and heals her troubled heart? Or will he stop at nothing to achieve his goal to be mayor?

# Sneak Peek into Beguiled

*New Orleans, 1895*

Sunlight glittered through the windows of the St. Louis Hotel, casting bizarre shadows over the dead body of Jean Cuvier. A sparrow trilled a happy song in the courtyard outside the posh hotel suite, the sound eerie and disturbing. Layla Cuvier stared at the corpse of her husband lying on the floor and knew that from this day forward, her life would forever be changed.

*No longer will I have to endure his touch.*

Her eyes confirmed what Colette, her servant, had told her. Jean lay sprawled on the floor, his brown robe wrapped around him, his face a peculiar shade of pink. Needing the confirmation of what seemed so obvious, she reached down and touched his hand. The feel of cool flesh beneath her fingers sent a shudder through her and she recoiled in revulsion.

"Mrs. Cuvier, a doctor is on his way and the hotel manager has sent for the police," said Colette, wringing her hands in an anxious manner.

Layla felt numb as she stared at the man she had shared a house with for the last year. As his wife, she should feel sorrow at his death, but relief and a sense of peace filled her. She had barely tolerated Jean's presence.

She rose and nodded to her servant and friend. "Please help me dress before the doctor arrives."

"Of course," the maid said, but glanced at her hesitantly.

"Did Mr. Cuvier say anything about feeling ill?" Layla asked, gazing at her husband's still form.

"No. But I went to bed before you retired," the maid said. "Did you hear him call out?"

"After I shut my bedroom door, I heard nothing last night," Layla said, knowing the sleeping draught had ended her insomnia. The draught created a dream world filled with people and color, and a world so different from reality. Yet she would have heeded Jean's call if she had heard his cry for help. "So many nights he slept in the chair."

And Layla loved the nights he left her alone.

"It's so sudden. How do you think he died?" Colette asked.

"I don't know. He hasn't been ill." Layla gave Jean one last glance, stunned at his death. Their last conversation was an ugly reminder of his evil ways and she couldn't help but wonder if his heart could have failed him. Though their marriage had been a farce, she had never expected him to die. "Let's hurry. I'd rather greet the authorities fully dressed."

"Are you all right?" Colette asked gazing at her worriedly as they entered Layla's bedroom. "You seem so composed."

Layla gave the woman a quick glance as she shed her nightgown. "I'm a little shaken, yet I feel strangely calm."

Calm and relieved, she hoped that now his ugly secrets would die with him and she could escape this farce of a marriage and return to her home.

Hurriedly Layla chose a black dress appropriate for a widow. She had barely gotten her ebony hair swept up off her neck in a coiffure that left wisps of curls swirling around her face when Colette opened the door to the police. They swarmed into the suite, covering the rooms like a bevy of ants.

Layla stepped out of her bedroom, and into the doorway of Jean's bedroom to watch with interest as a uniformed policeman leaned over Jean's prostrate body lying on the floor.

The voices of the officers seemed distant and removed and the scene before her surreal, like a colorful nightmare.

A short ugly little man dressed in a shabby brown suit separated from the others and walked toward Layla.

"Mrs. Cuvier?" he asked, his intimidating eyes focused on her.

"Yes?" She felt as if he stared deeply into her soul, but she had nothing to hide and met his gaze, undaunted by his beady gaze.

"Detective Dunegan of the New Orleans Police."

They walked the short distance to the lavishly decorated parlor of the suite.

"Please sit." She pointed to a chair in the small sitting area as she sat across from him.

"How did your husband die?" he asked. He took out a notepad and a pencil from his tattered coat pocket.

"I don't know. My maid awakened me this morning with the news that she'd found Mr. Cuvier lying on the floor of his bedroom. I hurried into his room, where I found him lying there, his body already cold," she said, clenching her hands in her lap. "I have no idea how long he's been dead."

Layla glanced toward the bedroom, half expecting Jean to walk through the door, laughing that he had fooled them all.

"When did you last see him alive?" the detective asked.

She thought back to the night before. They had fought fiercely and she had been determined to return home to Baton Rouge this morning. She had intended to meet with an attorney to see what kind of legal recourse was available to her, but miraculously nature had taken care of things.

Now she prayed the ugly truth would die with Jean and she could return to her previous life. She licked her lips nervously.

"The last time I saw Mr. Cuvier was around midnight," she said, remembering how she had left him in the parlor asleep in the very chair the detective occupied.

A man stood in the doorway to Jean's room with a stethoscope hanging around his neck. "Detective Dunegan, can I speak with you a moment?"

Through the open window, she could hear laughter in the courtyard of the hotel, the sound incongruous with the atmosphere in the suite.

The two men disappeared into the bedroom. Their muffled voices held an excited undertone, though she could not understand what they said. As the minutes passed, she sat feeling more nervous, wondering whom she should contact regarding jean's death.

"Now where were we?" he asked. "Oh, that's right. You said the last time you saw the deceased was around midnight." He paused and frowned at her. "Did you and Mr. Cuvier sleep in separate rooms?"

"Yes. My husband kept odd hours, and I have trouble sleeping and don't like to be disturbed."

"So, you heard nothing in the night? He didn't call out to you for help or assistance?"

"No, I took a dose of a sleeping draught not long after he came home." She gave the detective a puzzled glance. "Do you always ask these kinds of questions when a man dies?"

"I'm just doing my job, Mrs. Cuvier," he said matter-of-factly.

Layla glanced around and noticed that more and more policemen seemed to be filling the hotel suite. They stood around in little clusters talking, occasionally glancing in her direction. A few of the officers seemed to be combing the room as if they were looking for something.

"What are they doing?" she asked alarmed. She had never heard of the police doing this when someone died.

The atmosphere seemed charged with some ominous foreboding that she didn't understand.

www.ingramcontent.com/pod-product-compliance
Lightning Source LLC
Chambersburg PA
CBHW071733190726
48292CB00003B/737